A PRIVATE WAR II

ANDRE'S WAR

PERRY COCKERELL

ILLUSTRATED BY JUDITH GOSSE

ANDRE'S WAR:

A PRIVATE WAR II

Andre's War: A Private War II

By Perry Cockerell

Illustrated by Judith Gosse

Copyright © 2017 by Perry Cockerell

Second Edition Copyright © 2022 by Perry Cockerell

Library of Congress Control Number: 2022920706

ALLIANCE
PUBLISHING
Alliance Publishing LLC
Dallas, Texas

Printed in the United States

CONTENTS

PREFACE

*"A Private War," is the first novel in the trilogy of
the Private War series. In order to better prepare the
reader who might not have read the first in the
trilogy, we offer a short synopsis of the history of the
story in A Private War and characters that precede
"Andre's War: A Private War II."*

AFTER LOSING HIS FAMILY IN a mysterious house fire in 1930,
Andre Williams grew up with his best friend Booker
Thompson. Andre and Booker were raised by Booker's Aunt
Clara until Booker's Uncle George took custody of the boys.
Andre's wish to attend St. Peter's Catholic School after the fire
would not come to pass. He visited Sister Camille at the
school for years, and the kind nun educated him privately
before he and Booker joined the army in 1941. The young
soldiers were sent to the African Theater in 1942 aboard a
British ship. It was on that ship that they met Oliver Smith,
the first black journalist approved to cover the European
Theater and a reporter for the *Birmingham Defender*.

Oliver encountered other journalists along the way,
interviewed Josephine Baker, and met Franklin Roosevelt and
Winston Churchill. He was later joined by reporters Cub
Miller and Tatiana Phillips in London. The journalists
followed the Invasion of Normandy and reported the war
from France after the liberation of Paris.

Privates Andre Williams and Booker Thompson were
assigned to fight through the southern part of France through
Operation Dragoon. After the invasion, Andre was accused of
shooting and killing by Booker. A JAG investigation ensued

and Andre was charged with criminal negligence in Booker's death. Andre contended that the shooting was accidental and in self-defense during battle. Captain Jesse Weinstein defended Private Williams during the courtmartial. The prosecutor, Captain John Thomas, was convinced that Andre shot Booker Thompson because of the fire and Andre's family's death in 1930, having used the shooting as a cover for his real intentions. Capt. Thomas and Capt. Weinstein faced off in a dueling trial, testing the lawyers beyond anything they ever expected.

Oliver, Tatiana, and Cub became interested in the case and were torn over decisions regarding whether and how to cover the military trial.

After his release and return to battle, Andre returned home to Birmingham in 1946 and began to work for his Uncle George. Oliver paid a visit to Andre and reunited all of the characters, resulting in an offer to work at the *Birmingham Defender* and bringing a sense of closure to questions about Andre's childhood—or so he thought.

So for now . . .

PART A:
AT HOME

Chapter 1

———— ❦ ————

"MAYBE THERE'S WATER AT THE house," said a Union soldier as four men rode their horses through the cotton fields.

"Surely they have a well," said the second soldier.

A third soldier of Scottish descent was singing the Scottish song, "A Ramblin Soldier."

Then he stopped. "We need – that's it."

"Not me," said the fourth. "I'm going to rest."

"No, you are not," ordered the third. "We have to move on. It's just a matter of time before the troops are after us. Don't be stupid. We have no time."

"As soon as we're back, we ditch the uniforms. The war is over. The South lost," said the first.

"Lincoln's dead. The South will pay a price for that forever," said the second. "We will pay a price if we're get caught," said the third.

The men approached the home, tied their horses near the large tree in front of the home, and went to the front door. The third soldier, the leader, knocked on the door. No answer.

"Maybe they are sleeping," he said. Another knock.

The door opened. A young woman opened the door. She wore a white dress, as if she were going to church. Her two young children came to the door and looked at the soldiers.

"Is your husband around, Miss Lady?"

"Why yes, he's in back."

Not true.

"Well, good morning there Miss Lady. We mean you no harm. We would just like to get some water and food and then head on."

"I would like some water," said the third soldier with a Scottish accent. The soldiers laughed.

Chapter 2

❧

ONE YEAR LATER, THE CIVIL War was over and the home was abandoned. A free slave, who dreamed he would be a pastor finished his work in the cotton field and walked past the home with his son as the night began to fall. The wind blew through the porch that surrounded the home and it made a sound as it swept the dust onto the ground.

"Why is that house empty, father?" the son asked. "Something bad happened," he said.

"It's new," the son said as he ran up the porch and around one side of the home, looking into the window.

"Get down from there," his father commanded as sweat rolled down his forehead. His overalls and shirt were brown with dirt.

They walked away and nothing was said for fifty yards.

"Did someone die there?" the son asked.

"The story goes that a wealthy family moved here, bought the land, and built the house. When the war started, one of the sons went to sea for the Union, leaving his wife and kids. He didn't return. The wife never got over it and would sit at the back of the barn waiting for him to come back. Some said she became old and that the back of the barn was her wailing wall."

"What's a 'wailing wall?'" the boy wondered.

"It's a place where people pray."

"What happened to her?"

"Some say she grew old and was an old maid. But she wasn't; she was young and beautiful and had young kids."

"What happened to them?" asked the boy.

"Don't go in the house. It's bad luck." They walked to their home.

"Why won't you tell me what happened in there, father?"

"There's no need. If it's bad you would want to know why. If it was good you would want to know what it meant. Either way whatever happened, happened."

"You live with what happened?" the boy asked his father.

"Yes. As it is written in the Bible, 'In that I command thee this day to love the Lord they God, to walk in his ways, and to keep his commandments and his statutes and his judgments, that thou mayest live and multiply: and the Lord thy God shall bless thee in the land whither thou goest to possess it. But if thine heart turn away, so that thou wilt not hear, but shalt be drawn away, and worship other Gods, and serve them; I denounce unto you this day, that ye shall surely perish, and that ye shall not prolong your days upon the land, whither thou passeth over Jordan to go to possess it."

"What does all that mean?" the son asked.

"It means to be grateful to the Lord thy God, obey his voice and cleave unto him: for he is thy life, and the length of thy days: dwell in the land which the Lord swore unto thy fathers, to Abraham, to Isaac, and to Jacob, to give them."

"Are you saying that no matter what happens to us, we are to be grateful?"

"Yes, no matter what happens to you, good or bad, you are to be grateful to the Lord thy God for it. Remember that."

"That's all I need to do?"

"That's all you need to do," the father said.

Chapter 3

IN THE SPRING OF 1948, things were about to change at St. Peter's Catholic Church. Sister Camille, Sister Laurie, Sister Aude, and the rest of the St. Claire nuns at St. Peter's decided to restore the abandoned two-story plantation home on the church grounds near Mountain Springs, Alabama that once belonged to the wealthy family who donated money for the church. Rumor had it that the tragic event at the home had happened near the end of the Civil War. Father Webster meant to restore the home for years and never did.

The home and tired walls breathed new life after the sisters opened the windows. It was quite a home when it was built. It had a wooden porch that encircled the entire front and sides of the house. It had an office, a study, and a large dining room. The second story had three bedrooms with windows covered with old, musty drapes overlooking the front yard. The house also had an extensive basement.

The sisters enjoyed cleaning out the spooky place and removing the cobwebs and replacing some of the windows. The nuns planned to host a summer camp for Negro girls at the home and campus during a weekend in June.

A week prior to the camping event, Father Webster called Sister Camille, Sister Laurie, and Sister Aude into his office. Father Sanders was there also.

"I know the sisters have been working to renovate the old home and that is a good project. I wanted you to be aware of a letter that I received in the mail. It reads:

> *Dear Mr. Father, we know what yoos and them catholics are planning at that church of yours an event for some negro girls. We don't tolerate the mixin of races here in these parts. You will need to abide by our instructions.*

"Who would write such an atrocious letter," asked Sister Camille.

"They need a grammar lesson," added Father Sanders.

"That's not all. I read in this morning's paper of the *Birmingham Defender* that there was a raid by the Ku Klux Klan on a black Girl Scout camp yesterday," said Father Webster.

"Oh, my God!" cried Sister Camille.

"Lord help us," said Sister Laurie, crossing herself.

"God in Heaven, protect us from this evil," whispered Sister Aude.

"Two days ago at Camp Blossom Hill, a Girl Scout camp was raided by a group of hooded KKK members. A convoy of twenty cars demanded to know who was there and went through the belongings of the girls. The men warned the women not to remain another night. Some of the girls went home after that," said Father Webster.

"You will need to be careful with the children tomorrow. We don't have security for this kind of event," warned Father Sanders.

"God is our security," said Sister Camille.

"You don't need to remind us," said Father Webster. "We need to be careful over the next few days. This incident was reported nationwide. I would hate for something like this to come here."

Chapter 4

FATHER WEBSTER HAD REASON TO be concerned. The Ku Klux Klan was rising across the South. Some politicians endorsed their actions. Others joined to raise votes, not realizing what they were doing and staining their career in the process. For some, the stain was permanent. Others found a way to admit their involvement and move past their mistakes.

In Georgia, not seen since the 1920s, the Klan in full regalia burned a cross in front of the home of a high school coach. The Anti-Nazi League asked the new Alabama Governor Jim Folsom to revoke the Klan's charter on file in the Jefferson County Courthouse in Birmingham. Reports of these incidents made nationwide news.

In New York, Folsom appeared on a radio program with Editor Ralph McGill of the Atlanta Constitution and said that he was not ready to act against the KKK but reported that law enforcement had stopped most of the lynching. "Out of the twenty-eight attempted lynchings last year, twenty-seven were thwarted by local law enforcement officers," he said.

Chapter 5

UNDAUNTED, SISTER CAMILLE AND THE others went on with their plans for the weekend camp session. The house was comfortable after the Sisters renovated it. In her room, Sister Laurie kept a parakeet that she found on the front porch one morning, unable to fly. Sister Laurie named the bird Calista and taught it to say: "Jesus is watching you" which it repeated daily to anyone entering the room.

The next day, over fifty teenage Negro girls arrived at St. Peter's by bus for their weekend camp. Andre Williams visited Sister Camille the same weekend. It had been a while since he had last seen her. He looked forward to their visit.

"Andre, what are you doing here?" asked Sister Camille as he walked up the porch steps.

"Hi, Sister Camille. I hadn't seen you in a long time and wanted to see what is going on with you," he said, giving her a hug.

"That is so nice of you to come see me. How do you like working for the newspaper?" she asked.

"I like it. They have me working in the plant, doing everything—stacking, delivering, proofreading. I'm working hard to be a great journalist."

"That's great! That is so wonderful," smiled Sister Camille.

"I went to the church and they said you were here. What are you doing with this place?" asked Andre.

"This is a project of the sisters. The owners donated the land to the church. The sisters have been renovating the home. A lot of folklore came with th home."

"Really? Like what?"

"I'm told there was an unspeakable crime that took place here many years ago. No one knows what happened, but I believe there will be peace here."

"That is good," he said looking around.

"Come inside and look around," she said, leading him on a tour of the first floor and the upstairs area.

"This place is spooky," said Andre.

"It is at first, but you get used to it," said Sister Camille as she opened the door to Sister Laurie's room.

"Jesus is watching you," cawed Calista. "What was that?" inquired a surprised Andre.

"Just ignore him. That's Calista, Sister Laurie's parakeet."

The sounds of vehicles could be heard.

"Did you hear that?"

"Sounds like cars," said Andre. "The girls are arriving."

"The girls?" asked Andre.

"We are hosting a weekend camp for the young Negro girls at St. Peter's and other churches. It is our ecumenical outreach. We are including young girls of all faiths. This will be our first event here.

"Welcome to St. Peter's," said Father Webster. "May I introduce Father Sanders, Sister Camille, Sister Laurie, and Sister Aude. We hope you enjoy your weekend at St. Peter's."

"For now, leave your bags on the porch. We will attend the 4 o'clock mass.

After that you can pitch your tents and unpack," said Sister Camille. "My name is Leondra," said a young girl to Sister Camille.

"I'm Sister Camille, and who are the others?"

"This is Tasheeka. This is . . ." said Leondra.

"My name is Violet," said Violet, interrupting Leondra.

"It is nice to meet all of you," welcomed Sister Camille.

"You will have a wonderful time this weekend," said Sister Laurie.

"God will provide you with all of the benefits that you will receive here," said Sister Aude.

Violet looked at Tasheeka, "Does she always talk like that?"

"Be quiet," said Leondra. The girls giggled.

"We will have food inside after Mass," said Sister Camille. The night was perfect. The moon was bright and full.

"Are we going to see another supermoon like we did in January?" asked Violet.

"I don't think so. I think one that bright only comes every seventy years," said Tasheeka.

"They say the moon pulls the water, so it pulls all the water in your brain and that is why some people go crazy. They turn into wolfmen during full moons," said Leondra.

"That's silly," said Violet, rolling her eyes.

"Didn't you see the movie, 'The Wolf Man?'" asked Leondra. "Who has money to see a movie?" said Tasheeka quietly.

The evening stars began to come into view, accompanied by Venus, the first planet to appear. Before long the entire Milky Way could be seen from one edge of the horizon to the other.

Sister Camille stood on the front porch watching the girls settling in and pitching their tents. Sister Laurie and Sister Aude placed chairs in front of the home so that the girls could sit and listen to Sister Camille as the amazing stars spread all over the night sky.

"Girls, come gather around to hear Sister Camille," called Sister Laurie. "Good evening," said Sister Camille.

"Good evening," responded the crowd of girls.

"We are glad that you are here. I hope that while you are here this weekend that you come to realize that there is something extraordinary within each of you that you have not yet been trained to believe in. When you come to St. Peter's, you will find that you will go beyond yourself. If you would like to accomplish something, you must first believe in yourself and expect the result has already been given to you. Do you expect to have relationships in your life? Do you expect to marry a certain man? Do you expect to be President of the United States? Do you expect to travel to the moon?"

"What is she talking about?" Violet whispered to Tasheeka.

"Shut up," hissed Leondra. "I want to hear her."

"You must change what is possible for you. There is no beginning and there is no end. There is only now. Each of you have a part of you that is extraordinary. You can do anything that you believe in by having fait and having the feeling that the result has already occurred. There is a higher state of being that you have not been trained to believe in. A state where you begin to recognize your connection to Jesus.

"Do you believe that is possible to bring something from the world of the dream and into reality? Here you will begin to learn how to manifest your dreams into reality. What you think about and what you dream about will become your reality as long as you believe and have the feeling that you already have, what you wish to have. Jesus said, 'Ask and you shall receive. Seek and you shall find. Knock and the door will be opened to you.' You will know Jesus by expecting him to be here and feeling that he is already here and enjoying his presence as if you had expected it all along."

"Did she just say that I can have anything I want because I think of it?" asked Tasheeka in a soft voice.

"Something like that; we have to feel it, or believe that we already have it, said Leondra.

"I like this. All I have to do is think about it and then I have it. I want a big house. Where is it? I don't see it. I want it now. She said all I have to do is think about it and then I will get it," said Violet. "This is fun. Just think about it and you get it. No work."

"Shut up," said Leondra.

Chapter 6

THAT EVENING AT THE WEEKLY meeting of the Klavern 800 of the United Klans of America, a secret meeting took place in an abandoned home hidden deep in the woods not far from St. Peter's. Klansman Bennie Jackson stood before a dozen Klansmen and raged against the rise of the black race. He was the great Titan, the highest-ranking officer of the group in the southern half of Alabama. The white haired sixty-four-year-old had risen high in the Klan, despite being Catholic in an overwhelmingly Protestant organization that considered Catholics no better than infidels.

The Klansmen attending sat in rows of chairs. There was an altar-like shrine that stood in front of the room with a candle, a container of water, an open Bible, and an American flag with a cross laid across it. A Confederate flag stood in the corner.

"Your Excellency, the Sacred Altar of the Klan is prepared, the Fiery Cross illumines the Klavern," announced one of the Klansman to another.

"Klansman, what means the Fiery Cross?" asked Bennie.

"We serve and sacrifice for the right," answered all of the Klansmen. "We must discuss the Catholic church near Mountain Springs integrating the black girls."

The room continued their discussion. Eventually the men decided to drive to the church to end the integration.

Apparently, the church had not taken their letter seriously.

Chapter 7

THE GIRLS RETIRED TO THEIR tents and sleeping bags.

"Can you believe what that Sister Camille was saying? Something like, 'Here you will begin to learn how to manifest your dreams into reality.' Who talks like that?" asked Violet.

"Be quiet," said Leondra. "She's nice."

"And what about that Sister Aude? No one talks like that. Who abused her?" snapped Violet.

"I might be a nun someday," said Tasheka.

"Of course, you will. No one is going to marry you," said Leondra. "You're bad," giggled Tasheka.

"I don't think I understand what Sister Camille said," said Violet. "She makes it sound like if we just think about something long enough, then the universe brings it to us. Is that what she said? I mean, does that really happen?"

"I don't know," Leondra replied. "I dream a lot about things that I want and nothing happens. I think you have to do more than dream. I think you have to do something. You can't just sit there and think you have something and then it appears. You can't pass a test by dreaming that you passed it. You have to work for it. She makes it sound like all you have to do is dream about it and then it shows up later. That sounds like witchcraft."

"Witchcraft?" asked Tasheeka. "Do they still do that stuff?"

"There are crazy people who do that Voodoo. I don't know if it is real," said Leondra.

"I have an aunt who used to say 'Voodoo' all the time," offered Violet. "What'd she say?" asked Tasheka.

"She'd say, 'I've been doing some Voodoo down in Jackson.' She was my aunt from Jackson, Mississippi," said Violet.

"What was her name?" asked Leondra.

"Aunt Clara," Violet replied. "We all thought she was crazy, so no one would say anything."

While lying in their tent, the girls saw the lining of their tent light up. "What is that?" asked Leondra. She got out of her sleeping bag and looked out of the tent. A car was coming and its headlights stretched across the field heading their direction. Then another car and then another.

"I'm going to get the sisters," said Leondra. "I'm not staying here," said Tasheeka.

"I'm not staying by myself," insisted Violet.

The girls ran up the porch and into the home. They skipped up the stairs to the second floor and knocked on the door. Andre was still there, visiting with Sister Camille and Sister Laurie at the dinner table and having coffee. Sister Aude had gone to bed.

They heard the knock on the door.

"Who could that be?" asked Sister Camille as she got up to answer the door. "Sister Camille, there are cars coming," Leondra announced.

Sister Camille looked out the door and was aghast as she watched the cars drive up with their headlights shining.

"Andre, run up and get Sister Aude," she said quietly. "What is it?" he asked.

"I don't know. A bunch of cars," said Sister Camille, looking concerned. "My gosh," he said seeing the cars arriving. Andre walked quickly to find Sister Aude.

"Sister Aude, Sister Camille is asking for you downstairs. She thinks there may be a problem," he called to her from outside the door.

"As a servant of Jesus Christ, I will come. Jesus will protect us," said Sister Aude as she walked out of the room. Her hair was down and he hardly recognized her. She was the sister who tucked him in bed the night of the fire when he was six years old. He watched her as she walked downstairs.

Soon the cars stopped. Young and old men crawled out of their cars and stood in front of the tents and behind them. Some of the men were looking inside the tents. A few of the girls began to scream, frightened and confused with the commotion.

"Oh, my goodness," cried Sister Camille, looking out of the front door window. "The evil of some men. God expects His people to do the ridiculous so He will to do the miraculous."

The girls left their tents and ran into the home. "What are we going to do?" wept one of the girls.

"Have no fear. They cannot harm us," consoled Sister Camille.

"They aren't going to do anything," said Andre. "They are stupid, but not that stupid."

Andre went to the phone and called Cub at the *Birmingham Defender,* asking him to come immediately to St. Peter's. This was a story. He recognized a story when he saw one, even if he wasn't a journalist.

Cub Miller was working the night shift and answered the desk phone.

Andre told him to get to the church as soon as possible.

Cub grabbed his coat and hat and took the newspaper's truck to travel the thirty-minute drive to the church grounds. By the time he arrived, at least one hundred men in white robes stood in front of the home.

Some of the men entered the tents in their uniforms and pointed hoods that fell to their shoulders, finding no one in the tents. Sister Laurie and Sister Aude could see the men from the second floor.

"Andre called the newspaper," reported Sister Laurie.

"What? We don't need help. God will protect us," said Sister Aude. "We need the sheriff," said Sister Laurie.

The noise of the men converging on the home grew louder. Two hooded men posted a cross in front of the home, doused it with gas, and lit it. The fire raged. The hooded men yelled as the fire grew.

Father Webster heard the commotion and saw the burning cross from his quarters. He was stunned to see the grounds of the church covered with hundreds of cars traveling towards the home. He called the sheriff, who had no choice but to respond to Father Webster's request.

"Jesus Christ," Cub said quietly as he approached the scene, viewing the entire event from a reporter's eye seeing the burning cross from a distance. He parked and took cover behind the cars at the back and slowly moved forward. He could see the angry mob in front of the home.

"Come out. We know you are in there. No one is going to get hurt if you do what we say," shouted the Klan leader in his white robe.

"You can't go out there Sister Camille," warned Sister Laurie. "You shan't go," agreed Sister Aude.

"Nonsense," replied Sister Camille. She opened the door, walked out, and stood on the front porch with Sister Laurie following quickly behind her. The fire was raging and the white robes were flapping in the wind, creating a sound like of flock of birds flying.

"We have no quarrel with you Sister. If you stand aside nothing will happen to you. We can't have our laws disobeyed," ordered one of the hooded men.

"We mean you no harm, Miss Lady. We are not going to let this go on during our watch," said another hooded man."

"Let what go on?" she asked.

"Mixin' of the races. That is not allowed in these parts," said a Klansman. "Oh, for goodness sakes," sighed Sister Camille. "You take your men and leave this place. You have no right to be here. Leave now before God judges you here this day."

"Just come with us and you will not be harmed," ordered one of the hooded men.

"God chose the weak to shame the strong, the lowly and despised of the world, those who count for nothing to reduce to nothing, those who are something, so that no human being might boast before God," said Sister Camille. "What did she just say?" asked one Klan member in his deep southern accent.

"You can't let her talk to us like that," growled another.

"We can't let her get away with that. She needs to be taught," demanded another hooded Klan member.

"She has no respect!" said another.

"Yeah, no one can talk to us like that," said another.

"Well, at least they can talk," said Sister Laurie. The sisters smiled but they were cautious.

Another man shouted, "White women have no business having these girls here. We don't like it and the people around here don't like it. We mean to see that our orders are obeyed. We are not going to let the Catholic church poison this country. Do you understand that?"

The men converged on the front porch, passing the nuns and opening the door. The girls began to scream hysterically when the men entered the home, running throughout the home up the stairs and down the stairs to the cellar. Some ran outside into the woods. The sound of the sheriff's siren sounded in the distance and was coming towards the home.

"Come on, let's go," ordered the leader of the Klan.

The rest of the Klan followed and went to their cars. They began to leave as the sheriff drove up to the home. There would be no murder that night but the message was clear: there would be no mixing between the races.

The cross was still burning and smoke was permeating throughout the area. Cub made it to the front of the home and photographed the burning cross.

Sister Laurie and Sister Aude went into the home and came out with pails of water to douse the cross.

"I'm sorry this happened," said the sheriff as he kicked the cross and knocked it down. The fire stopped as the sisters finished it off.

"Can't you arrest them?" asked Sister Laurie.

"All of them? They are like rats. You have to kill all of them."

"Well, I would certainly hate to kill a rat," muttered Sister Camille. She paused as the sheriff looked at her with a raised eyebrow. "I didn't mean that," she said quietly. The sheriff grinned and smiled at the remark.

Father Webster and Father Sanders arrived and ran to the sisters' sides. "Thank goodness you are here," cried Sister Camille.

"What can you do about this?" asked Father Webster. "Can't you do something? This is trespassing."

"We are outnumbered and can't take them on here. We are taking down all of the license plates. When we match all the plates we will be calling each of them down to the station. They hate that." said the Sheriff.

"Maybe the rats can change?" hoped Father Webster.

The sheriff smiled and walked off the porch. "You must be an optimist." He grabbed the cross and put it in the back of his truck and drove off.

Cub returned to the newspaper and made calls to find a Klan representative. He found the number of the Klan office from their charter filed with the Secretary of State of Alabama. Eric Rainwater answered the phone.

"This is Cub Miller with the *Birmingham Defender*. Your Klan boys were at it again threatening nuns and the Catholic church and Negro children on a youth camp out. Do you have a statement?"

"Who is this?"

"Cub Miller from the *Birmingham Defender*."

"I don't have a statement for you."

"Ok. Can I call back?"

"I will call you back," said Rainwater.

Chapter 8

OLIVER WAS AT HIS HOME that night, taking notes while looking through a journal he had kept of his time during the war.

"What are you writing, my sweetheart?" asked Tatiana. "Just doing research about the war."

"I see. All work and no fun, pour toi."

"Not at all."

Oliver rose from his desk, grabbed Tatiana gently, and kissed her. "You don't waste any time, do you?" she asked.

"A writer never wastes time. I was writing about you. I always get what I write about."

"I've never heard that one. Yes, you do and my father will never forgive you for it," she said.

"Maybe someday he will." Oliver kissed Tatiana. "I'm going to bed now."

"Be there in a minute," said Oliver.

By the time he adjourned to Tatiana, his wife was already asleep. The two were not ready for a family yet. Their life was their work. The couple had married in Chicago only two months before and had a short honeymoon to New York City. They then returned to Chicago to pack her belongings for the long train ride to Birmingham, where they found a small home near the paper with a little backyard. Soon Tatiana had chickens strutting about the yard and packaged her own eggs to give away. "Tatiana's Fresh Eggs," she labeled them. While the endeavor was a hobby for Tatiana, others would enjoy and use the products of her labor.

The next morning Oliver and Tatiana left for work together. Tatiana picked up a newspaper on the way.

"Don't pay for that," said Oliver. "We get them free."

"I know, but I can't resist. I have to see my byline."

"You'll get over it. Plus, it gets expensive."

"Looks like Cub got the front-page article. Something about the Klan," said Tatiana.

"Not them again," sighed Oliver.

"They raided a girl's retreat at St. Peter's Catholic Church. Isn't that the church that your soldier friend Private Williams talked about during the trial?"

"It is."

"Looks like St. Peter's is in the news again," said Tatiana, shaking her head.

Chapter 9

ANDRE WOKE UP EARLY AND went out to bring in the morning paper after experiencing the events last night at St. Peters.

"*Klan Leader Denies KKK's part in Raid*" the headline ran with a byline by Cub Miller.

Andre read the article:

> *BIRMINGHAM. The president of the Federated Ku Klux Klan, Inc. says his organization took no official part in a nighttime raid on a Negro Girl Scout outing at the grounds of St. Peter's Cathedral near Mountain Springs, Alabama.*
>
> *Eric Rainwater, of Birmingham, issued a statement last night in which he said:*
>
> *"I categorically deny that the Federated Ku Klux Klan, Inc. as an organization incorporated under the law of the State of Alabama had any part in the incident at St. Peter's church grounds or any similar incident."*
>
> *The Klan official said members of his organization are not supposed to engage in any activity without his permission. He added that he gave no orders to "visit that camp."*
>
> *Rainwater said he doesn't "approve of mob violence."*

"Still," he added, "if I saw a mad dog or snake, I would shoot it. And some people act like mad dogs and snakes."

An estimated 100 hooded and robed men entered the camp on the night of June 10th and ordered three white women to leave within twenty-four hours.

The women, Sister Camille, Sister Laurie, and Sister Aude from the St. Peter's Cathedral near Mountain Springs, Alabama, were on the grounds running the camp for Negro girls. The camp closed the day following the incident.

Andre walked back to his apartment with the paper, to tell Sherry about the front-page story. She was still asleep. She had been through a lot with him. What would he do without her?

He entered the small kitchen in their one-bedroom apartment and placed the newspaper on the counter before he fixed their coffee. The smell would wake her. He brought her a cup and laid it on the desk by the bed. She didn't wake. He touched her hair as he sat down on the edge of the bed.

Despite being married and having a new job, Andre was depressed and was not over the war. His condition would have been called "shell shock" if he had served in World War I. Today it was called "combat stress reaction." He was undiagnosed and he didn't realize he needed help. Sherry, dealt with his moody behaviors at home and Andre masked his symptoms at work.

A married man should be happy and need no help, he thought. Andre had a promising career but he was missing something. He missed the excitement of the war and his life in Europe, but it also served as a traumatic memory at the same time. He wasn't carrying a weapon, the time zone was different, and he struggled at nights with restlessness and insomnia. At times, he felt alone and missed his time in the army, a place where he had focus and a sense of mission. Booker's death was always on his mind. Then his pathetic criminal trial, he thought, for accidentally shooting Booker – friendly fire. No one blamed him for Booker's death now, but he carried a stigma with him in his own mind that no one could see.

It fell on Sherry to take care of him. But Sherry was not an army wife and had no idea what to do. She had no experience with military service men returning home. Overwhelmed, scared, and exhausted, Sherry had no idea what she was walking into when she married Andre.

Sometimes at night Andre would cry out and she would wake him out of a nightmare.

"It's nothing," he would say.

Sherry didn't believe him. Nightmares stalked him, and Andre would not tell her about his dreams.

"It's nothing," he would say.

Sherry would wrap her arms around him until his breathing stopped and the tension left his body.

Andre had not shared anything about his tour of duty or his trial over the death of Booker with Sherry.

Where was the Andre who came to her porch and sang her a song years ago? Andre looked at Sherry as she slept and remembered their wedding. Uncle George had performed the ceremony. Sister Camille, Father Webster, Father Sanders, Aunt Clara, Sherry Hardeman and her family, and a few friends of the family attended. Mary, Booker's old girlfriend, also attended. Oliver, Tatiana, and Cub attended

Reverend George Thompson pulled out his Bible to begin the wedding: "Everything I learned in life I learned from this Book. Before I begin the vows, I would like to recall a story from the book of Matthew. It is my favorite passage in the New Testament: Matthew 18. Sometimes Jesus would be asked questions by people with a sincere motive and sometimes not quite so sincere. At this time, however, the disciples came to him and asked, "Who is the greatest in the Kingdom of Heaven?" He called a little child to him and placed the child among them and said, "Truly I tell you, unless you change and become like little children, you will never enter the Kingdom of Heaven. Therefore, whoever takes the lowly position of this child is the greatest in the Kingdom of Heaven. And whoever welcomes one such child in my name welcomes me."

"Praise Jesus," said Aunt Clara. George smiled. Everyone smiled. He continued:

"For a long time in my life I was confused about that passage in the Bible. I didn't know what that really meant. Jesus was not talking about us becoming childish, but instead, childlike. I think we are childish every day either in our homes, our jobs, driving on the road. It isn't difficult to be childish. All I have to do is focus one hundred percent of my attention on myself.

"But, those who are childlike are those who look at others. They walk into a room like this one and are amazed at the beauty and the traditions of this church. People who are childlike are those who see family and friends they have known for years and bring great joy to them. Jesus seems to be saying that a fulfilled life now is the best way to be childlike.

"This brings me to a story. You know Andre and Booker grew up together.

Their Aunt Clara and I raised them."

"Praise Jesus," repeated Aunt Clara.

George smiled again. "We did, didn't we Aunt Clara?"

"We did!"

"I remember once when I took Booker and Andre camping on a canoe trip," said George. "It was about ten years ago. I took them down the Choctawhatchee River. There was lots of flooding back then. The first night was the worst. We didn't know what we were doing. Trying to get our canoes from point A to point B, and by the time we got there we were exhausted. I had to make a meal for that night for the boys. I remember buying a treat for them at the store—some packages of chocolate pudding. I realized that we had to eat it all, otherwise bears or other animals might come in that night looking for food.

"I started eating the chocolate pudding and I spent a good portion of the evening trying to finish all of it, not leaving much for Booker and Andre. They were so tired and could have eaten all of it in a matter of minutes.

"So later in the trip, we took a day off from canoeing on a beautiful sunny day. We brought back fish and didn't finish all of it. So, we put the fish we didn't eat back in the water, and soon a white bird came and devoured all of the fish. "I can think of all the times in my life when I was childish, when I put my needs above my friends'. But I learned there is a different way and better way. "We should be excited for Andre and Sherry. They should enjoy being childlike and enjoy the things that are natural in life. That is the way God intended it, but we might have missed it because we were thinking about ourselves.

"Andre and Sherry have a wonderful opportunity to have a relationship that is filled with joy and honor, being excited about the whole thing and about the birth of a new family.

"Now let us pray. We thank God for the gift of life. We ask that you for your blessing on this new family being created."

After George performed the wedding, the couple exchanged vows.

As they were leaving, Oliver came up to Andre to shake his hand. "I don't know what he meant by the chocolate pudding story but I will never forget it. Congratulations, Andre and Sherry!" said Oliver.

"Yes, congratulations to both of you. I'm so happy for you, Sherry," said Tatiana, giving her a hug.

"Thank you," said Andre. "I don't know where he came up with that story. That's Uncle George. He said he wanted to say something that was off the wall." The families wished the couple well as they exited the church, rice flowing across the wind. Andre and Sherry were on their way to their honeymoon. Cub arranged to let them use the newspaper's truck for their honeymoon. They had no money to spare.

"Where did Reverend Thompson come up with the story at the wedding? What was he talking about? I started to think this was the 'chocolate chip cookie wedding,'" laughed Sherry as they were driving off.

"It *was* off the wall. You have to be careful what you say and think. Words can make such a lasting impression," said Andre.

"Where are you taking me?" asked Sherry.

"It's a surprise," teased Andre. But he knew that it was back to Mountain Springs, where they grew up.

Chapter 10

—⁂—

AFTER THE INCIDENT WITH THE Klan, Andre went to see Cub to congratulate him on the article. He couldn't believe that his story involved Sister Camille and the others from St. Peter's. But first he had to see Mr. Nelms.

Andre was greeted by Brandesha Yancey, Mr. Nelms' young, thin, and attractive office secretary and personal assistant.

"Are you new here?" asked Brandesha to Andre. "Fairly new. I'm Andre Williams.

"I've only been here a few weeks. It can get kinda crazy in here with Mr. Nelms wanting this, wanting that, then Mr. Smith wants this and that and now with his new wife, who wants everything now and done yesterday. I think she's too skinny and walks around like a glamour beauty with all that makeup. She's our new drama queen if you ask me," said Brandesha.

"You mean Tatiana?" asked Andre.

"Oh yes, *Tatiana the Great,* the lady who interviewed Eleanor Roosevelt. Whoopee! We have to throw out the red carpet out every time she walks in. Her father is the publisher of some big newspaper in Chicago everyone tells me so we have to be nice to her. She thinks she owns this newspaper," grumbled Brandesha.

"She's always been nice to me," said Andre.

"Oh brother. She's the Kleenex Queen nonpareil. Always writing some story about how horrible things are and how Alabama will never recover. Everyone has to cry. That's her thing—if she can get someone to cry and talk about how the world is coming to an end, then she has her story and then goes home.. There is only one side to her story. She's never heard of the other side, It's fake news, if you ask me," rattled Brandesha.

"You're pretty hard on her," said Andre.

The intercom interrupted Brandesha as she was lecturing Andre.

"What is it, Brandesha?"

"There is a young man to see you. His name is Andre Williams."

"Send him in. How are you Andre?" asked Nelms.

"I'm good, sir," answered Andre.

"You've been working enough in the plant now. It's time to start writing.

Are you ready for that?"

"Yes sir. I'm ready."

"First, you need to go back to school. You can't do this job without an education."

"I know.."

Nelms hit the switch on the speakerphone on his desk. "Have Cub come in here."

"Yes, Mr. Nelms," said Brandesha over the speaker.

"Mr. Miller, Mr. Nelms wants you in his office," Brandeesha announced over the intercom in the room. The newsroom was abuzz with typing and chattering.

"Now?" Cub asked.

"Now," Brandesha said with a voice that sounded like a missile as she motioned.

"All right," responded Cub as he rose from his desk. Andre was in the room with Nelms when he entered.

"Andre!" Cub exclaimed. "Thank you for calling me about the Klan story."

"You are welcome. It's great to see you, Shorty," said Andre.

"It's Cub Miller now."

"I see," said Andre.

"So, you got a job here?"

"I did," said Andre.

"He's going to start out just like you," said Nelms.

Cub looked at Andre. "One day I was shining shoes. Then the next day I was working at the paper. I never looked back," recalled Cub.

"You started out as a proofreader on the night shift. That's how you learn the language. If you can find mistakes, you would always remember them and won't repeat them when you write," explained Nelms. "Now I want you two to head out to the new college they have out there and audit a grammar class. I had Oliver check out the curriculum over there. Seems like a good place. What is the name of that place, St. Matthias? Who names a church St. Matthias?"

"St. Peter's," said Andre.

"St. Peter's," agreed Nelms. "Cub, I told you I wanted you in school a long time ago, and then the next thing you know you took off to Europe following Oliver. Then I had two reporters over there on that boondoggle that cost me a fortune keeping both of you in hotels and meals. You two head up there this afternoon."

"Yes, Boss," nodded Cub.

"You can take the company car to get up there and back."

"Come on, let's go," said Cub to Andre.

"Thank you, Mr. Nelms," said Andre.

Chapter 11

PRIVATE LANNY ELLIS FOUND HIS way to Birmingham. He knew Andre and Booker, during boot camp and in serving through Africa and Europe with them. He and Private Williams fought in the integrated 5th Platoon, J Company, 394th Infantry Regiment, 99th Infantry Division along with white soldiers to take the bridgehead at Remagen. It was the first integrated U.S. Army fighting unit since the Revolutionary War.

After the war, Ellis worked as a government contractor with the Federal Bureau of Investigation as a field analyst. His job was to investigate the Ku Klux Klan and discover their members and associations. He was in Georgia investigating the Klan after they attacked a high school coach. As soon as he learned about the raids of the Girls Scouts and the camp at St. Peter's, Ellis relocated to Alabama.

Ellis had a personal interest in his mission. His family had been traumatized for years by discrimination and actions of the KKK and white supremacy groups. He would bring down the KKK even if it meant capturing them, interrogating some of them, and then letting some of them go – something that the FBI had not authorized him to do. The FBI investigated crimes; it did not serve as a local police force.

Through a few calls, Ellis learned that Andre was working at the *Birmingham Defender*.

"Who are you?" asked Brandesha, looking up.

The voice of Brandesha did not bother him. Ellis was used to incoming missile fire.

"Lanny Ellis. I'm looking for Andre Williams. Tell him that Private Lanny Williams is here to see him."

"Lanny! What are you doing here?" asked a surprised Andre. "I came to see my good friend," said Ellis.

"I wasn't expecting you. You're the last person I would expect to see here," said Andre.

"I wanted to get the gang back together. Remember Remegen and how we took out the German battery?"

"Yes. I haven't seen anyone since I came back."

"You need to connect up. You know how it goes. The military guys end up being your best friends," said Ellis.

"I'm shying away from the military right now. I guess you know about Booker?"

"You don't need to go there," said Ellis.

"I have to work right now. Let's meet after work. There is a coffee shop down the street," offered Andre.

Chapter 12

———— ⟡ ————

AFTER WORK, ANDRE MET ELLIS at the coffee shop. Ellis was sitting at the counter when he arrived.

"So, how is it with you?" Are you married?" asked Ellis.
"Yes."

"Are you ok since the war?"

"Yes," Andre lied.

"Have you seen any of the other soldiers since the war?"

"No."

"Do you know about Hawkins?"

"No."

"I heard he got a job as a mechanic. He says he is going to have his own company someday."

"What about Adkerson?"

"I checked on him. He says he is going to go to law school."

"That is ambitious of him. What about Kirkpatrick?" asked Andre. "He says he is going to go to school and then into the Marines."

"Marines? Hasn't he had enough?" asked Andre. "What about Trimmer?"

"He got a job as an employee of some defense contractor in Fort Worth," said Ellis. "He says they are developing a new plane called a B-36 that will have propellers on the back of the wings."

"That's cool," said Andre. "What about Saller?"

"He went back home to Memphis and got married. He said he is taking his wife to Texas to go into the oil business."

"What are you doing now?" asked Andre. "I might go into the ministry," said Ellis. He lied.

"You, going into the ministry? I can't imagine that," said a surprised Andre.

"Why do you say that?" asked Ellis.

"Man, you were brutal to everybody on active duty, especially Booker."

"That's in the past now. I've changed."

"That's good. Hey, I was wondering why you came to see me?"

"The war is over. We care about our soldiers."

"That's what they say," muttered Andre, taking a sip of coffee.

"I read the *Birmingham Defender* article about the KKK. Did you work that story?"

"I tipped off the reporter. I was at the scene where it happened. I'm not an investigative reporter yet. I'm going to college. But I'm going to cover the Birmingham Black Barons baseball game this weekend," explained Andre. "do you want to go to a game?"

"Yeah. I can do that," nodded Ellis.

Ellis switched the subject. "Do they know who those guys were that came out to the girls' camp?"

"I saw the name of the leader who was quoted in the paper."

"Can you imagine that? They have a leader who gives a quote in the paper, like the KKK is some kind of legitimate organization," said Ellis, shaking his head.

"That is crazy," agreed Andre.

"Believe me, this KKK business is crazy. There are some well-respected white people out there who belong to it, but they are cowards and go around in masks, not showing their faces. The law is changing to make them take off their masks. I think you should do a story about who these people really are," Ellis suggested.

"A black newspaper publishing the names of the white KKK. Can you imagine what would happen if we did that?"

"I don't know," said Ellis.

"I know the paper is doing stories on the Klan."

"Can your paper give me some of the names of the Klan guys who are wearing the hats and running around acting like a bunch of goons scaring everyone?" asked Ellis.

"The Klan stories are by two of the experienced reporters, Cub Miller and Oliver Smith," said Andre. "Why do you need to know that?"

"What are you doing tonight?" asked Ellis, ignoring Andre's question. "Going home."

"Let's do something tonight. I haven't had any fun since the army," said Ellis.

"I can't tonight, but I'm covering the Barons on Saturday. You can go to the game with me. Meet me here and we will watch the team. A bus will take us to the stadium. We can do something after the game," offered Andre.

"You got it," said Ellis.

Chapter 13

NELMS CALLED IN THE REPORTERS to his Monday morning conference that morning and set out the week's schedule.

"Let's go around the room. Tell me what you are covering this week," ordered Nelms. "Good job on the Klan article by the way, Cub."

"Yes, good job," said Oliver. "That was great," agreed Tatiana. "Thank you," nodded Cub.

"Hold on. Before we do that, I do have some stories I want covered. Who can follow the election?"

"I can," Oliver volunteered.

"Can you believe the Republicans are going to nominate Dewey again?" asked Nelms.

"I think they have a shot this time," said Tatiana.

"I don't. I don't think they can unseat Truman. Dewey won't take on Truman and hit him like Truman hits him. He has to fight back if he wants to win but he isn't going to win. Dewey doesn't have anything to offer us," explained Nelms.

"That's right," Oliver agreed.

"Oliver, I want you to cover the race. I think Dewey will get the nomination and Truman will get the nomination. Then you have Wallace. The Southern folks are breaking away with those Dixiecrats with Strom Thurmond," said Nelms.

"Remember, our job as reporters is to explain what is going on and cover what matters, wherever the facts lead us. Truman is going to campaign like no other presidential candidate. By train across the country. Our job is the same at it always has been. We write about policy and how it affects the lives of people," cautioned Nelms.

He took a few moments and looked through a stack of papers on his desk. "Let's see. The House Un-American

Activities Committee is investigating Hollywood. See if there are investigating any black actors. You take that one, Tatiana."

"You want me to cover Hollywood, Mr. Nelms?" asked a surprised Tatiana.

"If the government thinks the Communists have infiltrated Hollywood, then I do. Just find out what the hullaballoo is about," Nelms replied.

"I don't think there are any black actors involved in that," said Tatiana. "Why would the communists do that?" asked Nelms.

"You're being facetious, aren't you Mr. Nelms?" asked Tatiana.

"Yes. We've never trusted the Soviets. That reminds me. We need an entertainment editor. Someone who can cover black entertainment. Tatiana, can you add that to what you are doing?" asked Nelms.

"I don't have any experience in entertainment, Mr. Nelms." Tatiana said. "You don't need any experience. Isn't that right, Cub?"

"Sure is, Boss," said Cub. Nelms looked at him.

"Cub, I want to do some features on people. Start working with young Andre and have him do the research. Have him report to me later today."

"Will do, Boss," agreed Cub.

Nelms gave Cub another stern look and said nothing. "Tatiana, can you do a feature on Alice Dunnigan?"

"I know her," said Tatiana.

"You do?" asked Nelms.

"Sort of. I met her in Washington when I was on my first assignment to cover the First Lady back in '43. She's a correspondent for the *Chicago Defender*, the competitor of my father's paper. Why are you interested in her?" asked Tatiana.

"She was named Bureau Chief of the Associated Negro Press," Nelms explained as he continued to sort through the papers on his desk, looking for ideas. "Cub, look up a young man from Atlanta. He is about eighteen and is going into the ministry at Morehouse College in Georgia. His name is Martin Luther King, Jr."

"Will do, Boss."

Nelms looked up at Cub and said nothing.

"Tatiana, can you write something on our new Olympic medalist?" asked Nelms, looking through some more pages on his desk.

"Here is something on Satchel Page. What's up with Jackie Robinson?

Check on him," Nelms said to Cub.

"Can I give that to Andre? He's going to cover the Birmingham Barons," suggested Cub.

"Yes, give that to him," agreed Nelms. "Will do," said Cub. "He will like that."

Nelms looked through a stack of papers. "Tatiana, can you get me some information on John Sengstacke, the new owner of the *Chicago Defender*?"

"John Sengstacke," said Tatiana. "You got it."

"He took over after Robert Abbot died. I'm going to meet him at the National Newspapers Publishing Association next month. I always want to know something about people before I meet them. And Oliver, can you write something on Truman's executive order desegregating the military?" asked Nelms.

"Yes, sir," nodded Oliver.

"Ok, let's get to work," ordered Nelms, restacking the papers on his desk. "Tatiana, can you stay afterwards?"

"Yes, Mr. Nelms."

Oliver smiled at her and got up.

"I wonder what that's about?" Cub whispered to Oliver as they walked out of the room.

"Probably some new assignment," answered Oliver.

"Tatiana, I didn't bring it up in there because I saw your reaction, but can you also do some reviews?" Nelms asked her.

Tatiana responded with a guarded smile. She was hoping for some national stories like Oliver. "What do you mean by 'reviews'?"

"Movie reviews," said Nelms. "Movies?" she asked.

"Yes. Brandesha was covering local plays, church plays, and community theater. She's going through some kind of rough time right now with a domestic relations case. She's trying to get custody of her kids and won't be writing anything for a while, at least until her case is resolved."

"I'm sorry to hear that. I hope it works out for her."

"Yes, I hope it does, too."

"Have you ever written a movie review?"

"No, sir."

"You can take Oliver with you," offered Nelms. "That sounds good," said Tatiana.

"Here is a list I've compiled from this year. Have you ever heard of *Ebony Parade*?"

"No."

"How about *The Fight Never Ends.*"

"What is that about?"

"Joe Louis. Maybe I should have Cub see that movie. He covered Joe Louis in Italy."

49

"That would be fine with me," agreed Tatiana. "I don't like boxing or any kind of violence. I would not want to participate in any activity like that might reflect negatively on the paper."

Nelms looked at her. Then he moved on.

"You might like this one. It is *Love in Syncopation* or *Miracle in Harlem*.

That should get you started. Sheila Guyse stars in *Miracle in Harlem*."

Chapter 14

TATIANA WALKED TO HER OFFICE. Oliver came in and closed the door. "What was that about?" he asked.

"He wants me to do movie reviews," Tatiana explained.

Cub knocked on the glass door and Tatiana motioned him to come in. "What was that about?" asked Cub.

"Movies," said Tatiana. "Our receptionist-slash-entertainment writer is going through some kind of personal trouble and he wants me to take over for a while. I volunteered both of us for the musicals. I gave the boxing movie to Cub."

"What!" complained Oliver. "Musicals? Come on."

"Yeah, musicals for you. Boxing for me!" Cub cheered. "Yes. You can do the Joe Louis movie," said Tatiana. "That's great," smiled Cub.

"Are you busy tonight?" asked Tatiana.

"If your plan is to take me to a musical then I am busy," said Oliver. "I don't do musicals. When people live their life, they don't suddenly start singing to each other. Not to mention the fact that we have tickets to the baseball game."

Tatiana smiled. "Good try. We can still make it for the first few innings of the game. You boys get to work. We have some movies—some work—to do tonight. They both start at the same time."

"Very funny," said Oliver. "See you later," waved Tatiana.

"You got lucky, Cub," mumbled Oliver as they walked out.

"Pre-dinner cocktails are at 7 p.m.," Tatiana called.

Oliver smiled.

Chapter 15

———— ⌘ ————

CUB AND ANDRE RODE TOGETHER in the newspaper's 1945 truck they used to deliver papers around the city. The men talked the entire way.

"I'm glad you got through that trial over there. What an ordeal that was. And that prosecutor, Captain Thomas. What a piece of work he was. I don't know how you made it. I don't think I could have withstood all of that," said Cub.

"Yeah," agreed Andre.

"Do you ever miss Booker?"

"Sure I do," Andre answered quietly.

"Must be terrible to have gone through that," said Cub.

"Do you ever miss Second Street Barbershop?" asked Andre, changing the subject.

"No way. There is no way that the whitemen, Lewis and Alvin would accept me now as a reporter. As a shoeshine boy I was just fine in there, as a reporter, no. If I walked in there today, they wouldn't talk to me unless I started shining shoes. It would be Shorty Miller all over again."

Andre laughed.

Cub and Andre arrived at the majestic grounds of St. Peter's Catholic Church and the new college located behind it. They were awestruck by the magnificent structures.

"So, this is it. This is where we take a grammar class?" Cub asked. "I guess it is. Somewhere around here," said Andre.

"Where did they get all that money to build this church during this Depression?" inquired Cub.

"I don't know. A Depression causes people to do great things," said Andre. "Very astute. That's one way to look at it," agreed Cub.

"Do you know this priest by the name of Sanders?"

"Who?"

"It says here on this sheet that Oliver gave me, 'Father Michael Sanders,'" read Cub.

"Father Sanders?" asked Andre. "You know him?"

"I know him," said Andre. "I thought he was a math teacher."

"What about him?" Cub queried.

"Nothing," said Andre.

Cub and Andre went into their classroom, late. The students were already in seats. Pupils registered for the class were undergraduate freshman taking a summer school course. Cub and Andre felt out of place. Andre had not even graduated from high school and was now enrolled in a college course.

Father Sanders entered the room.

Andre looked and rolled his eyes. He was sitting in a classroom with Father Sanders -the same Father Sanders that he had dreamed about with Booker disrupting the class. It was almost like Booker was in the class with him.

Father Sanders walked up to Andre and Cub. "Nice to see you, Andre."

"Father Michael Sanders."

"Cub Miller with the *Birmingham Defender*."

"And you are Andre Williams. It is nice to meet you again."

"Same here."

"Father Webster told me that the newspaper had enrolled you both in the class. I am looking forward to seeing you here. I know you are auditing the class, but I hope you can come as much as you can."

"We will," smiled Cub.

Father Webster went to the podium. "Let us pray," he said.

The students closed their eyes. Cub looked around and Andre closed his eyes and smiled. He was sitting in a classroom with Father Sanders and thought about Booker getting everyone to move their chairs up to the chalkboard the minute Father Sanders turned around.

Father Sanders ended the prayer.

"Thank you all. My name is Father Michael Sanders and I will be teaching this journalism course during the second half of the summer. I'll bet you didn't know that I was a journalist at one point in my life. I worked a few years for a paper in Duncan, Oklahoma, out of college before joining the priesthood. It was a small, but good paper, and we did some interesting stories back then. So, let me ask you: what's with the verb 'sunk'?" asked Father Sanders, standing behind the podium.

The uniformed young sophomores taking summer classes said nothing. "Tell me if this is correct." He turned to the chalkboard and began to write these sentences:

> *The economy was struggling even before the real estate market sunk.*

> *Hundreds are missing after a South Korean ferry carrying high school students sunk on its way to the resort island of Jeju.*

I got out of the car and lifted out the walker. It sunk in the snow.

Our economy sunk into a deep hole during the Hoover administration, but we're slowly digging our way out.

Apparently that simple idea never really sunk in.

Father Sanders finished writing and then turned around. "What do you say, Mr. Miller? Are these sentences correct?" asked Father Sanders to Cub.

"I say all of them are correct," answered Cub. "What do you say, Andre?" asked Father Sanders. "Sounds right to me," agreed Andre.

"Everyone agree?" asked Father Sanders.

"I don't," said Linda Beckwith, a young freckly faced sophomore on the front of the class. Her blond hair was perfectly coifed. She was smart and the perfect Catholic girl. She could be a future nun.

"I think they all should be 'sank'," said Linda.

"Anyone else agree?" asked Father Sanders. No one said a word.

"You are correct," said Father Sanders. "They should all be 'sank.'" He changed the word *sunk* to *sank* in each of the sentences:

The economy was struggling even before the real estate market sank.

Hundreds are missing after a South Korean ferry carrying high school students sank on its way to the resort island of Jeju.

I got out of the car and lifted out the walker. It sank in the snow.

Our economy sank into a deep hole during the Hoover administration, but we're slowly digging our way out.

Apparently that simple idea never really sank in.

"The word *sank* is the right choice for each of these examples," said Father Sanders. "The simple present is: *the boat sinks*. The simple past is: *the boat sank*.

The past participle is: *the boat had sunk*."

"Huh?" said Cub aloud to the class. Laughter.

"I need to go to college" Cub thought to himself.

"Let me ask you this: does a light year measure distance or time?" asked Father Sanders to the class.

"Time," replied Cub. "What about you, Andre?"

"Sounds good to me." Unsure of his answer, Andre agreed.

"A lightyear is a unit in measuring stellar distances. Specifically, it's the distance light travels in one mean solar year—about 5.88 trillion miles," explained Father Sanders. "It measures distance, not time."

"Huh!" Cub responded. Laughter.

Father Sanders turned around and looked at Cub and smiled. He didn't think his subject would provoke a reaction by anyone.

"You know, the government has been searching for Earthlike planets in our galaxy. It's just a matter of time before they locate a rocky surfaced planet that orbits a sun, allowing water to exist," said Father Sanders.

"Are we alone?" asked a student.

"I don't know," answered Father Sanders.

Linda Beckwith asked, "Will the universe end? What happens to us then?" Father Sanders looked at her and said, "See you tomorrow."

"That was complicated. I had no idea what I was going to learn today," Andre said to Cub as Cub drove them back to the newspaper.

"Next time, bring a notebook to class with a pen and paper. A reporter always carries something to write with and take notes," said Cub. "Never go anywhere without something to write or or write with."

"Yes, sir."

"When you start proofreading at night, you don't want a typo in an article. I hate that worse than anything else. After working all night on an article and then you get up the next morning and read it and there is an error on the front page, I cringe. If you can proofread the paper without a single error, then you're a hero. But if there is a single error, then you are a zero," Cub warned.

Chapter 16

ON SATURDAY, ANDRE AND LANNY went to see the Birmingham Black Barons play their opening game against the Cleveland Buckeyes. They took the bus from the downtown station to Rickwood Field. The smell of roasted peanuts and hot dogs permeated the air walked closer to the stadium.

"Wow, a lot of people out here today," said Lanny watching the fans buy lemonade and sodas as the two approached the stadium.

"Mr. Nelms said that over 12,000 would here," Andre replied.

When the Barons arrived, the crowd cheered. They even cheered for the Buckeyes as their cars arrived and their men walked to the stadium.

The grass on the field was green and the sky was blue. The lights in the outfield turned on at five-thirty. This was the signal for the Parker High School band to play the national anthem. The sky was still light but was changing color.

"This will be my first story," Andre announced. "How do you begin a story?" asked Lanny.

"Start with a lead to get the reader's attention. Answer who, what, when, where, why; things like that," said Andre.

"I don't know a thing about journalism," said Ellis.

"I try do some research for the story before starting it. My boss, Mr. Nelms says to do research and get more than one source. The Barons are part of the Negro Southern League started in the '20s. The league is a feeder for the Negro American League and Negro National League. Satchel Page played for them, said Andre.

"They say there is a young player about seventeen years old who is supposed to play for the Barons. I've heard he is good," said Lanny.

"What's his name?" asked Andre.

"Willie Mays," said Lanny.

"Mr. Nelms said that the Barons have a chance to win the pennant this year. He says they are drawing larger crowds than the white baseball teams and that some of the players are so good they are going to be signed into the white leagues," Andre replied.

"You know what that means if they do that?"

"What?" asked Andre.

"The end of the Negro Baseball Leagues," explained Lanny. "Why?"

"Television. Jackie Robinson signing in the majors. Now people don't have to come to see these games when they can watch the majors on television."

Oliver and Tatiana walked by. Andre noticed them, got out of his seat, and went down to talk to them.

"Oliver, Tatiana, I didn't know you were coming," said Andre.

"Hi, Andre. We are just here for the first few innings, then we are off to the movies. Where's Sherry?" asked Tatiana.

"At home. I'm covering the game."

"Who is that with you?" asked Tatiana. "Lanny Ellis. We served in the war together."

"Mr. Nelms is here tonight," said Oliver. "He's right up there. He always sits in the same place with Brandesha."

They looked up and saw Mr. Nelms with a bag of popcorn and Brandesha.

Brandesha noticed Andre and waived.

"Look, Mr. Nelms. There is Andre Williams with Mr. and Mrs. Smith," said Brandesha. Nelms waived back.

"Who's the guy with Andre?"

"I don't know. He came to the paper looking for Andre."

In the first inning Ed Steele, the left fielder for the Barons, hit his first homerun. As Steele landed his foot on home base and jogged to the dugout, the announcer called out: "Fans, we are stopping the game right now to announce the prizes to Ed Steele for making the first homerun of the season. Congratulations to Ed Steele. For the first home run Ed Steele is being given: two chicken dinners at Porter's Club, one chicken dinner from Brown Derby Café, a diamond studded watch, five dollars from Davenport and Hann, five dollars from Orange Bowl Drink Shop, and two dinners from Bob Red's Blue Bird Inn."

The crowd cheered after the announcement of the gifts.

As the game was playing, Andre took notes. Ellis watched and told Andre what was happening.

"You know Andre, we could do some good together," said Ellis. "Like what?" asked Andre, taking more notes.

"You might be interested in what I'm doing," said Ellis. "What exactly are you doing?" asked Andre.

"Doing a service to our nation," said Ellis.

"I thought you were going into the ministry."

"I will, when the time is right, but the time is not right," said Ellis. "With your connections with the paper, we could be a team. You supply me the names and I go after them."

"What are you talking about?" asked Andre.

"The Klan. What else?" said Ellis looking at Andre.

Then there was a hit and the crowd cheered.

"What do you mean? I know nothing of them."

"You saw what happened out at that Catholic church last weekend. You were there."

"I was there. I don't know any names. They are sneaky dirty rats who blow people up, bomb homes. They are bad, sick, and demented," said Andre.

"Exactly. They can't change. We need to string 'em up upside down and try them just like they tried our ancestors," said Ellis.

"What are you asking me to do?" wondered Andre.

"I say we take down a few of the Klan, some of the real bad ones. The real racists that can't change. We rough 'em up, figure out who they work with, and then what can they do? If they go to the sheriff or the police, they have to admit who they are part of the Klan. It is the perfect crime," said Ellis.

"The Sheriff probably already knows who they are," said Andre.

"Of course he knows, but he isn't going to do anything. If your paper names some of the prominent citizens on the front page and puts one of those hoods next to them, those people will freak out once they have been discovered," said Ellis.

"They would bomb our newspaper if we did that," said Andre. Ellis said nothing in response.

"Who do you work for?" asked Andre. "Is this why you came to see me?"

"Just think about it. We could do some good together—when you are ready," said Ellis.

"The only name I know is the one that was in the paper. The spokesman was named Eric Rainwater," said Andre.

The Barons won the game, 11 2.

After the game, Andre and Ellis were leaving. Someone set up a booth outside the entrance of the stadium with a sign that read, "Can you answer the million-dollar question?"

The lady had a scarf around her head and looked like a gypsy. She looked at Andre and asked, "Can you answer the million-dollar question?"

"Come on Andre, let's get out of here," prodded Ellis. "Would you sell your eye for one million dollars?"

"No," said Andre.

"Do you believe in Jesus Christ?"

"Yes."

"Do you believe that he died on the cross to save you from your sin?"

"Yes."

"Do you believe that you are saved by the grace of God?"

"Yes."

"Do you believe you can do or have whatever you want if you only ask, believe, and have faith?"

"Yes."

"Then you have answered the million-dollar question."

"What is the million-dollar question?" asked Andre. "You answered it. It is the secret of the universe."

She gave Andre an imitation one-million-dollar bill and a card. The card had three letters on it.

LOA.

"What is that LOA?"

"That is for you to find out now that you have answered the question."

"What was that about?" asked Ellis.

"I didn't know at first and then I realized what it was. If you answered all the questions correct, then she gave you a one-million-dollar bill and this card."

"That's a fake."

"Yes, I know."

"What is on the card?"

"It says 'LOA' on the front. Nothing on the back."

"That's garbage. You will believe anything," scoffed Ellis.

Chapter 17

LANNY AND ANDRE WENT TO a local bar and pool hall after the baseball game. "Sorry about Booker. I know he was your friend." Lanny shot at the one-ball and it bounced off the side and spun across the table, hitting three other balls.

"We grew up together," explained Andre.

"He was a good guy." Then Ellis zeroed in on his shot and hit the one-ball again. This time it nearly went in the right corner pocket.

"You hated him," recalled Andre.

"I didn't hate him. We didn't get along but I didn't hate him. I'm sorry about the trial. But it worked out in the end," said Ellis.

"That prosecutor was a piece of work. He deliberately went after me," said Andre. "Do you want to play a game?"

"Yes." Ellis racked the balls up and then shot, breaking the balls with a loud sound.

"What did he do?" asked Ellis, watching his shot knock in one ball.

"He put me on trial deliberately. He is judge here in Birmingham now."

"Bad deal. A JAG officer tried you when he had no case?" asked Ellis. "Yes. He tried me when he had no case," Andre repeated as she took a shot.

"What's his name?"

"His name was Captain John Thomas. What a name. Two inconsistent names joined together. One is the good apostle and the second is the doubting apostle."

"What are you talking about? You really have gotten into this religion thing. You need a shrink." said Ellis.

"No, I don't."

"So, this guy is now a judge in Birmingham?"

"Yes. He will get his justice someday. He might not get his justice today, but he will get his justice on judgment day."

"You need to cool down a bit there," said Ellis. "I know. It's the war."

"It will pass. But, you might be on to something.

"Like what?" asked Andre.

"Don't you see it?" asked Ellis. "If fits a pattern."

"What are you talking about?" asked Andre.

"Nothing," said Ellis.

Ellis had suspicions about Thomas. He would investigate him further. Andre had no idea that Ellis he just tipped off Andre. Was there a question about Judge Thomas's character? Why did Thomas insist on prosecuting Andre? Was it really over the shooting of Booker?

"What are you writing down?" Andre suggested.

"Nothing," said Lanny.

"You have a notepad and you took down some notes. It looks like you are the reporter."

"Just needed to make a reminder of something I thought about," said Ellis.

Andre was curious about Ellis's interest in his trial and why he would have a notepad with him. Ellis was clearly someone different than he appeared. Ellis was not there to get the gang back together. He was looking for information. "Who knows?

Maybe he's some kind of racist," suggested Ellis, slipping up. "What?" said Andre, not quite hearing what he said. The sound of the clashing pool shot and balls was too loud. "Nothing. I don't even know the guy," said Ellis.

"Let's go," said Andre. "I have to work tomorrow. I haven't done this since the war."

Walking out through the bar following Ellis, Andre thought to himself, *"Captain Thomas is a racist? Is that what he said?"* Totally dumbfounded by the accusation, Andre began to think that the allegation by Ellis made sense. Why did Captain Thomas prosecute him?

Chapter 18

"ANDRE IS THAT YOU?" ASKED Sherry.

"Yes."

"Who is with you?"

"This is Lanny Ellis. We served in the war together," Andre replied with his speech slurred. "This is my wife, Sherry."

"Nice to meet you, ma'am. I'm sorry about our condition."

"I'm glad to see that Andre has somebody to spend time with," said Sherry. "Do you need a place to sleep tonight?"

"Yes. That would be nice."

"You can use this couch." She went to get sheets and a pillow. "I will see you in the morning."

Andre and Lanny talked a while longer. Then Andre went back to bed. "Are you drunk?" asked Sherry.

"No. I'm not drunk."

"What did you two do tonight? Who is he?" asked Sherry.

"I've been doing some Voodoo down in Jackson. Do you know where the Old Testament is?" said Andre, making no sense.

"What are you talking about?" asked Sherry.

"It's nothing. Something that my Aunt Clara said to me. This was after she burned down our home."

"Andre you need help. I can't hear this now," said Sherry. She could smell Andre's breath. "You are weird. Go in and brush your teeth and take a shower. I'm not sleeping with you in that condition."

Sherry gave another blanket for Ellis to sleep on the couch. "I hope you are ok with the couch. That is all we have."

"I can sleep like a baby in a fox hole," smiled Ellis.

Sherry walked back to the bedroom. Andre was brushing his teeth. "So, who is he?"

"A guy from the army," he said. "What does he want?"

"Nothing. We did a lot of talking tonight. He's a good guy. We were in boot camp. He wants to get some of us back together again. That's all."

"I hope he's gone in the morning," said Sherry.

"He and Booker didn't get along. They hated each other."

Andre tried to kiss Sherry.

"No kiss tonight," snapped Sherry.

Andre got ready for bed. He took the card he received at the ballpark and put it on the night desk next to the bed. Sherry was asleep. He turned sideways and saw the card on the top of the desk. He turned it up and saw the letters, *LOA*.

"LOA. I wonder what that means."

He turned on his back and looked up at the ceiling. He said his prayers:

> *Our Father who art in Heaven, hallowed be your name. Thy kingdom come. Thy will be done. Give us this day our daily bread. And forgive us our trespasses, as we forgive those who trespass against us and lead us not into temptation but deliver us from evil.*
>
> *Hail Mary full of grace the Lord is with thee. Blessed are thou among women and blessed is the fruit of thy womb.*

Oh my Jesus, save us from the fires of Hell. Lead all souls to Heaven, especially those in most need of thy mercy.

Andre quickly fell asleep. He could hear a voice whispering to him:

Relax. Close your eyes and begin to breathe. Slowly and deeply. With each breath let your body relax. The ideas you are about to hear will become your own. There is no need to stay awake. The powerful affirmations you are about to hear will be absorbed by your subconscious mind even while you are asleep.

Now, relax and breathe and repeat in your mind as it is being said out loud. I will have no need. I shall not want. The Lord is My Shephard. Ask and it shall be given to you. Seek and you shall find. Knock and door will be open to you.

Everything you need in life is yours. Remove all negative thought of anyone or anything. You are successful. You know what you want. You know what to expect. You have it now. It is already present. You expect it. You have it. You feel it, believe it and it is already here.

From now on each day of your life is filled with abundance. You have to see it, believe it, and have faith that it is there. The universe is around you. You are part of the universe. The universe wants you to have abundance. You are creating your own vortex . . .

Andre dreamed. Later, he woke up and went outside in his bathrobe. Sherry was still asleep. He walked into the front room where Ellis was asleep on the couch. Andre opened the door to the apartment, walked out to the walkway, and stood by the metal railing. His apartment was on the second floor. The moon was large and bright. He could see the surface so clearly. Why didn't the moon turn like the Earth? He was impressed by the stars and the Milky Way. Then Andre decided to sit down on the stairs. While sitting down, his foot slipped and he slid down the stairway, knocking his head against the concrete and metal stairway.

Darkness.

Chapter 19

———— ❧ ————

AT WORK THE NEXT DAY, all Andre could think about was the card he picked up after the baseball game. His head hurt from his fall the night before.

"Is this a dream?" he thought.

He came home late that night. Sherry was making dinner in the kitchen and there was a wonderful smell of spaghetti permeating the room. He kissed Sherry from behind as she was standing in front of the stove, making the sauce with meatballs.

"You surprised me! I wasn't expecting that," she said. "So how was work today?"

"I like the new job."

Sherry was surprised by Andre's statement. "I'm glad to hear that."

"I attended a journalism class today. Some proofreading later," he said.

"They want you to start writing?" asked Sherry. "Yes."

"That is great! See my sweetheart, everything is working out for you and us."

"I know it is, but what if I'm not able to do my job?" he asked.

"Is anyone saying you aren't doing your job?" she asked. "No."

"What is the problem? Your job sounds fun to me. You could be working in a factory. I think you have one of the best jobs around. It has so much potential and you don't have a college degree," said Sherry.

"What if I mess up?" he worried.

"How can you mess up proofreading? That is nothing compared to what you did in the army. You have everything going for you right now."

"I still have the army on my mind. I have thoughts and still think about them and then I have strange dreams. They don't make sense."

"You will get over it."

"That is what war does to you. It never leaves you. You experience it every day. I feel like I came back yesterday," explained Andre.

Sherry paused and looked at him. "You are not the same person sometimes. Remember how you came to my porch with the guitar and said all those things to me before going off to the army? You sang. You made up songs. No one makes up songs like you do. They are nothing like what I hear. You joined the army and didn't even tell me! Just think of what you have now. Stop worrying about the past."

"I will try. I will, I promise."

Andre had periods of withdrawn behavior at family events and Sherry's mother, Phyllis, noticed his behavior one Sunday.

"What's wrong with him?" she asked, carrying plates into the kitchen. "He said nothing at lunch."

"I don't know what it is or how to deal with it. It has to do with the war."

"Thank goodness. I thought it might be something between the two of you. If he doesn't talk about it, he won't get better," said Phyllis.

Andre sat back on the couch. On the coffee table was an old copy of Literary Digest magazine that he had brought home from the newspaper. He opened it up and saw an article about Napoleon Bonaparte's novella *Clisson and Eugenie,* written by him before he was a famous general. He thought nothing further about it.

Chapter 20

ONE DAY AT THE OFFICE Oliver was visited by Roy Otwell, one of the black journalists that Oliver and Tatiana had met when they covered the war in Europe. Otwell was on assignment in Europe during the war for a white newspaper. He lived a life of privilege and knew many famous people. Oliver and Tatiana last saw him at their long dinner evening at the La Coupole Restaurant in Paris during the war.

"Oliver, you have a guest," said Brandesha through the speakerphone while putting on her lipstick and looking at her face in a compact mirror. The sound of her voice bounced off the wall, penetrating the room like a freight train.

"Who is it?" asked Oliver.

"He says his name is . . . what is your name?" asked Brandesha. "Roy Otwell."

Brandesha yelled into the speaker box: "He says his name is Roy Otwell.

Do you know him?"

Everyone in the office could hear Brandesha's screech as her voice carried like a missile attack in the newsroom. Otwell was embarrassed to hear his name projected with such a loud volume. His visit became the business of everyone. He looked around and saw others at their desks, looking at him.

"Roy Otwell? Send him in," said Oliver.

"Roy, what are you doing here? Been a long time."

"Traveling through. Just checking in on you. I didn't realize I would be welcomed with such a reception."

"That's it, just checking on me? It is nice to see you!" said Oliver. They hugged each other.

"Same here. I heard about your lady taking a job here. I left the *Amsterdam News* and went to the *Statesman*. Her father sent me here to check on her. Old man Phillips was upset about that. Looks like you really caused a stir up there when she decided not to come back to his paper," explained Otwell.

"I hoped that wouldn't be a problem."

"Yeah, he wanted her back. You must be doing something right. And her working for old man Nelms. That *really* got under Phillips skin. The story goes that he wanted you to meet her and then you would move to Chicago. Instead you stole her away from him."

"She came back here after the war. Nelms offered her a job on the spot. So, what are you working on?" inquired Oliver.

"I'm doing a story on the 5th Platoon, the integrated unit that served together in Germany near the end of the war and follow up stories on how they readjusted after the war."

"Those sound like great stories."

"So how is Tatiana? Does she really like it here?"

"Why not ask her yourself?" suggested Oliver.

"Hi Roy," said Tatiana, coming over to give him a hug.

"Tatiana, you look so great. Are you happy here and with this old man?"

"Sure am," she smiled.

"Let's go to dinner tonight. I have to work. Meet me at the Tower Club tonight," said Oliver.

Oliver punched his speakerphone switch and Brandesha answered. "What do you want?" she said.

Oliver grimaced.

"Would you get me a reservation for three at the Tower Club tonight?"

"You want me to do what?" she squawked.

Oliver could feel her words hit his coat.

"A reservation at the Tower Club."

"You want me to get a reservation at the Tower Club? Is that what you want?" asked Brandesha.

"Yes, for three people," repeated Oliver. "For how many people?" asked Brandesha. "Three people."

"For three people?"

"Yes, Brandesha, for three people."

"Ok, ok. You don't have to get snippy about it. I will get you a reservation for three people," retorted Brandesha.

"Whew," sighed Oliver, looking at Roy. Roy gave an awkward smile.

Chapter 21

AT DINNER, TATIANA LOOKED GRAND in a low-cut silver dress and heels. Oliver was dressed in a dark brown double-breasted suit and tie with a white shirt and cuff links.

"You look great, Tatiana!" admired Otwell. "Oliver, what are you writing about?

"I'm writing a book about the war," he replied. "What kind of book?"

"The experiences of the black journalists covering the war."

"Which theater?"

"The European theater."

"I might do a book someday. I've been thinking of writing a biography on Robert Abbott," said Otwell.

"Did you know him?" asked Tatiana.

"I didn't. He died in 1940. There is a lot of material there."

"My father knew him," said Tatiana.

"So, what do you know about the black journalists covering World War II?" asked Otwell.

"Let's see. The black weekly newspapers knew they couldn't compete with the dailies for hard news coverage of the war. They settled for features that came by mail and cables for the occasional blockbuster stories," said Oliver.

"Some for me. I could only cable a really good story," agreed Otwell.

"There were probably ten black journalists in North Africa," added Oliver. "What did you cover in Africa?" asked Otwell.

"The 92d Infantry and the 332nd Fighter Squadron mostly. Those were the only black fighting units," said Oliver. "I was also in Italy prior to France. Even while in France I covered the 92nd Infantry Division in Massa, Italy and through the Po Valley from November 1944 through the end of April 1945. Two soldiers were submitted for medal of honors, John R. Fox and Vernon Baker."

"Where did the other journalists go?" asked Otwell.

"Frank Bolden of the *Courier* went to Iran and the China-Burma-India Theater for ANP. Fletcher Martin of the *Louisville Defender* covered the South Pacific for NNPA. There were others who were divided up between the Pacific Theater and Northern Europe, and a few covering Burma, Russia, and Alaska."

"Oliver was the first accredited black journalist," boasted Tatiana. Oliver smiled at her.

"My paper promoted me as the first accredited black journalist to cover the war. I went to North Africa. I later found out that I was mistaken. The first black journalist accredited by the American government was Edgar Rouceau of the *Pittsburgh Courier*, who headed for Europe in 1942. The Russians accredited Homer Smith in 1939. Many black papers carried his dispatches from the Eastern Front long before Pearl Harbor."

"Anyone else?" asked Otwell.

"Vincent Tubbs of the *Baltimore Afro-American* was the first black journalist in the Pacific. He arrived in March 1943. Both the *Courier* and the *Afro-American* sent seven correspondents. The *Chicago Defender* sent four journalists and the *Norfolk Journal Guide* sent three," said Oliver. "And the *Birmingham Defender* sent two."

"You forgot me, Oliver," Tatiana broke in.

"I could never forget you," smiled Oliver.

"As I recall you were not working for the *Birmingham Defender* during the war.

Tatiana laughed. "I was supposed to go to France but I got sick in London. They wouldn't send me during the invasion of Normandy."

"That is a lot of information. Where did you two meet?" asked Otwell. "I picked him up in a taxi in London," laughed Tatiana.

"Cub and I got in a taxi and there was Tatiana," explained Oliver. "I knew her before that. I met her father at a conference in Washington on November the eighth, nineteen forty-one, one day after the day that will live in infamy. I will never forget. That was planned months before Pearl Harbor.

"I've heard the story of Mr. Phillips showing you Tatiana's picture at the conference," said Otwell.

"I didn't pick up on what he was doing," said Oliver.

"He doesn't pick up on anything," Tatiana inserted. "I kept clippings of his articles for two years."

"What does it take to get your attention?" aked an incredulous Roy. "A hit in the face, I guess!" said Oliver.

They all laughed.

"The real reason for the conference in 1941 was to get the black newspapers to be cheerleaders. The editors promised nothing. They knew that Hoover was afraid of the black press reporting on racial conditions of the black soldiers and whether they were being treated as labor instead of fighters.

The army was the one to make the greatest strides in integration. By 1941 there were 100,000 blacks in the army. One year later there were five times that many," said Oliver.

Otwell was impressed.

"I want to include the black contribution to all of the wars. Blacks fought in all of the nation's wars, beginning with the colonial militia engagements. Some 5,000 served as scattered individuals and in segregated units during the American Revolution. Several thousand blacks saw duty in the War of 1812, and 180,000 served in the Union Army during the Civil War," said Oliver.

"You've been doing your research," said Roy.

"Four regiments of blacks battled the Indians on the Western Plains and then the Spaniards in Cuba. In World War I, about three-fourths of the blacks served in labor units. The 93rd Infantry Division, attached to the French had a great record as did the regiments of the 92nd Division."

"Oliver, you need to slow down. This is too much information," interrupted Tatiana.

"Someone get him a drink to put the flames out over here," said Otwell. "Waiter, two scotches. Do you want a scotch Tatiana?"

"No. Just a white wine for me," said Tatiana.

"As I was saying," continued Oliver. "The Tuskegee Airmen in North Africa began flying combat missions in 1943. They were the glamour units of the war through Sicily and Italy. The Navy was not integrated and had Jim Crow, as I saw it. The black sailors were mess men, although there were a few token ships with predominantly black crews. The Marines ended its white policy in 1942. The 761st Tank

Battalion came through France to Germany and the Buffalo Soldiers drove through Italy."

Otwell smiled. "You *do* need to write a book."

"I *do* need to write a book," agreed Oliver. "We *all* need to write a book," said Tatiana.

The three laughed and the waiter brought their drinks. "Cheers," said Otwell. They drank their scotch and wine. Dinner was served.

"Remember that trial you covered back in Paris? The one where one of the soldiers was accused of shooting his friend?" asked Otwell.

"Yes, I remember it," said Oliver.

"The soldier works for the paper now," said Tatiana. "He does?"

"Yes, do you want to meet him?" asked Oliver.

"Yes, if possible. I'm doing some research on some of the soldiers and I'd like to do some follow up on them about their adjustment back home. How did he get to St. Raphael?"

"Through *Operation Dragoon*," explained Oliver.

Otwell reached into his pocket and pulled out a notepad. "I have a few names in my notes. I was wondering if you know these guys. Do you know the names Adkerson, Hawkins, Trimmer, Saller, Kirkpatrick? There are others."

"No," said Oliver and Tatiana.

"These were white soldiers who fought with an integrated unit in Germany near the end of the war. I thought this might make an interesting story. I understand that Private Williams was in that unit after the court-martial," said Otwell.

"You can meet him. He works as a proofreader and a stacker, and is going to cover a few things—sports, I think.

We're sending him to school so we can get him started writing," added Oliver.

"When I was working on the story I stumbled across a private who was in that unit and was familiar with the shooting of Private Thompson. Did the name Private Ellis come out at the trial?"

"No. Never heard of him," said Oliver, shaking his head.

"I interviewed a soldier by that name who said that he knew Private Thompson. He reported that Williams and Thompson weren't the only ones out there. Ellis said that Williams and Thompson were temporarily lost overnight and that was when the shooting occurred. He said no one interviewed him during the court-martial."

"I hadn't heard that," Oliver said. "We do know what happened, though. Private Williams accidentally shot Private Thompson. End of story. He has already been through hell and back and he is just getting started here. He doesn't need to be reliving that scenario again," said Oliver.

"I don't know where this will lead, but I got the impression from Private Ellis that there was more to this story than what came out at the trial."

"More to it? What more can there be to it?" asked Oliver.

"I don't know yet, but this Private Ellis knows what went on out there regarding the shooting of Booker Thompson," said Otwell.

"I think this case was investigated thoroughly. When I was in France I went to St. Raphael and interviewed a priest and a nun, and they told me how Williams collapsed there. They didn't say anything about anyone else."

"Did you investigate the platoon that Williams was with?"

"No," said Oliver. "I just reported the trial," explained Oliver.

"So, what else brings you to Birmingham, Roy?" asked Tatiana, changing the subject.

"I guess you heard about the Klan showing up at the Catholic church grounds?" asked Otwell.

"Yes. I'm working those stories with Cub. Cub was on duty the night that the Klan raided the girls camp at the Catholic Church," said Oliver.

"It was front page news," added Tatiana.

"Did you hear about the Klan in Georgia?" asked Roy.

"Yes, some kind of attack on some football coach? What was that about?" asked Oliver.

"Not sure. Did you read some of the white newspapers the next few days?"

"No. A white guy went missing after that. A prominent citizen. A lawyer in Montgomery," said Roy, pulling an article from a folder he had in his carrying case. "Take a look at this," he said, showing the article to Oliver and Tatiana.

Oliver read out loud:

> MONTGOMERY. *A prominent lawyer is missing and efforts to locate him have been unsuccessful. He is well-known in the community. Anyone with information should contact the Montgomery police.*

"So, a white guy goes missing. What does that have to do with what you are working on?" asked Oliver.

"I have some sources. I was tipped off about the Klan's gathering in Georgia. I went to investigate. There are guys on the inside of the Klan working to bring it down," said Roy.

"Good," said Tatiana.

"What kind of sources?" asked Oliver. "You know."

"No, I don't," said Oliver. "The Deep State," said Otwell.

"That sounds weird," said Tatiana. "What is it?" asked Oliver.

"Every prior administration leaves embedded agents to make sure the new administration doesn't do something crazy. If they do, they alert the national security agencies to make sure no president or his aides ever go rogue. They leak to the press. The press is the final check on the government. They are the unknown soldiers whose job is to preserve the nation as they see fit," said Roy. "They provide tips for FBI investigations. So far no reporter has ever been prosecuted for using leaked classified information."

"I see," nodded Oliver. "I learn something new."

"You didn't know that?" asked a puzzled Otwell. "No," said Oliver in a concerned tone.

"You mean that really exists? I thought that was some crazy fantasy of Republican right wing extreme groups," said Tatiana.

Otwell looked at her.

"No. It's real. What I learned is that the Klan throws a rally and then one or two of their guys go 'missing' after that. Then they are quietly returned. No questions asked. No charges are filed. The white guys can't go to the police to complain because they would have to admit they are members of the Klan," reported Otwell.

"It's a crime that they can't do anything about. That's sounds good," said Oliver.

"Yes. These guys are taken some place and interrogated and then the government pieces together who they work with an eventually the feds figure out a way to prosecute them because

86

the white juries always let them off. This is a guess. But I believe the FBI is quietly taking some of these guys down and getting them to confess. It has to be done. We have to know who these people are and rid the society of them. They are just rats," said Otwell.

"You think the FBI is kidnapping them?" asked Oliver.

"I think they are hiring private citizens to do that, ex-military, people who understand combat and then using "snitch money" that can't be traced back to the FBI. Then the FBI can deny all responsibility," suggested Otwell.

"The FBI would do that?" asked Tatiana.

"Who else could it be? You know its not the local sheriff. When you can't take them down legally, you have to do some thing to get them to bring down the kingpin," explained Roy.

"Why do they need to do that?" asked Tatiana.

"The federal government can't engage in illegal searches or seizures and can't use the evidence from those arrests in federal court. They call it the 'fruit of the poisonous tree.' The state governments can do that because the Fourth Amendment does not apply to actions by state government agents. So, the feds wink and look to the state government or private citizens to bring them evidence of a crime. As long as they have nothing to do with the illegal search, the evidence is admissible in a federal court."

"But if they are privately recruiting people to do that, wouldn't that be attributable to the federal government?" asked Tatiana.

"Yes, if they prove there is a connection. Right now, they are just figuring out who the enemy is," said Otwell.

"I guess that is one way to fight a war. The Civil War never ended," mused Oliver.

"The only way to break the Klan is to figure out who they are and bring them down. These people are so stupid they go to rallies in their cars and the FBI records the license plate information on their cars. Then someone picks off a few of them. Each time they have a rally, one or two of their guys go missing," said Otwell.

"Sounds like there need to be a few more rallies so we can eliminate all of them," said Oliver.

They laughed.

"What could possibly be running through the mind of someone who dresses up in a Klan outfit and mask and then raids a girls' camp, just so they can separate some white nuns from the Negro girls?" asked Tatiana.

"Who knows what goes on in the mind of the Klan member, if there even is a mind up there," said Oliver.

"That's the problem. There is a mind up there. Some of those guys are sophisticated citizens acting out like that. These white supremacists are scary," said Otwell.

"That whole hood thing really makes my skin crawl. That should be illegal," shuddered Tatiana.

"It should be," said Otwell. "Let me get back to the story I'm working on. I was in Georgia working on a way to unmask the Klan when I figured out something about that Ellis guy—the same Private Ellis who was with Private Williams. It looks like he found another war. After fighting the Nazis, he is now fighting the Klan."

"Are you saying that you think it is this man named Ellis who is doing the kidnapping?" Tatiana thought out loud.

"He might be. I put together that he was in Georgia where the last Klan rally was there. Now he is here in Birmingham after this Klan raid," said Roy.

"Sounds like you are spying on the federal government," said Oliver. "Good spying, it sounds like," said Tatiana.

"I don't really think he is FBI. I think he was recruited by the FBI or some government agency like DOJ to figure out who the Klan is so they can take them down," said Roy.

"Let him do his job," said Oliver.

There was a pause in the conversation. The music from the band was playing low in the background and some started to get up to dance. The band consisted of a saxophonist, pianist, drummer, and a bass fiddle.

"So, what else are you two covering?" asked Roy.

"I'm going to cover some entertainment news and Oliver is going to cover the '48 campaign," said Tatiana.

"That's great," said Roy.

"Would you like to dance?" asked Oliver, offering his hand. "Yes," Tatiana accepted.

He took her hand and they walked to the dance floor with the others. The music flowed through the room and they could see the entire downtown Birmingham from the top of the Tower Club through the glass windows.

"So, what do you make of his stories? Do you believe what he was telling us?"

"Not a word of it," said Oliver.

"His talk about there being a 'Deep State' in the media makes my skin crawl. I think that's the scariest thing I've ever heard in a while."

"Very strange," said Oliver.

"So why did he come here, Oliver?" asked Tatiana.

"I think he came to check up on you for my father-in-law, Andrew Phillips," said Oliver.

"No, he didn't," Tatiana shook her head. "My father would not do that." Oliver smiled. "Of course, he wouldn't."

Then the pianist began to sing:

There's a grand old maid across the sea...

Oliver kissed Tatiana as the pianist sang the last line.

Chapter 22

⎯⎯⎯ ❦ ⎯⎯⎯

THE NEXT MORNING, ROY DECIDED to visit Andre at the paper before heading back to Chicago.

"Andre, how do you like working for the newspaper?" asked Roy. "Fine."

"You recovered since active duty?"

"Yes."

"It's good to have a job. Do you like journalism?"

"I do. I have a lot to learn. Mr. Nelms has me attending a journalism class."

"You think you'll like being a journalist?"

"Yes. Mr. Nelms has me covering the Black Barons."

"That is quite an assignment. They have a lot of games this year," said Roy. "Seventy-six games. Maybe one road trip. I cover the home games," said

Andre. "Where do you work, Mr. Otwell?"

"The *African American Statesman*," said Roy.

"Really?" said Andre. "Did you know Robert Abbott?"

"No. I know he started the *Chicago Defender.*"

"You mean like Mr. Nelms?" asked Andre.

"Yes, like Mr. Nelms. How did you know his name?"

"Mr. Nelms had me research his background."

"Abbott died in 1940," said Roy. "Everyone in journalism knows about Robert Abbott."

Andre pulled out a notepad and pencil from his back pocket and began to take notes.

"Hey, that's good you are taking notes. Robert Abbott was probably the single greatest force in Negro journalism."

"Where was he born?" aske Andre.

"I think Savannah, Georgia," said Roy.

"Did he go to school?"

"Let me think. The Institute in Virginia. He was influenced by Booker T. Washington. There were few trained egro journalists back then. He recruited personnel from porters to barbers to bartenders."

"That's how Shorty got his job."

"Who?"

"Shorty Miller. Mr. Miller. He used to shine shoes in Mountain Springs before working for the *Birmingham Defender.* I met him when I was fourteen and working weekends at a store downtown. He moved to Birmingham and Mr. Nelms offered him a job."

"That's how it's done," said Otwell. "Abbott influenced the migration of the Negro to the North. Nearly one million migrated north to Chicago. The *Chicago Defender* had a lot to do with it. Abbott was poor but he became one of the first Negro millionaires in the United States. His salary was so high that the IRS made him cut it back. His skills were not in the business side. His strenght was journalism."

Andre scribbled down notes of the conversation. "How are you doing after the war?" asked Roy. "I got married," said Andre.

"That's great!"

"Thank you."

"I've been talking around. Some soldiers have trouble adjusting after the war," said Roy.

"Do you know a soldier by the name of Private Lanny Ellis?"

"I served with him. Do you know him?"

"I interviewed him. He mentioned your name. That's how why I came to see you."

"He mentioned me?"

"Yes. He said some nice things about you," added Roy.

"We were in boot camp together and later in Germany in one of the integrated units," said Andre.

"That's why I'm here. I want to write a book about the integrated fighting units in Germany. What was it like fighting with the white man?" explained Roy.

"I was with the unit right before the war ended."

"I want to know more about that," said Roy. "How do you know Mr. Smith?" asked Andre.

"We met in Paris. I met his new wife at the same time."

"I will be tracking down some of the white soldiers in the unit to hear what they have to say. Did you know privates Adkerson, Hawkins, Trimmer, or Saller?"

"We were in a platoon together. Our leader was Lt. Kirkpatrick. We took out a German battery along the way. I joined them after my cour-martial. I was with the black soldiers who were trained in France."

They talked for a while, then Otwell changed the subject. "I'm curious— how did you and Private Thompson get separated in St. Raphael?" asked Roy. "I don't remember. It was just for a short period. We would have found the

unit after a white but when Booker was shot we had to stay there."

"Were there others in the woods?"

"I think so. I thought there were Geramns. We could hear fighting," said Andre.

"Private Ellis says that he and others in the platoon went looking for you and Thompson."

"They did?"

"He said that they found Thompson but not you."

"I didn't know that."

"How well did you know Private Ellis?" asked Roy.

"We were in boot camp together and served later on in Africa. When you are in a war you get to know people," said Andre.

"Ellis said that you and Thompson were diverted temporarily under fire until they could get back to you."

"We were trying to find out way back to the platoon," said Andre. "According to Ellis, they saw Germans in the woods and Ellis fired his weapon at them just like you did."

"I didn't know that. I thought we were by ourselves."

"This fellow Ellis was cautious when I talked with him. He said that he and a few others who found Private Thompson were in Paris but were later transferred back out to the field. He said that they were interviewed by a JAG officer about your case."

"My attorney probably knew that. Ellis and Booker never got along. They fought a lot. Drill Sgt. Robert Mills had them box during boot camp to get it out of their system. We made bets on who would win."

"Who won?" asked Roy.

"It was a tie. I don't think either one of them beat the other. It was a tough fight."

"I hope they got it out of their system," said Roy.

"There was other stuff. Verbal sparring, abusive jokes. Guys can be brutal to each other. They don't mean anything by it. We needed the Army to straighten us out. In the end, we looked after each other."

"Did Ellis testify at your trial?"

"No. My lawyer, Captain Jesse Weinstein did his best. He lost the trial but won the appeal. He's in Montgomery now. I heard that the prosecutor is now a judge in Birmingham."

"When was the last time you saw Ellis?" asked Roy. "The other day. We've been hanging out."

"He came to see you? "Yes," said Andre.

"Are you still in the service?"

"I was released from active duty and have two years of reserve commitment."

"Do you think he knows what went on out there? I mean about the shooting of Booker Thompson?"

"I don't know."

"He was jumpy when I talked to him. What was he doing in Birmingham?" asked Roy.

"He said he came to see me."

"Thank you. I guess I'd better go," said Roy.

Chapter 23

TAKING ANDRE'S TIP FROM THE newspaper, Ellis and his partner Coggins were staking out Eric Rainwater, the spokesman for the Klan. Ellis planned to take down the Klan spokesman to send a message to the Klan.

"He owns a dime store downtown," said Ellis. "How can make any money there?" asked Coggins.

"Not a thing," said Ellis. "I know when he leaves. He parks in the back. No one will be around."

They parked and waited for over thirty minutes. At exactly 5:30 pm, Rainwater came out of the building and walked to his car.

Ellis exited the car and approached him. "Mr. Rainwater?" said Ellis.

"Yes?"

"I would like to . . . hit you," said Ellis, punching him in the stomach.

Coggins drove over and Ellis threw him in the back seat.

"What are you doing?" asked Coggins. "We were supposed to interrogate him; just ask some questions. Nothing else."

"Stop around the corner. I'm going to hide him in the trunk," said Ellis. "My God. What have we done?" said Coggins.

"Drive out of town," said Ellis.

After loading Rainwater in the trunk they drove out of the town and entered wooded area in the countryside. Coggins veered the car off the main road and on to an access road. They stopped. Ellis got out and pulled a groggy Rainwater out of the trunk.

"Do you know who I am?" he asked.

"No idea," said Rainwater. Ellis took out a knife and stabbed him in the stomach.

"What did you do that for?" asked Coggins.

"He doesn't deserve to live. He is a pathetic loser and always has been. I wouldn't let this guy clean my toilet," said Ellis.

"We aren't supposed to kill anyone. Just find out who the Klan is and then send that information to our contact. I can't do this."

"Yes, you can. You have no idea what their people did to my people. They will blow you up in minute. We have to kill them before they kill us. We have to vet these people. It has to be extreme to send a message. I should have taken him to a tree and hung him, just like he did my ancestors. That's what I'm going to do with my next one."

"No, you are not. What are we going to do with him?"

Ellis dragged his body off the road and into the woods. There were plenty of leaves to cover him up.

Coggins got back in the car and Ellis followed. They said nothing. Coggins didn't know if he would turn Ellis in or not. He would think about it. *One less Klan member was a good thing*, he thought. *But taking a life.* He had to think. "He wasn't even the head of the Klan and not much of a believer either," said Ellis.

"How do you know?" asked Coggins.

"He was the spokesman. They don't make the head of the Klan as the spokesman. No. The head is someone bigger.

Someone you would never expect. The least likely guy. Someone so obvious that no one would have a clue and wouldn't believe you if you figured it out. They would deny, deny, and deny. I will figure out who the snake is and I will take off that snake's head. I will hang him from a tree for everyone to see. His feet will not touch the ground. Justice will be done."

"You're crazy," said Coggins.

Chapter 24

BETTY JONES WAS THE NEW Adult Director at the First African Baptist Church where Uncle George was the minister. She wanted to stimulate the church and produce a play to raise money for new choir robes.

When she heard about Betty's plans, Sherry thought that if Andre participated in the play it might take his mind off of the war. Sherry visited the Birmingham Public Library and searched many books and plays looking for ideas. She found nothing. She went back to the apartment and got herself a glass of water and sat on the couch. She noticed a copy *Literary Digest* sitting on the coffee table. She looked at the cover and there was the article about a book written by Napoleon Bonaparte.

"So that's what he was reading," she thought to herself. She read the article about *Clisson and Eugenie*, a tragedy in which General Clisson, husband to Eugenie, goes to war and sends an aide back to take care of his wife—who then falls in love with the aide. In a state of remorse, the general leads his men into battle to die after learning that his wife had betrayed him.

"This story would make a wonderful play. I'll bet Mary will do this with me," she said to herself. But her friend Mary wasn't into music or plays. She wasn't a thespian like Sherry and was not into music like Andre. She was like Booker. She was strong, self-reliant, and independent and did not need add a play as part of her life.

Chapter 25

———— ⬥ ————

ONE DAY AFTER CLASS, ANDRE went to see Sister Camille. Cub did not attend that day and Andre had the truck to himself.

"Hi, Sister Camille," said Andre. "I meant to come earlier."

"It is so nice to see you again," greeted Sister Camille. "How is Sherry?"

"She's fine. I couldn't believe the Klan came out here and harassed the girl's camp. That was bad."

"I can't believe the evil that some men will do," said Sister Camille. "How are things going at the newspaper?"

"Fine," he said.

"Did you come all this way just to see me?" asked Sister Camille. "Just to see you. I wanted to see how you were doing."

"Everything is fine with you now?"

"I have a good job and I'm looking forward to writing and getting my name in print. I like that part of the job. But since I came back from the war and got the job and got married, things are not like they should be. I'm having these moments of feeling quite upset. Like I'm angry at something. I've started to take a drink here and there. Sherry is getting pretty upset over it and told me to go talk to someone. Then she said to come up to talk to you about it."

"That was good of her to mention me but it sounds like you need to talk with a professional. Doesn't the army have something for post-war veterans?"

100

"I should. I came home over a year ago and this is still with me."

"I think all you need to do right now is pray. Close your eyes and let your mind wander and think about what is on your mind. Try to remove all negativity from your thoughts and then pray. Take a mental picture of your heart's desire and place it with your will, and then imagine that you already have what you have asked for and be thankful for it and thankful to Jesus. He will supply all our needs," consoled Sister Camille.

"I will do that," nodded Andre.

Chapter 26

ANDRE SAID HIS GOOD-BYES TO Sister Camille and returned to the paper. Later, Nelms called Andre and Cub into the office.

"How are the journalism classes?"

"Good," said Andre.

"Pretty good, Boss," fibbed Cub.

"You are learning something?" asked Nelms. "I am," said Andre.

"I am too," said Cub, not looking directly at Nelms.

"Just so it's not a waste of time. How is it going down in the plant, Andre?"

"I'm learning my way around. I've been proofreading a lot. I stack, then I go on some of the deliveries. Then I help with the press," reported Andre. "There's a lot to running a newspaper," said Nelms. "Andre, to understand the media you have to know who the players are."

"Yes, sir."

"I meant to give you some more names. Let me know if you know who they are. Cub, you can jump in here," said Nelms.

"Okay."

"Okay, go do your research and get back with me."

"Booker T. Washington."

"Of course, sir. Everyone knows who Booker T. Washington is," Andre said.

"Jim Folsom."

"Isn't he the governor?"

"Yes," said Nelms.

"*Joe Louis.*"

"Sure. Everybody knows who Joe Louis is."

"I covered him in Italy," said Cub.

"*Satchel Paige.*"

"Yes, sir."

"*Mahala Ashley Dickerson.*"

"No, sir."

"*Ralph Abernathy.*"

"No, sir."

"*Nat King Cole.*"

"Yes, sir."

"*Alice Coachman.*"

"No, sir."

"*Helen Keller,*"

"Yes, sir. I've heard of her."

"*Hugo Black.*"

"No, sir. Is he a black man?"

"No, he's not. He's on the United States Supreme Court and from Alabama. Look him up. Look for a man named Ray Sprigle. He's a white reporter who won a Pulitzer exposing Black's membership in the Klan."

"Yes sir," said Andre.

"Check on these names: *Silas H. Hunt.* He was the first African American admitted to the University of Arkansas after Reconstruction. I just read that the University of Arkansas announced that it was going to admit black students to the law school. Another student attending at Howard University named *Clifford Davis* is trying to transfer to the University of Arkansas but they are wanting him to pay full tuition. So far

Davis hasn't budged. The school had a press conference announcing that if Davis shows up then he will be admitted. I guess the law school dean there, a guy named Leflar, figured out he couldn't charge Davis full tuition in advance if the other white students weren't having to pay in advance."

"Yes, sir. Mr. Nelms," said Andre.

"Now, I have it on good authority from the NAACP that Sprigle is in the South posing as a black man. He plans to write a book about what it's like living in the land of Jim Crow with its oppression, cruelty, and discrimination. Can you imagine that, a white man posing in the south like a black man."

"Is he using his own name?" asked Cub.

"No. He's going by the name of James Rayel Crawford from Pittsburgh," said Nelms.

"How did you find out?" asked Cub.

"Friends. I have my sources. Let me see. Where was I? Do you know what the 13th, 14th, and 15th Amendments are?"

"They are rights under the Constitution," answered Andre.

"Yes, we have those rights but there is this idiotic racist law called the Boswell Amendment that is denying the right to vote to African Americans. The Civil War was fought over eighty years ago and we are still fighting it," said Nelms.

"I don't understand. If voting is granted by the Constitution, how can the states deny that right?" asked Andre.

"They come up with all kinds of ways, tricky state laws to remove voters from the rolls. I met Dr. Lawrence Nixon and his wife Tandy back in the 30s."

"Who are they?" asked Andre.

"A black doctor from El Paso, Texas, who couldn't vote in the Texas Democratic Party primary because the courts did not consider it to be an election. He sued and the case went up to the U.S. Supreme Court. The Court held that the Texas Democratic party could not exclude blacks from voting."

"What happened after that?" asked Cub.

"The Texas Democratic party changed the law so they could exclude anyone from voting in primaries to get around the Supreme Court decision," said Nelms.

"Did that fix things?" asked Andre.

"No. He sued again and the case went to the Supreme Court a second time. This time the court held that the Democratic Party couldn't exclude Negroes from voting in the primary," explained Nelms. "They finally eliminated the white primary in a different case. I follow the justices. The second *Nixon* case was written by Justice Benjamin Cardozo, who was appointed by . . .?"

"Roosevelt?" guessed Andre. "Hoover," said Nelms.

"You really know the law, Mr. Nelms," said Andre. "You sound like a lawyer."

"When you cover the courts, you learn a few things. Cub, I want you to cover the courthouse beat," said Nelms.

"Sure will, Boss," said Cub. Nelms said nothing.

"Alabama is not abiding by the rule of law," said Nelms. "Under this Boswell Amendment, every prospective voter must read and interpret any section of all of the United States Constitution to the satisfaction of a local registrar, and the opinion and decision of the registrar is final. It doesn't mention race. They could exclude a white person if they wanted. In most counties in Alabama, a large number of Negroes have never yet been able to interpret any portion of

105

the Constitution to the satisfaction of the registrar—even those who can read or write."

"We have the right to vote, but the local authorities set up a law that is designed to stop the black vote without mentioning race? Cute," said Cub, shaking his head.

"Here is how it works. Month by month all year, Negro registration climbs. Then in midsummer, with Democratic primary election day looming in September all over the state, county commissions proceed to 'purge' the list of registered voters. Notices are sent out to thousands of voters, black and white, notifying them to appear at the courthouse based on irregularities, they say. Upon showing up, the voter is giving a 'hearing.' That is enough to scare off most Negro citizens. Most don't even appear. Those who do show up get shafted, and the whites go back on the list whether they appear or not."

"I didn't know this was going on," said Andre.

"Now you have homework. Go figure this out in your spare time. Go up to the research room and you will find all kinds of information. Ask one of the librarians up there to show you how to research. We will meet again when you figure out who they are."

"Thank you, sir."

"Are you covering the Barons this weekend?"

"Yes sir!"

"Ok. See you there," said Nelms.

"Maybe I can do an article about all of those people," offered Andre.

"Do that. If it is good, then I will print it," said Nelms. "You never know.

You might interview the president someday." Andre gleamed.

Chapter 27

THAT NIGHT AT HOME, ANDRE lay on his bed to rest and meditate as Sister Camille suggested earlier in the day. His mind wandered and as dark pulsations of light filled his mind, he fell asleep. Thrust back into time he began his first presidential interview.

"Mr. President, the young reporter is here to see you," said the White House protocol officer. Andre entered the Oval Office. The new U.S. President offered his hand to him. The 5' 8" president was strong, muscular and with obvious stamina. He wore impeccable clothes and had a commanding presence with self-confidence and determination.

President Andrew Johnson was stiff and formal. His hair was combed back and he was slightly balding on both sides at the front. His black and gray-sprinkled hair fell halfway over his ears and curled in a direction back to the front, a popular style during that time.

They shook hands.

"You are the young reporter from the *Birmingham Defender*. Your editor, Mr. Nelms, said he was sending you to interview me," said President Andrew Johnson.

"Yes sir, Mr. President. This is a great honor."

"What would you like to ask me?" offered the president.

"What is it like being president?" asked Andre, with his notebook and pencil ready to take notes.

"Take a seat," said the president, pointing to a chair. Johnson walked around to take a seat behind his desk. "You should know the story. I was always a campaigner. I could wear out any opponent. Opposition only drove me further towards my goals. Compromise is alien to me and defeat makes me fight harder. I never give up," said the sixty-year-old president.

"During the first 100 days, what has surprised you the most about this office? Enchanted you the most from serving in this office? Humbled you the most? And troubled you the most?" asked Andre.

"Now, let me write this down," the president said, pulling out a White House feathered pen and dipping it in ink. "I've got . . ."

"Surprised, troubled ..."

"I've got—what was the first one?"

"Surprised."

"Surprised," repeated the president. "Troubled," said Andre. "Troubled," repeated the president. "Enchanted."

"Enchanted, nice," said the president. "And humbled."

"And what was the last one, humbled?"

"Humbled, Thank you, sir."

They talked and talked.

Chapter 28

⚯

ANDRE'S DREAM CHANGED. HE SAW a young man on the street. It was Andre, in overalls. There was a gang of white boys on the street kicking a can. One had black hair and deep dark eyes. He was a wild youngster.

"Hey, you," said the black-haired boy to Andre. "Come with us."

"Ok," Andre said. "Who are you?"

"We are the Jesse Johnson's boys," one said. "Let's play ball," one said.

"We can fish," said another.

"Can I come with you?" asked Andre. "We've played with mulattos before."

The other boys, including his brother William, were running and kicking a can down the dirty street.

"What's your name?" asked Andre. "Andrew Johnson," he said.

"Where do you go to school?" Andre began his interview.

"I don't go to school," he said. The other boys continued to laugh and kick the can down the street while the young Andrew Johnson broke off from the others to talk with the curious black boy.

"Come with me," he said.

Andre and Andrew, followed by the other boys, went to a home known to be owned by a Mrs. Wells, who had two daughters in the home.

"A lady named Mrs. Wells lives here with her daughters. I don't like her," Andrew said. "But I like her daughters."

It was a Saturday night and the young Andrew Johnson began to pelt her home with pieces of wood. His brother and the others began to take part. They kept throwing wood sticks at the window to see if the girls would come out. Andre watched.

A lady came out. "Who is that out there? Is that Andrew Johnson? You are nothing but a ringleader of a gang of worthless white trash. I'm going to sue you back to your shanty house. Your Uncle Jesse is going to hear about this," she said, yelling off of the front porch.

Andrew ran off. "Come on," he said to Andre. "I know a shortcut."

Andrew took Andre along the path of a wealthy landowner by the name of John Devereux in Raleigh, North Carolina. Only minutes after leaving Mrs. Wells' home, he was now facing Mr. Devereux, who saw the boys and sent his coachman with a whip after them.

"We gotta go," Andrew said to Andre. They ran while the coachman chased them with a whip in his hand, flying amidst the green farmland.

Then they walked by a stream running into a pond in the wooded area. Andrew picked up a rock and threw it across the stream, watching it skip along the water. Andre did the same. The other boys had run off in different directions. The two fifteen-year-old boys walked along the stream. The sun was almost down and the orange sky was coming through the clouds. They watched the sunset.

"Who was your mother?" asked Andre.

"Polly," he said. "She is 'Polly the Weaver'," he said. "What does that mean?"

"She is a seamstress."

"Who is your father?" asked Andre.

"He was Jacob Johnson. He died when I was three years old. I never knew him."

"My father died when I was six," said Andre. "My whole family died when I was six." Andrew said nothing.

"Yeah, I was told that there was a newspaper publisher named Thomas Henderson who was having a fishing party on Hunter's Mill Pond. He took some people out on a canoe and when the boat got near the pier, it rocked and the passengers fell out. My father jumped in to save them. He died sometime after that ringing the town bell. They said that he never recovered from the accident."

"That's too bad," said Andre.

"We can stay at our place tonight."

Andre followed him.

The next morning Andrew and his brother William were packing to leave.

They heard that Mrs. Wells had placed an ad in the morning's newspaper. "Where are you going?" asked Andre.

"Carthage," said Andrew. "It is about fifty miles away. I can find work as a journeyman tailor."

The newspaper ad read:

> TEN DOLLAR REWARD. Ran away from the Subscriber, on the night of the 15th instant, two apprentice boys, legally bound, named WILLIAM AND ANDREW JOHNSON.

The former is of dark complexion, black hair, eyes, and habits. They are much of a height, about 5 feet 4 or 5 inches. The latter is very fleshy, freckled face, light hair, and fair complexion. They went off with two other apprentices advertised by Messrs. Wm & Chas. Fowler. When they went away they were well clad in blue cloth coats, light colored homespun coats, and new hats. The maker's name in the crown of the hats is Theodore Clark. I will pay the above reward to any person who will deliver said apprentices to me in Raleigh, or I will give the above reward for Andrew Johnson alone. All persons are cautioned against harboring or employing said apprentices, on pain of being prosecuted.

JAMES J. SELBY, *Tailor*

Raleigh, N.C. June 24, 1824

Chapter 29

━━━━━━━━ ✺ ━━━━━━━━

ANDRE WAS BACK IN THE oval office.

"You know when I was your age I played with everyone. I was poor and white but we still felt like we were better than blacks, slave and free. It was racism. It was practiced. We disliked non-whites. I don't know where it came from, but it was there. We were racists. We didn't know why we were like that. We just were. I was poor but I always felt that I should be rich and that I *would* be rich someday. I had no schooling but I had a thirst for knowledge and I always read anything I could. That was how to get educated. We selfeducated ourselves. I was always determined to be something greater than I was. I had no idea I would end up being the president," said the 17th President of the United States.

Andre was amazed as the sitting president openly acknowledged his racism and white supremacy. He was raised that way and didn't know why. He followed a Civil War where more than 600,000 soldiers died and a president who was killed over ending slavery and preventing the South from seceding from the Union. How strange that Abraham Lincoln's legacy was succeeded by someone who would oppose his reforms.

"How did you get into politics?" asked Andre.

"I became mayor of Greeneville, Tennessee. I eliminated the requirement that someone own property to hold office or to vote. Then, as you should know, I was in the legislature in the House and Senate and then governor of Tennessee, and on to the U.S. Senate. After that, I was the military governor of Tennessee."

"Why were you chosen to be vice president?"

"Lincoln wanted to move to the middle and Hamlin brought nothing to the ticket. The anti-slavery voters in Maine knew they had to vote for Lincoln. Lincoln wanted a war Democrat who could appeal to the border state people.

There weren't many. I was the only southern governor who chose not to secede and supported the Union."

"That took a great act of courage," said Andre. "Thank you."

"So you, as a Democrat from the pro-slavery party, were the vice president to a Republican president who was anti-slavery," pondered Andre. "That is amazing."

"We are elected separately, not as a team. But, we formed the National Union Party so we could attract Republicans and Democrats."

"Did you know him before you ran for office with him?"

"Not really. I was military governor of Tennessee and reported to him but we didn't have much contact. We had a few things in common. We were both from border states. We both were poor and self-taught. Men at the tailor shop gave me books. I taught myself how to read."

"Who is your family?"

"You don't know?" asked the president.

"I do. I just wanted you to talk about them."

"I married Eliza McCardle when she was sixteen years old. We were married by the Justice of the Peace. She was the daughter of a shoemaker. Martha, Charles, Mary, and Andrew

Jr. are our children. Martha serves as the White House official hostess since Eliza stays mostly in Greenville."

"What was it like, rising to become president?"

"I could out-travel and out-speak anyone. I never lost the energy and drive. Over time, my tailor shop expanded and I ended up selling it but keeping the shop. I owned a farm and some real estate ventures and became wealthy in my own right. I even had a few slaves. Dolly was one. She was being sold at a slave auction and she came up to me and asked that I buy her. She liked the clothes I was wearing. I spent $500 on her. I bought her half-brother Sam after that." Andre was taken aback at how casually the president spoke about slavery. "Yes, Dolly had a son William Johnson, he called himself. He had a sister as well. I used to put both of them on my knees and play and laugh with them and rub their heads together."

"Mr. President, I don't understand why you are opposed the 14th Amendment after the country fought a war and adopted the 13th Amendment. The Republicans may want you out of office because you are impeding the progress made by President Lincoln," said Andre. Andre was nervous. He knew that Andrew Johnson would be impeached but the president had no clue what was coming. Maybe he could persuade him to change and to change history.

"I might be from the South, but I don't believe a state has a right to secede. I'm still a Unionist. I believe that all of the laws are to be applied to all of the states with absolute equality. The authority of the federal government over the states was due to having to deal with a hostile force, and that authority ended with the end of the war. I believe that this is a country of white men and, by God, as long as I am president, it shall be a country for white men," said the president.

Andre was sickened and stunned by his response.

"Mr. President, do you really believe that?" asked Andre.

The president didn't respond. How could he have said that so soon after the end of the Civil War? Racism was institutionalized and Andrew Johnson was a man with deep-seated racism. Lincoln's successor was about to impede the progress being made by Congress. The White House was occupied by a racist. He could understand why the Republicans moved to impeach Johnson: he was standing in the way of the 14th and 15th Amendments.

"What is the best thing you have ever done?"

"I assume you are here today, October 18, 1867, because today is the day that the United States takes possession of Alaska. I signed the treaty on May 28. They called it Seward's Folly. Can you imagine purchasing country like that for $7.2 million dollars? That is less than two cents an acre."

"That sounds like a gold mine," said Andre.

"What is the worst thing you have done?" asked Andre. "I'm sure you know what it is," said the president.

"I don't, Mr. President," said Andre.

"It was my speech after I was sworn in. It was the worst day of my life," he said. "I poured three tumblers of whiskey before giving my inauguration speech. I walked out and gave a thoroughly humiliating and degrading speech.

I ranted, screamed, and whispered. I called on each cabinet secretary by name until I couldn't name any more. I had to leave town for weeks to recuperate. It was a terrific black mark for me. It put me in a terrible light."

"I'm sorry," said Andre.

"It was not uncommon for people to say, 'Oh well, Andy's been drinking again.'"

Chapter 30

———— ❧ ————

"JESUS CHRIST," ANDRE SAID TO himself after conducting his first presidential interview albeit in his dreams. "How could that president have been so racist? One minute he is holding black kids on his knee, and then he is talking about how this was a white man's country."

"What are you talking about?" said Sherry, waking up and rolling over. "What is this about, my sweetheart?"

"Sherry, you wouldn't believe it. I dreamed that ... no, you don't want to hear this."

"Where is my coffee? I need some coffee." Andre brought her coffee.

"That's good. Now, I need to tell you something before you go to work," said Sherry.

"What?"

"With what you have been going through after the war, Mary wants both of us to be in a play at the church. That will get your mind off of the war. I might even sing a song."

"You don't sing. Why would you sing a song?" asked a surprised Andre.

"Yes. I can if I work on it. It is a play we are writing from a book written by Napoleon Bonaparte. We are going to add music to it, too."

"Is this real? A play from Napoleon Bonaparte and you are turning it into a musical? I look forward to that. Why should I be in it?"

"To get your mind off the war and whatever you are thinking about, the trial, that prosecutor, that judge, whatever. It will be good for both of us. Just don't laugh at me up there," said Sherry.

"I won't," said Andre.

"The play is about two women and one soldier. You are the soldier."

"What is the name of the play?"

"*Clisson and Eugenie*. It's a love story."

"Did Napoleon Bonaparte really write a book?"

"He did. You are going to play Clisson."

"We will see."

"And another thing—your Aunt Clara called yesterday. She wants you to come visit her."

"What about?" asked Andre.

"She didn't say; something about some papers that she received. She wants you to look at them. I told her you would go see her."

Chapter 31

———— ✦ ————

THE NEXT MORNING ANDRE WENT to see Mr. Nelms. "Come in, Andre. How is the article coming?"

"I'M RESEARCHING ALL OF THE people you gave me."

"I always tell Cub, have a good lead. Do you have a good lead?"

"Not yet, Mr. Nelms. But I know who Robert Abbott is."

"Tell me about him."

"He established the *Chicago Defender.*"

"What do you know about him?"

"He was born in Savannah, Georgia, and educated at the Hampton Institute in Virginia. After studying the printing trade, in 1905 he started a weekly newspaper with twenty-five cents."

"He was imaginative," said Nelms.

"He created something from nothing," contributed Oliver, walking in the room with Tatiana.

"I was just about to call you. Where is Cub?"

"He's coming," said Oliver.

"His paper is the competitor of my father's," said Tatiana.

"Andre is doing some research for me. What else did you find out?" ask Nelms. "His paper appealed to the Negro because of the headlines, satire in the cartoons. It appealed to the masses," said Andre. "Who did that?" asked Cub, walking in the room.

"Robert Abbott. You should know him," said Nelms.

"My friend Roy Otwell worked for his paper. He came to see me and said he might do a book about him someday," said Oliver.

"I met Mr. Otwell. We talked about Robert Abbott," said Andre."He said he had the genius of Booker T. Washington."

"Is that how you found your information? Through an interview?"

"Yes," said Andre nervously.

"You didn't do any research on him?" asked Nelms. "Not yet."

"You need more than one source. Add more to that and start writing," said Nelms.

Chapter 32

THAT EVENING SHERRY CAME HOME late from rehearsal. "I wondered where you were," said Andre.

"We were at play practice. I can't believe it. Our script is so lousy. They will laugh us off the stage."

"Good luck with it," said Andre. "I volunteered one of your songs."

"What?"

"We decided to use one of your songs in the play."

"I guess you can do that," said Andre. "What song did you pick?"

"Something about, 'If that's the way you feel.'"

"Not that one. Booker said that was the worst song he had ever heard."

"He never liked music," said Sherry.

"I made that song up the night at the recruiter's office after joining the officer. Booker took my guitar and said, "get serious."

"You took the guitar off the porch that night? I wondered what happened to it ... I liked the middle part of that that song," said Sherry.

"It's different. You sing one line of the song and then you go up until you have reached an entire octave—like you are stair-stepping up the piano," said an enthusiastic Andre.

"You feel better about yourself now?" said Sherry. "I did, for a moment."

Chapter 33

"NOW, HERE ARE THE SCRIPTS," said Betty. The cast consisted of the choir members, church youth, and young adults. "The play is set in 1795 and is about a soldier and his wife. Everyone knows who Napoleon Bonaparte is, don't they?"

"Waterloo" said John.

"Yes, but this is not about Waterloo. He wrote this book before he was famous. It's called *Clisson and Eugenie*. It has been turned into a short play. We are going to add music. The choir will help. Thank you for coming today."

"Here, here," said one choir member, taking a bow. "A musical?" said John.

"Yes. This is a good play. Let me read this summary about it. It says here it is about a soldier named Clisson who was attracted to war and dreams of going into battle. He wants to rise high in the military ranks and has a lot of success, but envy and petty jealousies and his growing reputation often stifle genius and bring false accusations against him. His cool head and moderation in the face of these attempts to sully his name serve only to increase the number of his enemies."

"This is a terrible play," said Mary. "It doesn't sound like a play that a church would put on."

"We will update it. Reverend George says we can do what we want with it. We present it at a special performance at St. Peters for a girls' summer camp group on Halloween night. We have several months to get it ready. Sherry has songs that she is going to include in the play. One was written by Andre."

"Good grief," said John.

"I've heard his songs. They are weird," said Mary. Everyone laughed.

"Sherry will play Eugenie," said Barbara. "Who will play Clisson?" asked John.

"I haven't decided yet," said Betty. "There is a character named Amelie."

"Who will play her?" asked Mary. "You are," said Betty.

"I don't want to be in this play," said Mary as she got up. "Don't leave Mary, you will like this play," said Betty.

"Mary, It won't be the same without you," said Sherry.

While the cast was talking, Betty took John into a room by himself. "Andre can't act," Betty said to John. "Sherry wants him to play Clisson to get his mind off the war. He served in World War II and we are to feel sorry for him because he claims he was mistreated — or something like that. She said he served in the war and needs to get his mind off it and the play will help him. She says music was what he once liked and now he doesn't sing or play his guitar anymore. She says she wants him to get out his quote—depression—unquote, from the war. It must be some kind of male thing."

"He has a job at the newspaper. What's the big deal?" asked John.

"Just let him take this role. We know you would be better in the lead. I will go out there and say he will play the part better. We both know he will be terrible. You congratulate him. If we don't give him the part he will quit and we don't have enough males to be in the play."

"The lead role going to someone who can't act. If that's what you want, then ok. I still would have been better in the role," said John.

"I know you would have. It's a stupid play anyway. Who would have thought of putting on a play of Napoleon Bonaparte and putting it to music? Sherry is going to make a fool of herself and him. We just let it happen."

"The music—it's like something I've never heard before. Totally different from the music of the 1940's. Napoleon Bonaparte will come back from the grave if he sees how his play is being tortured like this," said Betty.

"Yes. He met his Waterloo," said John. They laughed.

"John, you play the part of Beville. He steals the wife of the lead character," said Betty.

"I'm good with that," said John.

Sherry was in the hall listening to every word. How hurtful this will be to Andre, she thought. How could Betty do this? How petty. But Sherry had a p[lan and she walked in on them.

"I thought I heard you," said Sherry innocently.

"Yes, we were just talking about how much we love the play and the music, and how both you and Andre will do a great job in it. I'm so glad you picked this play," said Betty.

"I can't wait to see both of you in it," said John.

"I can't either," said Sherry with a smirk. "I love the music in it." John and Betty looked at each other. Sherry said nothing.

127

Chapter 34

———— ❧ ————

"ANY NEWS OUT THERE?" ASKED Nelms during a morning meeting.

"The police reports show a man was found murdered outside of town. I recognize the name. He was Klan. He was the Klan spokesman," reported Cub. "The report didn't say he was Klan."

"One less Klansman.Good," said Nelms. "What do you have Oliver?"

"Nothing."

"Here's an interesting story about Alabama's Justice on the Supreme Court."

"What is it?" asked Oliver.

"Seems like the Justice approved of an order solicited by Abe Fortas that prevents a federal district court from investigating voter fraud and irregularities in the 1948 Democratic primary in Texas," said Nelms.

"What election?" asked Cub.

"The primary race between Coke Stevenson and Lyndon Johnson," said Nelms.

"What does that have to do with us?" asked Oliver.

"Voter fraud. Find out what it is about," said Nelms.

"Hugo Black is a changed man," said Oliver.

"He disavowed the Klan and regretted his membership. He is proof that people change. By bringing up his past, we changed him," said Nelms.

Chapter 35

THAT NIGHT, ANDRE WAS PROUD that he had the personal attention of Nelms.

"You look happy," said Sherry.

"Mr. Nelms called me to his office to research a famous man."

"Who is it?" asked Sherry.

"Robert Abbott."

"Who is he?"

"He started the *Chicago Defender*, a newspaper that was responsible for the black migration from the South to Chicago."

"That is great! I'm glad you are feeling better. I will make something for dinner."

Sherry served her delicious spaghetti. Boiled spaghetti pasta, tomato sauce with ground beef and spices. It was cheap, easy, and fast.

"Andre, I have news for you," said Sherry. "What is it?"

"You have the lead in the play as Clisson."

"How can I do that? I can hardly do my job."

"That's not true. You are doing great at your job. The play will take your mind off the war. You can focus on something else," said Sherry.

"You sound like Sister Camille."

"I'm no Sister Camille. I have no idea how those women can wear the habit, but all power to them," said Sherry.

"You know I can't act. I will be the worst actor up there," sighed Andre.

"I have an idea," she said. "What is it?" asked Andre.

"Have you noticed that when you watch a foreign play, that since you can't tell what they are saying, you can't tell if they are good actors?

"Yes. What are you saying?" asked Andre.

"Betty and John want us to look like fools on stage. They don't like the play. They are going along with it so we end up looking stupid up there."

"How do you know?"

"I overhead them."

Andre said nothing.

So, I have an idea."

"What is it?" asked Andre.

"This story of Napoleon's was written in French, right?"

"I guess it was," said Andre.

"We do some of it in French."

"I didn't think of that," said Andre.

"Betty wanted John to play Clisson. So Betty is giving you the part so she can prove that John would have played it better. That's what I overheard."

"What if we quit the play?"

"No. I want to outsmart them. We practice the play in English during rehearsal but speak in French on the night of the play. When an audience hears a foreign language, they can't tell if the acting is bad."

"I don't know if I can memorize my lines in English and in French. What about Mary?" asked Andre.

"She will go along with it."

"So the crowd comes to a play thinking that they will watch a show in English, and then they hear it in French and the entire cast won't know until the play is over? That could be a disaster."

"No one would think our acting is bad. Even that song that you made up—no one will think it is bad because they will hear it in French."

"We can't do the entire play in French—you just sing that one song in French."

"Okay," said Sherry.

"This is a coup or we will all die in battle."

"Yes, that is how it is at the church. All these petty jealousies come up," said Sherry.

"You don't see any of that stuff at the St. Peter's. Those people worship and then leave. They go to Mass and pray, get their communion, go to Confession, and then they are done for another week. The priest says a short homily. No one gets blasted from the pulpit by a preacher telling us how we are going to hell," said Andre.

"George doesn't scream like that," Sherry insisted.

"He came up with the off the wall sermon at our *chocolate pudding wedding*," recalled Andre.

"No one gives a sermon at a wedding. I wanted him to talk about good things and then he came up with that. I will never forget that," said Sherry.

"I don't know where he came up with that but now I can't forget it. He was saying that we should be childlike instead of childish. No one remembers what anyone says at a wedding. I will never get that out of my mind," said Andre.

"You're funny," smiled Sherry.

"I will do the play," Andre relented.

"I have a confession to make. Mary didn't ask me to be in the play. I had to drag her in the play kicking and screaming. She's like Booker. She hates music."

That night, Andre kissed Sherry before going to bed. "Bon nuit," he said.

"Look at you!" she cooed, kissing him back.

Chapter 36

"WHERE ARE YOU HEADED?" CUB asked Andre.

"To class. Aren't you coming?" said Andre.

"I forgot. Take notes for me. By the way, Nelms wants to see you. He told me to cover the voter fraud story in Texas involving the Senate race between Lyndon Johnson and Coke Stevenson," said Cub.

"What about it?" asked Andre.

"I will handle that story. He said for you to look up Hugo Black," said Cub. "Mr. Nelms told me to do that yesterday and to look up a man named Ray

Sprigle," asked Andre.

"Black used to be a U.S. Senator from Alabama. Roosevelt appointed him to the Supreme Court in 1937. That's all I know," said Cub.

"I will check the library after the class," said Andre. "Say hi to Father Webster," said Cub.

Andre went to St. Peter's for the journalism class. During the class, he pondered why Lanny Ellis appeared in his life. Now it made sense. Otwell interviewed Ellis and now Ellis wanted to see him. What was Ellis up to?

In the library Andre perused the books, looking for information on the United States Supreme Court. He ran across a section devoted to the United States Presidents. There was the book he checked out about Andrew Johnson. He looked at the back at the card. There was his name, Andre

Williams. The date was October 10, 1941. People would think that he was crazy is they knew that he had interviewed Andrew Johnson in his dreams. In dreams anything is possible, he thought.

Andre found a book about the United States Supreme Court. Hugo Hugo Lafayette Black was born in 1886.

"Appointed in 1937. He's been up there eleven years," said Andre to himself.

He read further. Black was a senator from Alabama from 1927 to 1937.

"A U.S. senator from Alabama. That's why Mr. Nelms had me look him up. Black is from Alabama."

Black was nominated to the Supreme Court by President Franklin D. Roosevelt and confirmed by a vote of 63 to 16. He was the first of nine Roosevelt nominees to the Court. Six Democratic senators and ten Republican senators voted against him.

"Black is a staunch supporter of liberal policies and civil liberties. He advocated a textualist reading of the United States Constitution." said Andre, reading from the book.

Black successfully defended E.R. Stephenson in a sensational trial for the murder of a Catholic priest, Father James E. Coyle. Then he read that Black was a member of the Ku Klux Klan and exposed by Ray Sprigle of the *Pittsburgh Post-Gazette,* who won the Pulitzer Prize for his series of articles revealing Black's past with the Klan.

"That's why he asked me to look his name up. Black was involved with the Klan and a reporter discovered it. He's teaching me how reporters investigate."

Andre left the library and went to find Sister Camille at the old home. He walked through the fields to see her.

"Hi Andre, I saw you walking from a distance. What have you been doing? Are you enjoying school?" asked Sister Camille.

"Yes. I was in the library doing some research."

"Do you like your journalism class?"

"Yes. I like Father Sander's class."

"He was a journalist before he became a priest."

"A friend of mine from the army came to see me at the paper," said Andre. "An army buddy? That's great," said Sister Camille.

"I had a great time with him. I had too much to drink. Then I figured out later that he a reason to see me. He said he was going into the ministry."

"The priesthood? That is great. Good for him."

"I don't think he meant the priesthood. He's not like that, Sister Camille. There is another reason. There is always a motive behind everything he does."

"After a while you figure out who are positive relationships and who are negative relationships."

"I'm learning. It seems like the ones I think are positive turn out to be negative. The ones I think are negative turn out to be positive. How do you figure out who is a positive and who is negative?" asked Andre.

"Are you talking about one person?" asked Sister Camille.

"Probably. In the war, I was prosecuted by a guy I believe was a racist. I hate him. I can't understand where those people come from, so I try to see if I can understand them."

"I'm sure you weren't prosecuted by someone who was a racist. You have to forgive."

"Okay."

"You were talking about negative relationships? Negative relationships bring out the negative aspects of you. Positive relationships bring out your positive aspects. You should avoid negative things and negative people. They are easy to pick out. They bring up your flaws, pick at you. They try to control you. All they talk about is themselves. They think what they talk about is important and what you talk about is not important. They constantly bring up the past. They never really forgive or forget. They are always wanting you to do something for them. You get very little in return. Many times, people don't even realize that the person they think is positive is really negative."

"That is a lot to remember, Sister Camille. Have you had some problems with people?" asked Andre.

"No."

"You've never had a negative relationship?" asked Andre.

"Of course, but I find something positive in it. I'm told that if you can find something positive in any situation, then you can rise to a high state of intelligence. I admit that it is hard for me to think something positive when I think of those criminals who raided the girls' camp. You know what went on out here. But I realize that even rats need to live." Then she stopped. "Oh, maybe rats don't need to live. Oh, I shouldn't have said that."

"You are right. They should all be dead."

Chapter 37

————— ⌖ —————

"CONGRATULATIONS ON GETTING THE PART of Clisson," said John to Andre at rehearsal after work.

"Thank you," said Andre. "You have the part of Berville. How do you like that?"

"I like it. He gets the girl in the end," smiled John. "Who cares?" said Andre smiling back.

Betty was on the stage with Mary and Sherry, showing them where they should enter the stage.

"Cast, in the first part of the play Andre, playing Clisson, meets Eugenie and Amelie. He is at first drawn to Amelie instead of Eugenie. It says here that he is drawn to Amelie by her fresh face and beautiful eyes. So Mary, since you are playing Amelie, try to lure Clisson," said Betty.

"I can do that," said Mary batting her eyes.

"Now lights, camera, action," announced Betty, singing the word *action*. "We don't have a camera," said John.

"I know that," said Betty. "Can't you tell when I'm kidding? Now, Lights, No Camera, and Action!"

ENTER CLISSON, EUGENIE AND AMELIE:

Andre was holding his script.

CLISSON: *May I escort both of you to your country home? I would like to see you sometime.*

"Andre, exit stage left. For everyone—that is house stage right. Got it?" clarified Betty.

"Yes," said Andre as he exited stage left.

"Sherry, as Eugenie, look at Clisson as he leaves," directed Betty. "Mary, you are Amelie here and you are to be upset with Eugenie."

AMELIE TO EUGENIE: *You know you must learn to hide your feelings when you are displeased with a man.*

"Cut," said Betty. "Very good. Very good indeed. In fact, wonderful."

Betty walked up to Mary and said, "Amelie, the script says you are '*to upbraid*' Eugenie because Eugenie is displeased by the approach of Clisson."

"How do I upbraid her?" asked Mary. "Give her a scolding look," said Betty. "I can do that," said Mary.

The cast laughed and Andre smiled.

"At this point Clisson likes Amelie, but he leaves her and is attracted to Eugenie. So Andre, you have to show some attraction to Eugenie," said Betty.

"I can do that," Andre nodded. Laughter again.

"Sherry, you are to remain quiet. You want him to be attracted to you without giving him a sign. You want him to feel like he wants something he can't have. You know how that is. It is a typical male thing—they want what they can't have. We can't have that, can we?" said Betty.

"NO WAY!" said all the women in the cast and choir. "WAY TO GO! YOU GO GIRL!" said Mary.

John laughed. The other men did not.

"Now, where was I?" said Betty with a dramatic flair. "Yes, Sherry, you are to be noticeably displeased with Clisson.

There are no lines here for you but do something with your face to show that you don't like him."

"You already told me that," said Sherry.

"Yes, I did. Ok, where are we? I've lost my place. I must be dying. Oh, God help me, I must be dying," said Betty, acting as if she was in a Shakespearean tragedy.

"You are not dying," said Mary.

"Ok. Ok. Where am I? Let me get my composure," said a flustered Betty.

The cast looked at her, saying nothing.

"Now, let's go to scene two. This is where Amelie wants Eugenie to go to the spa."

The cast looked at her. No one said anything.

Then Mary piped up. "A spa? They had a spa back in the 1800s?"

"Yes, the people publicly bathed in the 1800s. I can't imagine anyone going to the spa in 1948 and bathing with a man. That's disgusting," said Betty.

This time the entire cast laughed, except for John.

"Now, lights, camera, and *action*," said Betty. Betty sang the word *action*

and looked at John. She whispered, "I know. We don't have a camera."

> **AMELIE:** *Eugenie, can you come to the spa with me today?*
>
> **EUGENIE:** *I can't go.*
>
> **AMELIE:** *Don't make me plead my case with you.*
>
> **EUGENIE:** *I must ask you then, are you wanting to the spa for you, for me … or for the gentleman?*

AMELIE: *We were invited by the gentleman. I can't go.*

EUGENIE: *You were invited by the gentleman?*
AMELIE: *We were both invited by the gentleman.*
EUGENIE: *But it is you that must go.*

"Cut. Very good. Very good indeed. In fact, wonderful. Wonderful indeed.

I think I'm going to cry," sniffled Betty. "I thought we stunk," said Mary.

Some in the cast laughed.

"Tomorrow we rehearse scene three. That is where Amelie meets Clisson and they talk for hours. Amelie is to come back and convince Eugenie to come to the spa the next day. Eugenie doesn't know whether to hate Clisson or to be impressed by him. Learn your lines," said Betty.

"That's one weird play," said Andre to Sherry on the way home. "And what's with the director, Betty? I thought she was going to freak out on stage up there. I thought I was a bad actor. I don't think this is a good play. Something is not right about this whole thing. I can feel it."

"Can't you read her? She is telling us that we are wonderful when she is probably thinking we are terrible. But I'm on to her. Nothing is going to happen with this play. We will make it great, despite her. Just wait and see.

"We are going to thrill everyone on Halloween," said Sherry.

"Scare them on Halloween is more like it," said Andre.

Chapter 38

"SISTER, I HAD A DREAM that I was in the White House." Said Andre.

"The White House? Did you see Mr. Truman?"

"No. I saw Andrew Johnson."

"President Andrew Johnson? The President after President Lincoln?" exclaimed Sister Camille. "The only president to be impeached? Why wasn't it Mr. Lincoln or Mr. Roosevelt? Why Mr. Johnson?"

"I don't know."

"Did you read something about him? Your mind does that to clear things," suggested Sister Camille.

"I read book about him a few years ago."

"About this dream," continued Sister Camille. "Your mind recalls what you think about. Your thoughts are like electronic vibrations sent into the universe. The universe brings to you what you think about. That is how you connect with God. God is energy and broken down to the tiniest parts of the universe we are all energy. God is within us. We are made in the image of God. Be careful what you think or ask for because the universe responds to what you ask for. Your mind is the most powerful tool on the planet."

"It's that simple?" asked Andre. "You just think about it and then it comes?"

"You have to want it, believe it, and have the feeling that the wish is already fulfilled."

"I see, we work for what turns out to be reality and what we don't receive is just a dream," said Andre.

"That is quite right."

"I told you how I wanted to understand how racists think? The next thing, I'm interviewing the President of the United States who was a racist."

"Your mind is taking you to whatever you think about," said Sister Camille. "Is it ok to have a dream interviewing a racist president? I mean, who dreams that kind of a dream?" asked Andre.

"It's harmless fun. You are a journalist and you are conducting an interview of President Andrew Johnson. You read a book him and it is logical that you would dream of interviewing him. It was not real because there is no record of Andre Williams interviewing President Johnson."

"What were you saying about God and the universe?"

"The Scriptures explain in simple terms how the universe works. A nuclear physicist can figure out how the universe works by reading the Bible."

"I see," nodded Andre. "Life is nothing but a stage and there is no difference between a reality and a dream?" Andre pondered.

"Dreams are not reality but there are dreams that can be reality. For the universe to work, you have to have faith, belief, works, and an emotional feeling as if you already have received what you are asking for. All you need to do is decide you already have it, believe you have it, expect it, have gratitude, and give thanks to God. Then it comes to you when you take steps to work for it," said Sister Camille.

"This sounds like witchcraft," said Andre.

"You make me laugh," smiled Sister Camille. "Everything was imagined at some point in time. We are living a life of imagination. Take that new device that they call the television. How do you think they brought those images to that screen? One day everyone will have one in their home. They imagined it and created it."

"What is life about?" he wondered.

"Life is about creation and change. God created the Heavens and Earth. We create as well. We manifest something from nothing. It is the nature of life to solidify into form and to find our true purpose and why we were placed on this earth," explained Sister Camille.

"That is deep," sighed Andre. "But what are you creating by being a nun?"

"I think I can make St. Peter's a place well known across the world. What if we could broadcast our message to everyone? What if people could hear and see what we do here with one of the new televison sets? That would really be imaginative," mused Sister Camille.

"Yes. I predict that St. Peters will be broadcast over the entire world."

"Do you study any famous people?" asked Andre.

"Why yes. I do. I've been fascinated with a French priest by the name of Paul Couturier," said Sister Camille.

"Who is he?"

"He was born in the 1880s in Lyon and lived in Algeria. He was influenced to become a priest in the Society of Saint Irenaeus. He became interested in reconciling the Catholic Church with the Orthodox Church after helping thousands of Russian refugees who fled to Lyon after the Russian Revolution."

"What did he do?"

"He helped find food and shelter for them and tried to understand the great division in the church. Instead of trying to convert them to the Roman Catholic church, he came up with a concept of ecumenism where we are drawn closer to Christ even though we are separated. We are all at different points at the bottom of the pyramid and then come together at the top," said Sister Camille.

"That is interesting," said Andre.

"It is a way to forge common ground with those who are different," said Sister Camille.

"Do you have dreams like the one I had?" asked Andre.

"Once I had this dream and it was in the future—it was 2075 or something like that. This entire facility had a television ministry that reached the entire globe, and it started right here at our old chapel. The world saw Mass every morning. I dreamed that the Pope had a great reconciliation conference in Rome. The Protestants ended their reformation and rejoined the Catholic Church. They added the six books of the Old Testament back into their Bibles."

"Really?" exclaimed Andre. "That would be a big deal. It sounds revolutionary."

"There were other changes. Priests could marry. St. Peter was married, so why do priests have to be celibate? The Pope made peace with the Orthodox Church and with the Muslims. All of the mosques taken over by the Muslims hundreds of years ago were given back and are now shared by all the religions. Now there are Catholic Churches in Saudi Arabia—even in Mecca. No longer do the Muslims call us "infidels" and want to kill us. In fact, the Pope celebrated Mass at a mosque in Mecca and Muslims use our churches when there are no mosques. Not only is religion practiced freely in the world, it is practiced freely within the same churches."

"That's how it's done in the army. One hour there was a Protestant service and the next was a Catholic service using the same chapel. You really do think big," said Andre.

"That's what they always say. If you are going to dream, then dream big," said Sister Camille.

Sister Camille had a great imagination and she could always make the greatest challenges seem so simple. Maybe she was responsible for his imagination and was the reason he began to dream all of his dreams.

Chapter 39

ANDRE TOOK A BUS TO Mountain Springs to visit Aunt Clara. After walking through downtown and reminiscing about his time there, he walked to Aunt Clara's home. He and Booker played at her home. He hadn't seen her since she tried to pin the burning of his family's home on him after the war.

"Come in here, my precious Andre," gushed Aunt Clara.

"Yeah, yeah," said Andre. "Sherry told me to come see you. She said it was about your home."

"Andre, I can't believe what I've done."

"What did you do?" asked Andre. "I'm going to lose my home."

"Why?"

"Because men are coming to take out all my stuff."

"Why would they do that?"

"I got this letter in the mail and it says I have to leave."

"Let me see that," said Andre.

Andre perused the letter. A company who held her a lien on her home for burglar bars had foreclosed on her home. She was about to be evicted.

"I thought your home was paid off," asked Andre.

"It was, but I was being robbed and people were sneaking in my home and I signed papers to put burglar bars on my home." Now I have to leave. I didn't pay for the bars. I didn't have any money."

"We have to do something," Andre said. "I bet I can get Mr. Nelms to run some stories in the paper. You need a lawyer."

"Oh, thank you Jesus, thank you Jesus," cried Aunt Clara. "Don't thank him yet," said Andre.

"You and Booker used to play all the time over here. Then we left for along time."

"That was George's fault. I was raising you and Booker, and he took both of you away from me."

"Yes, I know the story," said Andre.

"Then you know I would've never abandoned you. When the home burned down I went to the Catholic church and took you back. Your mama wanted you to stay up there and get an education. She knew you had to have an education to make it in this world. I couldn't raise you and Booker by myself."

"I know," said Andre.

"I don't blame you," said Aunt Clara. "What was that?" asked Andre.

"I don't blame you for the fire in your home. It's time to forgive yourself," said Aunt Clara.

*Comeon!*Andre thought to himself under his breath, almost about to laugh.

Not that again. My crazy aunt strikes again.

"No one blames you for the fire. You need to move on," said Aunt Clara. Andre smiled. He wasn't going to let Aunt Clara get under his skin again. "I don't know why I signed those papers," she said.

"I don't know what I can do about this, but you need a lawyer. I know the lawyer who represented me. I will see what I can do," said Andre.

"Oh, thank you, thank you, Jesus. I don't want to lose my home. You know I don't want to lose my home."

"Yes, I know what it is like to lose a home," said Andre. Aunt Clara said nothing.

"Stay here tonight. I will fix you dinner just like old times."

"Ok."

That night on June 24, 1948, they turned on the radio and heard Thomas Dewey accept his nomination for the Republican Party

You, the elected representatives of our Republican Party, have again given to me the highest honor you can bestow—your nomination for President of the

United States ... Mere victory in an election is not our purpose, it is not our task. Our task is to fill our victory with such meaning for mankind everywhere, yearning for freedom that they will take heart and move forward out of this desperate darkness of today into the light of freedom's promise ... The ideals of the American people are the ideals of the Republican Party. We have tonight, and in these days which preceded, here in Philadelphia lighted a beacon, in this cradle of our own independence. We have lighted a beacon to give eternal hope that men may live in liberty with human dignity and before God, and loving Him, stand erect and free.

"Would you vote for him?" asked Andre.

"Gosh no. Mr. Truman will win the election," declared Aunt Clara.

Chapter 40

ANDRE LEFT AUNT CLARA'S AND went to downtown Mountain Springs. Talking with people would help him with his mild depression. There was something about finding out about someone new and asking questions that stimulated him. He wanted to see a story written by him in print with his name in a byline. That was worth more than a paycheck, he thought. Money didn't interest him. Journalism was his passion.

Andre stopped in at Second Street Barbershop. He hadn't been there in years. Would Lewis and Alvin be there? What would they look like? What about Cousin Carl? Would he be there? He walked in. Cousin Carl wasn't there. The barbershop looked different at 4 p.m. in the afternoon, rather than the early Saturday mornings with people bustling and coming and going. The town was wide awake. After 4 p.m. it was quiet and settling down. Lewis and Alvin were sitting in their barber chairs.

"What are you doing here?" demanded Lewis as Andre walked in. "I can't cut your hair. You have to go down the street."

"I'm not here for a haircut," answered Andre.

"You want to shine? He'll be back later," said Alvin.

"No, I don't want to shine. Don't you recognize me?" asked Andre. "No," said Lewis.

"Do you recognize me?"

"No," said Alvin.

"I'm Andre. I used to come here all the time when Shorty was here."

"You are Andre? The black kid who came here on weekends? Boy, have you changed."

"Yes, he's changed," said Alvin.

"I don't think that's Andre. Andre was always crying and looking for Shorty.

That isn't Andre, is it Alvin?" said Lewis.

"No. I don't think that's Andre," said Lewis. "I think Andre would still be short and still be looking for Shorty."

"Yes, he would be looking for Shorty. He would say '*Is Shorty here? Is Shorty here?*' Isn't that right, Lewis?"

"Yes, Andre had a girl he brought in here I think it was his sister. Wasn't that his sister?"

"Yes, that was his sister," said Lewis. "Andre didn't like girls, did he Lewis?"

"No. Andre didn't like girls," said Alvin. "Ok, Ok," said Andre.

"What are you doing now?" said Lewis changing the conversation. I'm a reporter now. I met Shorty at the *Birmingham Defender.*"

"You are a reporter?" asked Alvin.

"You can't be a reporter. You tell Shorty to get back here on Monday!" said Lewis.

"What does he do down there? Shine shoes?" asked Alvin. "No. He is a reporter. He covered World War II," said Andre. "Shorty can't write. Isn't that right, Lewis?"

"That's right. He can't even write his name," said Lewis.

"Do you want to report on shining shoes?" Alvin laughed at his own joke. "Ok. I get it," said Andre. "I want to interview you."

"You want to interview me?" asked Alvin. "Lewis, he wants to interview me."

"He wants to interview you? He can't interview you. He has to interview me first," said Lewis.

"Ok. Now let me ask you my first question." Quiet.

"I would like to know how a racist white guy like you became the owner of this barbershop?"

Silence.

"What do you think about that Lewis? He called me a racist," said Alvin. "You are a racist," said Lewis.

"We are both racists. We've always been racists. We don't know why. We just are. We were taught," admitted Alvin.

"Now that is the first straight answer you have given me," said Andre, taking notes. "You weren't taught. You were born that way."

Then Andre began his first interview of Lewis and Alvin, asking how they began Second Street Barbershop and how they found Shorty.

Chapter 41

AFTER LEAVING THE BARBERSHOP, ANDRE head the sound of the old lady begging in the street and singing. He went to see her. She had not changed. The same man was with her, sitting on the sidewalk with a hat in front of him. People dropped coins in the hat as they walked by.

"Can I ask her some questions?" Andre approached the man. "Ask her," he nodded.

"Can I ask you your name?" inquired Andre.

"You know, you know," then she said something that he could not understand. "You are with the paper?"

"Yes," said Andre.

"I remember you. I remember everyone. You were the boy at the Bargain Barn. You played at the barbershop on Saturdays."

"You remember?"

"I remember everything," she said. "What do you want to ask me? I may not be able to see but I know what goes on in this town."

"Where are you from?"

"Here."

"How long have you been doing this?"

"Ever since I lost my legs."

"I'm sorry. How did you lose them?"

"Polio. Just like Roosevelt. I could no longer walk. I thought I was the only one who had it. What else did you want to ask me?"

"Let's see. Did you vote in the 1944 election?"

"No."

"Are you voting in the election this year?"

"No. I don't vote."

"Do you favor Truman or Dewey?"

"Dewey? God almighty. That party, it worries me. They are so disorganized and so out of whack. Hmm. I think they need someone to come in that party to shake them up. You know maybe, that might do 'em some good, but not with Dewey. They should have nominated someone else. He doesn't get upset about anything and he's not shaking up anything. He has the same smile for everything. He has no emotion. They are comparing him to Hitler with that mustache of his. They need someone to shake them up from the outside. It might do them some good."

"Would you vote for him?" asked Ande.

"Would I vote for him? Hell no. It wouldn't happen. I know what needs to happen. We just got to convince them up there that this is the way it is. We are all in it. I think we are all in it. We're people. We all live together. People got to do what they got to do. Do I appreciate it? Not really, you know. Do I understand it? I think I understand that you have to do what you have to do. Do I hope? Yes. You know. You know. Somebody up there is going to do the right thing. We vote for hope. But I don't vote."

Andre was scribbling notes. He couldn't understand what she was saying, but the last sentence made sense to him. She didn't vote. How could she vote being blind.

"Give her some money," the man said. "You already took enough of her time."

"Yes, of course," Andre agreed. He reached in his pocket and threw fifty cents in the hat.

"Thank you."

Andre left and went to the bus station to travel to Montgomery to find Captain Weinstein. On the trip, he remembered: I forgot to go to Zero Pawn Shop.

Chapter 42

———— ❧ ————

WHILE ANDRE WAS IN MOUNTAINSprings, Sherry visited Oliver at the *Birmingham Defender*. Could he tell her about Andre's time in the war? "Oliver, you have a visitor," announced Brandesha, chewing gum and fixing her hair while looking in the compact's small mirror. Her voice penetrated the newsroom like an incoming missile.

"Who is it?" he asked, putting his finger on the button of the speaker box on his desk.

"Sherry ... what's your name?"

"Sherry Williams. I'm Andre Williams' wife."

Brandesha repeated the announcement in her speaker box so the entire newsroom could hear. "She says her name is Sherry Williams. She's Andre's wife."

"Send her in," said Oliver.

"Hello Sherry, what a surprise. What brings you here?"

"I hope you don't mind me coming here to talk to you Mr. Smith, but I have to talk with someone."

"What about?"

"About Andre. You spent time with him when he was overseas, right?"

"I spent some time with him, yes."

"Do you know something about him that I need to know?" asked Sherry. "What do you mean?"

"I know he had a trial over there and it must have been traumatic. He doesn't talk about it and I know nothing of it except that Booker was involved and was accidentally killed over there. That is all I know. He won't tell me but he is in great turmoil over the trial and the death of his best friend. You know we all grew up together."

"I think Andre is the best one to talk about his military tour with you. I don't think it would be appropriate for me to have a conversation with you about it," said Oliver.

"I thought you would say that. But it is just that Andre still thinks of the war even though he is here and has a new life. It is as if he never left the war. It is constantly on his mind. I think he wants to go back over there or wants to be in the service. He says that was the only place where he felt engaged. He talks a lot about how they had work to do and everything was taken care of for them with the medical, dental, food, housing, money. We are really struggling right now and he feels the pressure."

"I'm sure all servicemen go through that. Even the reporters went through that. There is a withdrawal period you go through. You identify with the soldier. When you are fighting, you fight for a cause. It gets in your blood and it is hard to get out. I'm sure it is just a matter of time before he gets back to his old ways."

"He used to sing a lot. His family sang a lot from what I know and that is still with him, but he hardly sings or whistles or anything. He has a guitar and I try to get him to play it. He won't."

"I'm sure he will be fine," Oliver reassured her.

"No, he won't. You are not listening. He has fits of depression and sometimes I'm quite astonished by his behavior. He has nightmares and dreams a lot. I think he has some kind of outrage or disgust or something over the way he

159

was treated during the war. Something happened over there and I want to know what it is."

Oliver looked surprised.

"And don't give me this, 'I am surprised' look. I'm sure you have noticed that he is outraged."

"I haven't. I don't spend time with him. Cub is the one that spends time with him. Is he outraged at you?"

"He is outraged at the system. It is as if the system was dirty to him."

"What do you mean the system was dirty to him?" asked Oliver. "The trial. Something about that trial was unfair."

"It *was* unfair. There should have never been a trial in the first place. He took the witness stand and exposed his entire life history before the world when none of that was necessary."

"Why did he do that?"

"There was a JAG officer over there who took a special interest in abusing him during the trial."

"What do you mean abusing him during the trial?"

"Not believing his story, for one. He wasn't guilty of anything. The prosecutor thought there was more to the story than just an accidental shooting. He thought Andre deliberately shot Booker Thompson."

"What?" said Sherry in disbelief.

"You didn't know that? He was supposed to be on trial for negligently shooting Booker Thompson and then the whole trial blew up over who burned his home. The prosecutor thought that Andre shot Booker for burning down his home that killed all of his family."

"I had no idea," said Sherry quite taken aback by the relevation. "No wonder he must be suffering. He was put on trial for shooting his good friend Booker Thompson, when it was an accident? I knew Booker Thompson all my life. He was one wild and crazy guy but he would never deliberately harm anyone. He was just one uncontrollable kid at times. Quite the opposite of Andre. That's how they balanced each other out. Andre was always attracted to things that were completely opposite of him. That curiosity was what made him different from the other boys at the school."

"Did you ask him to get some help from the military? They must have some kind of transition program for soldiers," suggested Oliver.

"I know very little about being an army wife. I'm ashamed of that. I should know more. I will find out. You know, I did suggest that he go back out to that church to see the nun friend of his, Sister Camille, and ask her about it."

"I imagine the Catholics have a cure for what he might be dealing with," agreed Oliver.

"I don't know. He's the Catholic at least I think he is. I just went along with it because I know that matters to him. We still go to Booker's uncle's church. He said he wanted us to join that church."

"I thought that the Catholic church was important in both of your lives," said Oliver.

"No. He goes up to St. Peter's to do that Catholic thing from time to time, but we haven't pursued it together. He visits there after those classes he takes with the other reporter who goes with him."

"Have you met Sister Camille?"

"I only met her that one time in the offices when we were all together. You were there. Did you know why we were all brought to that meeting?" asked Sherry.

"No. It was a surprise to me when Tatiana walked in the room with Mr. Nelms," recalled Oliver.

"How fun. I thought you two were the ones who planned that meeting out."

"No. We left Europe as friends. I thought I would never see her again. I hadn't seen her since Europe."

"I had no idea," said Sherry. "I remember something about the meeting that stuck out in my mind. You said something like *you don't have to answer that.* I was wondering what you meant by that?"

"That was about the trial. I think it would be best if you talk to him about that."

"Is he doing fine at the paper? He very much wants to be a reporter. He says he can't wait to do an interview of someone. He even dreamed that he interviewed the president of the United States. He wants to see his name in print. That other reporter, Cub, seems to put lot of ideas in his head. They go way back," said Sherry.

"He dreamed of interviewing the President of the United States?" asked Oliver.

Sherry paused. "Well yes, he did. In a way he did."

"Which president was that?

Sherry stopped. "I meant to say that he dreamed of interviewing a president."

"I see. He is ambitious," said Oliver.

"Or a dreamer," said Sherry.

The buzzer rang. "Mr. Smith, Mr. Nelms needs you and Mrs. Phillips to come to his office," said Brandeesha.

Oliver cringed from the incoming sound of Brandesha's voice pounding through the intercom box. Sherry stepped back when the blast of Brandesha's voice came into the room. She grimaced.

"Does she always talk like that?" asked Sherry.

"Don't worry about her," said Oliver. "I have to leave."

"Thank you. I can find my way out."

Chapter 43

———— ✥ ————

UNITED STATES ARMY CAPTAIN JOHN Thomas left the war with many honors and made his home in Birmingham, where he worked for a downtown law firm. It was only a matter of time before the governor appointed him to an open civil district court bench. His court had jurisdiction over criminal, civil, and family law cases. Thomas was content with civil law, but he loathed the family law cases and thought they were beneath him. Criminal law was Thomas's favorite. Someday he would be a federal judge, he told himself.

After the war, Captain Jesse Weinstein returned home to Illinois with his wife, and within six months took a job in Montgomery, Alabama, to start a new life in the satellite office of the firm Crane & Bass.

Andre located Captain Jesse Weinstein, now in private practice and made a trip to see him in the Montgomery office. Weinstein had the same pictures on his desk that he had in Paris. It seemed familiar to Andre to see him again. "Captain Weinstein, I can't believe I found you," said Andre.

"We settled here. The job offer was too good to turn down," said Weinstein. "When did you get out of the army?" asked Andre.

"Last year. I kept my reserve commission. How did you find me?" asked Weinstein.

"I did some checking with the lawyer's associations and tracked you down," said Andre.

"Have you recovered from the war?"

"I think so."

"What brings you here?" asked Weinstein. "My aunt."

"What about her?"

"She's in trouble."

"In what way?" asked a curious Weinstein.

"She signed some paperwork for some burglar bars on her home and they took her home from her. She has to move our or they will evict her."

"They can do that? I guess they can. Was that her homestead?" said Weinstein.

"Her what?" asked Andre. "Was it her own home?"

"Yes."

"What do you want me to do?" asked Weinstein. "Represent her. Can you?"

"You want me to represent her in the eviction and get her home back?" asked Weinstein.

"Anything is better than nothing," said Andre.

"I don't know. I've spent my time doing criminal work and JAG duties. That is federal law. I'm still learning the Alabama civil law. Can she pay me to represent her?"

"She doesn't have any money."

"Where does she live?"

"Birmingham."

"That's Jefferson County," said Weinstein.

"I work at the paper. We could cover the trial. You would get a lot of publicity," said Andre.

"Interesting. Let me think about that."

"I have another matter to talk about also," said Andre hesitantly. "What is it?"

"One of the ladies that works at the paper is having a rough time. She lost her kids to her ex mother-in-law. She wants to get custody back now that she has remarried," said Andre.

"You want me to take that case too?" asked Weinstein. "Can you?"

"Who will pay for that?"

"I can ask Oliver Smith and see if the paper can help," said Andre.

"You sure ask a lot on your first visit. Give me your number and I will call you there. Take care and let's meet up when we can talk further."

"Thank you, Captain Weinstein."

Chapter 44

---※---

OLIVER TRAVELED TO PHILADELPHIA BY train to cover the 1948 Democratic Convention. He was impressed by the Mayor of Minneapolis, Humbert Humphrey, who urged the Democratic Party to get out of the shadow of state's rights "and walk forthrightly into the bright sunshine of human rights." The convention adopted the civil rights plank by a close vote. As a result, twenty-two members of the Mississippi delegation and thirteen members of the Alabama delegation walked out.

That evening, President Truman accepted the nomination for the President of the United States.

I can't tell you how very much I appreciate the honor which you have just conferred upon me. I shall continue to try to deserve it.

I accept the nomination . . .

I would like to say a word or two now on what I think the Republican philosophy is; and I will speak from actions and from history and from experience...

The situation in 1932 was due to the policies of the Republican Party control of the Government of the United States. The Republican Party, as I said a while ago, favors the privileged few and not the common everyday man. Ever since its inception, that party has been under the control of special privilege; and they have completely proved it in the 80th Congress. They proved it by the things they did to the people, and not for them. They proved it by the things they failed to do . . .

Now my friends, with the help of God and the wholehearted push which you can put behind this campaign, we can save this country from a continuation of the 80th Congress, and from misrule from now on . . .

I must have your help. You must get in and push and win this election. The country can't afford another Republican Congress.

Chapter 45

"HERE, MR. NELMS, A PRESENTfor you from my backyard," offered Tatiana, arriving early for the Monday morning meeting.

"Eggs?" he asked, surprised. "Yes, 'Tatiana's Fresh Eggs,' it says here. Thank you, Tatiana. I didn't know you were a businesswoman."

"I knew it was your birthday," she explained. "How did you know that?" he asked.

"A good reporter will find out," said Tatiana with a grin. "Thank you, Tatiana," said Nelms.

"Happy Birthday," said Oliver. "Yes, happy birthday," said Cub.

"How was the convention?" asked Nelms.

"It was fine. Truman made a good speech. The mayor of Minneapolis did a good job, too. He is a comer. They adopted a civil rights agenda that will alienate the South," reported Oliver.

"Hubert Humphrey did a good job?" asked Nelms.

"Yes."

"They want the black vote in the big cities up North," said Nelms.

"The Dixiecrat Convention is today," added Cub, walking in the office.

"Who is going to cover it?" asked Nelms.

"I'm going there today to see if I can get in," said Oliver. "Good," said Nelms.

"What about you, Cub?" asked Nelms.

"I thought I would go with Oliver."

"That's a good idea. No telling what kind of disaster that's going to be," said Nelms. He turned to Tatiana.

"What have you found out about Hollywood, Tatiana?"

"Well sir, there are stories about the communists infiltrating Hollywood. Congress is investigating and wants to expose the communist actors. The president of the Screen Actors Guild, is an actor named Ronald Reagan, who said something to the effect of not letting fear or resentment compromise our democratic principles."

"Ok," said Nelms.

"That's the problem going on right now," said Oliver. "They know the communists are here, but how to fight them is the problem. Many are asking Dewey to condemn the Communist Party. He doesn't agree with the party but won't support a law to outlaw them."

"Some politicians want an outright ban," said Tatiana.

"How is the young Andre?" inquired Nelms changing the subject.

"I was thinking that Cub and I might take him hunting," said Oliver. "Hunting? What brought that on?" asked Nelms.

"Just something I was thinking of," said Oliver.

"I hunted when I was a kid," said Nelms.

"Let's all go somewhere to get away. Did you hear they killed a mountain lion in Alabama recently?" asked Oliver.

"A mountain lion?" asked Tatiana.

"I heard it was in St. Clair County," said Cub.

Tatiana frowned. "Poor lion. I hate the killing of animals. I think it's inhumane. I hate any kind of violence towards animals. We have to respect the creatures. I hope you don't encourage young Andre to kill animals. I find that highly offensive and if our readers learned about what you all were doing why they—"

"Yes?" said Cub.

"Why, if they hear about all of you hunting and doing that … why … why…"

"Yes?" said Cub.

"We don't know what they would think about that. The paper would never be the same. It would be a setback for the paper."

"It would be?" asked Cub.

"Yes," said Tatiana.

"That bad?" said Cub.

"And we have no idea what affect that might have on the wider community," said Tatiana, walking off disgusted with the newspaper men talking of hunting and shooting animals.

Oliver, Cub, and Nelms looked at each other. They didn't know what to say.

Brandeesha walked in the office, noticeably expecting a baby. There was a pregnant pause.

"Mr. Nelms, someone is here to see you," she said. "Ok, let's get back to work," said Nelms.

Chapter 46

—⟨❦⟩—

"I DIDN'T KNOW YOUR WIFE was anti-hunting," said Cub as they walked into Oliver's office. "What brought that on? I thought you were doing some good for Andre."

"She is opposed to killing or war of any kind," said Oliver. "Is she anti-military?"

"I don't think so," said Oliver.

"I would like to duck hunt, but it's still a while until duck season. We used to get down in the blind near the water and cover up. The ducks came in and then we blasted away," said Cub.

"Did I tell you that Andre's wife Sherry came to see me? She's the one that made me think about going hunting," said Oliver.

"Why's that?" asked Cub.

"To get his mind off the war and on work," said Oliver.

"That sounds good. I know a place where we can go dove hunting since that is coming up in a few months," said Cub. "There is milo, millet, corn, sunflower. When we hunted the mourning dove, we would spread the feed by hand. Did you hunt growing up?"

"Yes. We hunted. I heard that Alabama still has black bears in some parts," said Oliver.

"I didn't know that. We hunted in our family. We had to. We hunted deer, turkey, quail, hogs, ducks, rabbit, squirrels, doves, anything to survive. I would go with family members.

Some would show up and take the first position under a shade tree. The skilled dove hunter will scout out a field for opening day and observe the flight paths in areas, food, roosting sites, and water. When I find those, I set up near the water," said Cub. "Do you have a gun?"

"No," said Oliver.

"The best place to find a gun is to go to a pawnshop. Women hate guns, so when their husbands die, the first thing they do is take them to the pawn shop and collect the money to get rid of them," said Cub.

Chapter 47

ANDRE MADE IT BACK TO Birmingham in time to make the play rehearsal that evening.

"I'm glad you made it back in time. I was worried," said Sherry. "You look good. I missed you," said Andre, giving her kiss.

"What's gotten into you?" asked Sherry.

"Nothing, yet," said Andre. "I got a lot accomplished over the last two days. I think Captain Weinstein might take Aunt Clara's case."

"Great!" said Sherry. "That will make her happy."

"So, what have I missed?" asked Andre.

"Besides me? Just the same rehearsal," said Sherry. "Betty acting crazy sometimes directing the play. Sometimes she gets into it and gets lost. It has really gone to her head."

"Ok, let's go to the next scene," said Betty. "Sherry, come over here. Nice to see that you are back, Andre. I hope you don't go out of town again. We have to have you here for play practice."

"I will be here," said Andre.

"Now, where was I? Oh yes. Sherry, come over here and stand on this spot. You and Mary are to walk down the aisle with Andre. Andre is supposed to be enamored with Sherry. So Andre, when you play Clisson walking down the aisle, pay attention only to Sherry, who is playing Eugenie."

"Ok. I can do that," said Andre.

"Any questions Sherry or Mary?" asked Betty. "No," said Sherry.

"No," said Mary. "Andre?"

"No questions."

"Ok, lights, camera, and action," said Betty, singing the word *action*.

> **EUGENIE:** *What's the matter with him? How somber and pensive he is! His glance has all the maturity of old age, but his physiognomy reveals the language of adolescence.*

"Hold it," said Sherry. "Are these lines for real? I mean, are we really going to say this? What did I just say? I have no idea what this character said. What is physiognomy? No one says 'physiognomy.' We need to change that."

The cast laughed.

"You don't have to say that. Say 'his physical appearance reveals the language of adolescence'," said Betty.

"Still, what does that mean? His physical appearance reveals the language of adolescence," said Sherry, looking at Mary. "That sounds weird."

"Say—he looks young," said Andre, applying his journalism skills.

"No, we are not deviating from the script! My gracious. My gracious. God help us from this injury. You never, never deviate from the script," said Betty.

"Are you ok?" asked Mary to Betty.

"Yes, let me get my composure. Now, where was I? Where am I? Who am I? Now I remember. This was set in the 1800s. That is how they talked back then," said Betty. "Let's try it again. We can't deviate from the script."

"They spoke french. This is a french story," said Sherry. "Continue," said Betty.

Sherry continued as Eugenie:

> **EUGENIE:** *What's the matter with him? How somber and pensive he is! His glance has all the maturity of old age, but his physical appearance reveals the language of adolescence. Has he been to war?*

Mary said her lines as Amelie:

> **AMELIE:** *Yes, he has been at war and is not recovered. He looks to one of us for comfort. We must attend his needs.*

"Good," said Betty. "That was really great. You did that so well. I am so proud of you."

The cast looked at Betty and said nothing, not sure what to think. Then Andre read his lines:

> **CLISSON TO AMELIE:** *My darling. I am so happy to see you. I have been at war for years and I feel at home with you. I do not remember anything that happened before. I remember only you. I remember only now. There is no future. There is no past. There is only now. The future is what we believe it can be. I feel it; therefore, I feel it coming.*

"Sherry, on the next line, you are to be upset at Clisson for embracing Amelie," said Betty. "Now say your line as if you are made at Clisson." Sherry said her line:

> **EUGENIE:** *I'm so tired I have to go back home. I'm not going to listen to that. I'm going to break his neck.*

The cast laughed.

"Cut. Now the next scene will be at the home where the doctor comes to examine Eugenie. John is playing the doctor. John, you are to ignore Clisson when you come to see them," said Betty.

"That won't be hard to do," said John. Laughter.

Andre looked at him and said nothing. Sherry said her line:

EUGENIE: *Ask the doctor to come in.*

John entered stage left with a doctor's bag and walks past Andre, saying nothing.

Mary said her line:

AMELIE: *This is Monsieur Clisson.*

John, as the doctor, examines Eugenie while Clisson and Amelie watch at the edge of the bed.

Sherry continued:

EUGENIE: *Excuse me. We have heard so much about you, Clisson. I understand that you have been at war for the past few years. I would like to hear about your past experiences.*

Andre said:

CLISSON: *I have been at war fighting throughout the great lands. Now I am home ready to pursue my dream of being a writer. I plan to write a novel. A love story.*

Sherry:

EUGENIE: *A love story.*

Andre:

CLISSON: *Yes. A love story.*

"At this point, Clisson, you are to become interested in Eugenie," said Betty.

"Duh," said Sherry. "He's already interested."

"Yes, now where was I before I was rudely interrupted," said Betty.

Some laughter.

"Yes, your eyes are to meet hers and he is to fall in love with her," said Betty.

"I can do that," said Andre.

"Sure, you can," winked Sherry.

"Gross. You two stop it," said Mary.

"Ok, you two stop that. This is serious," said Betty.

Andre:

> **CLISSON:** *I feel our hearts are fused as if we were made to love each other.*

Sherry:

> **EUGENIE:** *But we hardly even know each other.*

Andre:

> **CLISSON:** *But I sense it. When I saw you, I knew you were what I wanted. I set my sights on you and believed in you and I could feel the universe was bringing you to me. I had faith.*

"Are you sure that's in the script?" said Sherry.

"No, it's not. I just said that. Somehow it came to me and it felt right," said Andre.

"Ridiculous," said John to himself, disgusted at the scene of Andre sharing his love for Sherry.

"Isn't that kind of soon for him to say that? It seems like they just met," asked John.

The cast laughed.

"No deviating from the script!" said Betty. "I'm going to die."

"You aren't going to die," said Mary.

"Ok. Where are we? Just read the part for now, because in the book there is supposed to be a long interval between scenes so it would be normal that he had more affection for Eugenie. We will figure something out. Maybe this is where we can put some music in the play. We have a few songs in mind," said Betty. "Sherry, you and Andre go ahead and finish the scene."

Sherry spoke her line:

> **EUGENIE:** *I dedicate my heart to friendship but I believe there is more than that.*

Andre:

> **CLISSON:** *There is more to us I know. I can feel it. The world is bringing us together.*

Mary:

> **EUGENIE:** *You sense it too?*

Andre:

> **CLISSON:** *I do. I used to pity myself the way I was treated by men, enemies but not with you. Now I live only for you. I no longer think of the past.*

"That was actually quite good. Very good, as a matter of fact. I'm starting to believe we can do this. When I first came here, people asked why couldn't we do a Shakespeare play? I said 'are you kidding? We can't even do this!' But now I think we can. I am a believer. I believe we can do it. I feel it. Therefore I believe it."

180

"You are using lines from the play, Betty," said Mary. "No, I'm not! I believe it! I believe in us!" said Betty. "She believes in 'us,'" said Mary.

"Well, my imagination is taking over. See you tomorrow," said Betty, singing the word *tomorrow.*

Chapter 48

"BRANDESHA, WHEN I WAS IN Montgomery I spoke with Captain Jesse Weinstein. He might take your case," said Andre.

"Who is Captain Jesse Weinstein? I'm going to have a navy captain represent me?"

"He's an army captain. He said he might take it," said Andre.

"That is great! Thank you! Thank you!" cried Brandesha. Everyone could hear the conversation in the newsroom.

Andre then went to Oliver's office to see if the paper could help Brandesha and his Aunt Clara.

"I don't know what the boss will think about this. This is a personal matter and Brandesha needs to be the one talking to the lawyer, not you." suggested Oliver.

"I think there may be more than just Aunt Clara's case. There were others on the same street who put burglars on their homes and they lost their homes after they couldn't pay for them. There might be a story there," said Andre.

"That's different," said Oliver. "I will talk to Nelms about it. There could be a public interest there. "It sounds like white investors taking advantage of black folk for the purpose of acquiring their homes. One way is to foreclose a mortgage on them."

Oliver told Nelms there might be a bigger story. The company were making contracts with people who could not pay back the cost and then foreclosing on the property. Nelms thought that this would be a good story for Tatiana.

Almost fuming, Tatiana left Nelms' office and went to see Andre in the basement, where he was proofreading the paper.

"Andre, this is where you work?" asked Tatiana. "Yes."

"I just got out of Mr. Nelms' office and he says that I'm to write a story about some company who is foreclosing on your aunt's home. I'm right in the middle of a story about the governor and I'm to drop everything to investigate this story. Thanks a lot."

"I didn't know he was going to give it to you. What about Cub. Can he do it?"

"You want me to ask Mr. Nelms to reassign the story to Cub?"

"No."

"I didn't mean to upset you. I will do the story but next time tell me before you drop a bomb in the boss's lap," said Tatiana.

"I will."

"What do you know about the company?" asked Tatiana.

"It is some fly by night company that installed burglar bars on homes in the black community. None of the people could pay the monthly payments so the company took their homes from them. There should be a law against that," said Andre.

"Does your aunt have a lawyer?"

"She's not really my aunt. She's Booker's aunt."

"Whatever. Does she have a lawyer?" asked Tatiana. "It might be Captain Jesse Weinstein."

"The same Jesse Weinstein who defended you?"

"Yes."

"Small world. Where is he? How did you get him to represent her?"

"He's in Montgomery now. I went to talk to him. He didn't say yes or no.

He said he would think about it," said Andre.

"Let me know if he decides to represent her," said Tatiana.

Chapter 49

———— ❦ ————

ANDRE PAID A VISIT TO Mr. Nelms.

"Mr. Nelms, I know why you had me look up Hugo Black."

"What did you find out?"

"He was a member of the Klan. A reporter named Ray Sprigle discovered that he was a member of the Klan and he won the Pulitzer Prize, just like you said," said Andre.

"That was some reporting. That is what reporters are supposed to do. How would we have known that had a reporter not figured it out? He wasn't going to tell us. Sometimes exposing someone's past like that ends up changing them, as painful as it might be," said Nelms.

"I hope I find a story like that someday," said Andre.

"You never know. You may interview the President of the United States someday," said Nelms. "Oliver met Franklin Roosevelt and Tatiana interviewed Eleanor Roosevelt. It will be your turn someday."

"I hope so," said Andre. Andre did not dare mention his imaginary interview of President Andrew Johnson.

"You know, Andre, if you want to be a real journalist, you have to do whatever it takes to get the story.

"Your job is no different than a politician who has to reach across the aisle to pass legislation. You have to look past your differences. Sometimes to do that, you have to understand the other side in order to work with them. When you understand them then you find out they aren't that different. They are just human beings struggling and trying to make sense of the world from their own perspective," added Nelms.

The phone rang. "I need to take this call," said Nelms. "Thank you. I'm going to class today," said Andre.

Nelms nodded his head. "Hello?" he answered to the phone.

On his way to class, Andre pondered the wisdom that Nelms gave him and how such an older experienced journalist was willing to share his knowledge with him. He had no idea how valuable it was to have a man of his age as a mentor.

Chapter 50

ANDRE VISITED SISTER CAMILLE AFTER his journalism class followed by a religion class taught by Sister Aude.

"How are you doing Sister Camille?" asked Andre. "I'm great Andre! And how are you?"

"I came to see you because I need a reason to smile," said Andre. "That is great. I enjoy talking with you. How is Sherry?"

"Sherry is doing fine."

"What are you two up to these days?"

"We are in a play together at our church."

"I'm aware of the play. The one being held on Halloween. I didn't know you were in it," said Sister Camille.

"I have the lead roles," said Andre.

"I know why Sherry came up with the play."

"Why is that?"

"So I will get over the war and my trial."

"You are still thinking about it?"

"Yes. The prosecutor—I hate him—I think he tried me for no reason."

"You must forgive him. He probably thought he was doing the right thing."

"You are right."

"Are you still doing a lot of dreaming?"

"Yes, I still do that."

"You must have a lot on your mind. Dreaming is a good thing. It shows that you are in a deep state of sleep. Dreams are your mind processing the information you are taking in," Sister Camille explained.

"I dreamed about boot camp and sometime later one of my Army buddies showed up."

"Boot camp?" said a surprised Sister Camille.

"Yes. The guys you were with—you never forget them."

"I suppose not," nodded Sister Camille. "Did you dream of anything else?"

"Nothing like my visit to the White House."

"You're funny."

"I enrolled on one of the religion classes at the school. We are learning some deep things."

"Like what?" asked Sister Camille.

"Like proof that Jesus is the son of God? That was one of the questions Sister Aude asked today in our religion class."

"She didn't tell you the answer?"

"No. She doesn't give answers to questions like that."

"That's simple, Andre. Look to the book of Luke, Chapter 9, verse 28. There you will see where it is written that Jesus took Peter, John, and James and went up to a mountain to pray. While he was praying, his face changed in appearance and his clothing became dazzling white."

"It says that?" said Andre.

"Yes. Then two men, Moses and Elijah, appeared and conversed with Jesus.

Can you imagine the look on the face of Peter, John, and James?"

"No, I can't."

"A cloud came and cast a shadow over them and they became frightened when they entered the cloud. Then from the cloud a voice came and said, 'This is my chosen Son: listen to him.' God could have changed what would happen to Jesus if he wanted to, but he did not interfere. There is your proof right there. In the Old Testament, God spoke through the prophets. Now you can speak directly to Jesus and God. You can have a personal relationship with Him."

"You make things so simple, Sister Camille," said Andre. "Thank you. So how is it going with the newspaper?"

"I've been interviewing anyone who looks at me. Now no one will talk to me at the paper because they think I'm conducting an interview."

"That will stop," smiled Sister Camille. "Are you enjoying the journalism class with Father Webster?"

"Yes. Sometimes it is hard. Like knowing when to use 'that' or 'which.' That is a hard one," sighed Andre.

"I know that one. When the clause is what they call 'restrictive' and needs the rest of the sentence to make sense, then you use 'that.' When the clause is surplus and not needed, then you use 'which'," explained Sister Camille.

"That's right, but then he gave us all these examples and I still couldn't tell the difference in any of the sentences," said Andre.

"That is a difficult area in English grammar," Sister Camille agreed. "Since I've been at the newspaper I can't read anything without wanting to make changes. I carry a pencil wherever I go. I underline words I don't understand. I went to Mass the other day and looked at the reading. I brought this with me. Listen to how they write things in the daily readings. They wrote, *'May the heavenly nourishment we have received, O*

Lord, we pray, transform us into the likeness of your Son, whose radiant splendor you willed to make manifest in his glorious Transfiguration. Who lives and reigns with you for ever and ever. Amen.' After being at the newspaper I would have written, *'May we receive your heavenly nourishment and transform us into the likeness of your Son.'* See how simple that is? I can understand that," said Andre.

"You are funny, Andre. I'm sure the Vatican will appreciate you."

"I have another question to ask you. How do you know if you are on the right path?" asked Andre.

"That's easy. Do you know where the path leads to?" responded Sister Camille.

"No. I took the path because it excited me and interested me."

"Like a ride in a park or carnival interests and excites you?"

"I think so."

"When the ride is over, where are you after that?"

"In the same place you started out," answered Andre.

"When a ship leaves a harbor, it knows where it is going to go before it leaves. If you pick any path, then that path will take you where it wants you to go."

"What if you think you are on the right path and it excites you and interests you, but you are not getting to where you want to end up?" continued Andre. "That's easy. Do you like your job? Are you unhappy with the job? Can you ever run the organization someday? Is it bringing you to new places and new people? If it is not, then you have to get off that path even if it is the best road built. It is not the right path for you," advised Sister Camille.

Chapter 51

———— ⌘ ————

AT PLAY PRACTICE THE NEXT night, Andre and Sherry decided to change the play without telling Betty. Andre remembered the song he would sing to himself, "*You Are My Window*," when he was in Paris waiting for his trial. He remembered visualizing a trip to the top of the Eiffel Tower with Sherry. He remembered Oliver Smith looking at the photo of Sherry when he and Booker were serving in Africa. Booker and Andre were naked, washing their mess kits and clothing in gasoline cans heated over an open fire.

"You guys doing ok?"
"Yes," said Booker.
"I am," said Andre.
"Aren't you the two guys from Alabama?" asked Oliver.
"We are," said Booker

. . .

"Is that your girl?"
"Sure is," said Andre. "I have something to go home to. She's my window to the future. She say's I'm a dreamer, and I say she is my window."
"Your girl is a window?" asked Oliver.
"She's my window to the future," explained Andre.

"Let's put 'You Are My Window' in the play," Andre said to Sherry. "That's fine with me. Betty shouldn't mind," said Sherry.

At rehearsal that evening, Andre and Sherry changed their lines:

CLISSON: *Our life together now seems like only hours. I remember when I first saw you at the spa. We now have children and we are deeply in love.*

EUGENIE: *I love you and you have loved me. We have no sorrow or pleasure that we share separately. Our nature gives us the same ear and feelings. You are still a dreamer, Clisson.*

CLISSON: *You are my window.*

"Cut, cut!" said Betty. "Where did that come from? That's not in the play. Eugenie doesn't say *'you are a dreamer,'* and Clisson doesn't say, *'you are my window.'* Where did you two come up with that?"

"We added it to the script," Sherry explained innocently. "We didn't think you would mind."

"Andre and Sherry. Andre and Sherry. What have I done?" said Betty about to cry.

The cast's eyes were all on Betty.

"All this work ... All this work. What have I done," said Betty. "What's wrong?" asked Sherry?

"There's no deviation from the script. Napoleon Bonaparte will come back from the grave and down this play. I know it. I feel it. This is real," chided Betty.

Some in the cast laughed. Betty recovered.

"Andre, say your line," said Betty. Andre said:

CLISSON: *I have faced the injustice of men. I have faced cowardly leadership. I have faced men who have lied, stolen, cheated and have no honor. Men* and bullies with dark secrets using their power to abuse others for no other reason than who they are. They will have their justice someday.

Sherry:

EUGENIE: *You have suffered an injustice. What is it and who was this man who injured you so that you cannot forgive?*

Andre:

CLISSON: *It is a man with a dark past. Whether he was born that way or was taught to be that way; that I cannot tell.*

Sherry:

EUGENIE: *Do you know this man?*

Andre:

CLISSON: *It is one so obvious that we know him but do not know him. He is in our future; he is in the past.*

Sherry:

EUGENIE*: What will you do, my Clisson?*

Andre:

CLISSON: *I will do battle against this wickedness and this man. The dark forces of the past that separate man from man and men from men will rise once again and he and his evil forces that pollute our society will be vanquished. They will be hung. I will see to it that we rid these evil forces of those that slaughter others for no other reason than they exist. For me I must do my part. For now, I must dream...*

193

Sherry:

> **EUGENIE:** *Some may think of you as mad by the way you so often dream and have this need to seek justice against this man, whoever it is who has wronged you in the past. You must tell me who this person is.*

Andre:

> **CLISSON:** *My beloved, my wife, happy mother my children, why Eugenia are your beautiful eyes wet with tears?*

"That was good," praised Betty. "Very good, in fact. I'm impressed. I am so impressed." Betty was fibbing.

"You can't be serious," asked Mary.

Chapter 52

———— ⌗ ————

ONLY A MONTH AFTER VISITING Jesse Weinstein, Aunt Clara was evicted from her home. Tatiana ran a story on the front page of the *Birmingham Defender* showing Aunt Clara being removed from her home in handcuffs. The photo was shocking and peaked interest across the city. Even white people felt it was unfair to see an old woman evicted from her home that was paid off because a contractor could place a lien on her home for the cost of burglar bars whose cost was significantly less than the value of the home.

Andre told Sister Camille about Aunt Clara's plight. Sister Camille told Father Webster, who thought the circumstances were a display of immorality. "Morally it is about as low as you can get," said Father Webster to Sister Camille. "I'm going to do something for her. The idea that you can sign a piece of paper and then the next thing you know you are being evicted from your own home. What an outrage! I will thunder from the pulpit," said Father

Webster sounding like a Baptist preacher.

Father Webster had Aunt Clara brought to St. Peter's and given a room in the old home that the nuns had renovated.

"I remember this home. I never thought I would stay here," said Aunt Clara. "It reminds me of the fire and I had to bring the boys here. I know Andre's mother wanted him to stay, but I had to take him back. I didn't think that he and Booker should be separated. We were his only family."

"I remember tucking him in that dreadful night. He asked me if I would take care of him. I know that must have been terrible for you," said Sister Aude.

"We have just the place for you now," said Sister Laurie.

"We are helping the girls who are coming to events here. We need someone there to watch the place, someone who can live here fulltime," said Sister Camille.

"Am I a nun now?" asked Aunt Clara.

"Of course you are," teased Sister Laurie.

They laughed as they walked her into the home.

Chapter 53

"ED, I HAVE BEEN DOING some further investigation on the trial that Andre went through during the war," said Oliver, walking into Nelms' office.

"What do you mean?" asked Nelms, typing. "Are you writing a story?" asked Oliver.

"Just some work," said Nelms as he turned around to his desk. "Now, what is it about the young Andre?"

"A reporter over there, Roy Otwell, came to see me and said that one of the soldiers said he was near the house where the shooting of Booker Thompson occurred. He did some investigation and gave his work to me," explained Oliver.

"What is there to do? He was tried, convicted, and then his conviction was reversed on appeal. Case over. What is there to investigate?" asked Nelms. "This new source says that he and his men were shooting around the same time and he discarded his weapon when it wouldn't work and took Andre's weapon that was left on the ground. I think we can find out what really happened."

"What do you mean, 'what really happened'?" asked Nelms. "We already know. He shot and the bullet hit the other soldier."

"What if it was the other soldier who actually shot Thompson? There might have been other witnesses."

"How would that change anything?"

"It means he should have never been tried."

"Do you have something to go on?"

"I might. One soldier says that he saw the shooting."

"So, go interview him."

"There is more. There were two women at the shooting and they might know something."

"Can you call them?"

"Not sure how I can do that. They are in France."

"I know where this heading. You're not going to France."

"I want to investigate further. I talked to them last time and I didn't go far enough. I want to fix that."

"You want me to fly you over to France at our expense so you can talk to them four years later? You don't have time for that. I don't have time for that. We don't have the money for that."

"We have the money for that," insisted Oliver.

"We do? Then you should run the paper," said Nelms.

"I mean I will pay my way," explained Oliver.

"Now you are talking. How long will you be gone?"

"Just a few days."

"I don't think that is a good idea. You might decide to stay over there," said Nelms.

"No, I wouldn't. I have a reason to come back."

"I think you are personally involved. Why not send Tatiana? She's not personally involved."

"I hadn't thought of that." Oliver paused. "There is something else."

"What?"

"I think Andre should go over there too. He needs to go back and face the reality of this and get this off of his mind. His wife came to see me. She says the war is not over for him."

"That would stir his mind back up," said Nelms.

"I think he has is 'shell shock." The way to deal with it is to confront your fears," said Oliver.

"So, are you proposing that we send Tatiana and Andre over to France to re-investigate the shooting of Booker Thompson? That sounds like a book, *'The Shooting of Booker Thompson.'* What are you going to tell her?" asked Nelms.

"To do a travel story while Andre investigates. "No longer than one week, tops," said Nelms.

PART B: RESOLUTION

Chapter 1

OLIVER WAS STRETCHED OUT ON the bed while Tatiana was getting ready for bed that night. He broke the news to Tatiana about her trip to France.

"How would you like to go to Paris?" Oliver asked Tatiana, brushing her teeth in the bathroom.

"Paris? I thought you would never ask! When are we leaving? Remember the La Couple restaurant? I can't wait," cooed Tatiana, sliding into the bed.

"Don't get too excited. I can't go. Nelms wants me to stay here. He wants you to go."

"Me? Alone? Why just me?"

"You and Andre Williams."

"What? I'm already covering his aunt's foreclosure. I'm doing entertainment news. What does he think I am? A travel writer?"

"Yes. He wants you to do a travel story."

"A travel story? You mean go to hotels, take the free service and write a good story about the experience?"

"You would never do that. Cheap hotels," said Oliver. "What's bringing this up now?"

"I have been looking into the shooting of Booker Thompson."

"We already know how about that. What is the point of bringing that story back up?"

"Roy Otwell gave me some new information. We don't have the full story."

"So what? He was acquitted. Who cares?"

"*He* cares. Otwell thinks another soldier knows a lot more. He has his theory that the bullet from the other soldier's weapon is the bullet that killed Private Thompson. Do you realize what the might mean? It means Andre did not shoot Thompson."

"That would be a breakthrough. Why does he need to go back to France?

Can't he interview the soldiers here," said Tatiana.

"I thought by sending him back over there it might get this event out of his system. His wife came to visit me and said he is still suffering from the war. That's why Cub and I were talking about taking him hunting. We didn't know you were going to object to that."

"I'm against any kind of violence against animals," said Tatiana. "How do you like your steaks?" aske Oliver.

"Don't change the subject."

"Can you go see Weinstein and find out what you can from him about the court-martial."

"I will do that. I have to see him anyway to see if he is going to help out the lady named Aunt Clara."

Oliver kissed Tatiana and then it was lights out.

Chapter 2

─────── ❧ ───────

SISTER CAMILLE CALLED ANDRE TO see if he knew an attorney who could help Aunt Clara. Andre told her that he had spoken to Captain Weinstein.

"Would it help if Father Webster called him?" asked Sister Camille. "Yes, it might," said Andre.

Sister Camille spoke to Father Webster, who promptly called Captain Weinstein to see if he could help Aunt Clara.

Weinstein examined Alabama law and discovered that the lien by the burglar bar company was invalid because those kinds of liens cannot be placed on a home if there is not a prior lien on the property for the purchase of the home. This meant that the foreclosure was invalid. It was his first civil suit and it would take place in Birmingham in Jefferson County.

Weinstein told the mortgage company attorney that the foreclosure could be set aside. The company advised that the property had already been sold. Weinstein would sue the company for money damages.

Chapter 3

TATIANA DROVE TO MONTGOMERY AND found Weinstein's office in the building with a sign on the door that said *Crane & Bass*.

"Hi there, Mr. Weinstein, do you remember me? I'm Tatiana Smith. I used to be Tatiana Phillips when I was in Paris. That was when I covered the Andre Williams' trial during the war—the one you defended."

"I do remember you," smiled Weinstein.

"I've been assigned to cover the foreclosure of his aunt's home. Did you take her case? Thank you so much for your service to his aunt. What can you tell me about the case? Tatiana sked.

"They are some fly-by-night company that buys up these mortgages that these burglar bar companies obtain from low income property owners, virtually all black people. When they don't pay they foreclose on the home and buy the property real cheap. It is a scam."

"That's just awful," said Tatiana. "How much damage do you think this company has done to the local community?"

"What?" asked Weinstein. "I don't know. I imagine there are many others like Clara Thompson out there."

"Do you think the community will ever recover?" asked Tatiana.

Weinstein didn't know how to answer that question either. "I hope so," he said. Weinstein's interest was in the specific law pertaining to Aunt Clara's case.

"How does it make you feel?" asked Tatiana.

"How does it make me feel? I think that would be a question for Aunt Clara. I'm just doing my job."

"For free, I understand? I heard the Diocese asked you to represent her," said Tatiana.

"Yes, they did. I'm going to take it on a pro bono basis."

"That is good, particularly at this time. Let me ask you, what should the federal government be doing to stop this kind of activity on the poor and low income families? Is the federal government doing enough?"

"I don't know. This is state law issue. They sold the property for basically nothing and I think the lien is invalid which means the property could not have had this kind of lien on it in the first place. It is called a "secondary mortgage" and it must be subordinate to a first lien. This property didn't have a first lien which made the burglar bar lien invalid." Weinstein explained.

"Is there something you want to get out of this yourself?" asked Tatiana. "I'm always willing to help," said Weinstein, perturbed by the question.

He did think about the question. Why was he helping Aunt Clara? It wasn't to make money. Now he realized that no matter what case he took, whether it was a paying client or a pro bono case, he needed to understand why he would spend his time on a particular case and client. He needed to understand that even for a pro bono client.

"Fair enough. I have another reason for calling," said Tatiana. "What is it?" asked a curious Weinstein.

"Do you have time to talk about the trial of Andre Williams?"

"I do. What about it?"

"Andre and I are making a trip to France."

"To do what?" asked a curious Jesse Weinstein. "To remember it, I guess," said Tatiana.

"Why? He was tried and convicted and his conviction was overturned.

What difference does it make now?" asked Weinstein.

"It makes a lot of difference to him. He isn't over it," explained Tatiana. "He needs to move on. The prosecution of the case was flawed in the first place. The premise that Andre shot Private Thompson over a house fire years ago was far-fetched. If he thought Thompson was responsible for the death of his family, Andre would have shot him a long time ago. The prosecutor knew better. He could have stopped the trial. I never understood why he wouldn't and why he put Andre through that ordeal."

"What do you mean?"

"His duty was to seek justice, not to convict."

"Maybe we are looking at this case in the wrong way. Instead of focusing on the facts, we need to focus on Thomas. Is there something in his past that is helpful?" asked Tatiana?

"Besides not paying his bar dues, negligently allowing witnesses to be transferred out of the theater and misplacing the burden of proof in a criminal proceeding, there isn't anything on Thomas."

"What was that?" asked Tatiana.

"He forgot to pay his bar dues in one state where he was licensed and his name was posted in the bar journal as being suspended from the practice of law. He had to jump through all kinds of hoops to get his law license reinstated. He blamed it on his service in the war. The bar examiners gave him a pass and said he did not have to take the bar examination again. He was embarrassed when word got out in the DOJ. Now the records are sealed."

"That's embarrassing," said Tatiana.

"I think he should have been required to take the bar exam again. Thomas always has an excuse for his behavior and looks out only for himself." He paused. "Forget I said that."

"You two fought like cats and dogs during the trial," recalled Tatiana.

"He was brutal to me and I was brutal to him. Brutality breeds brutality. One thing I learned in the military is that you can never trust anyone who is hostile towards you."

"Mr. Weinstein, there is some other information that I have learned that you might not know about," said Tatiana.

"Like what?"

"Oliver told me that another reporter was doing a story on the soldiers after they came home, and one started talking about the shooting. He said that he and some of his buddies saw the shooting. These soldiers were not called to testify."

"Was that Private Ellis? He was one that I tried to have called to the trial. I made a request to Capt. Thomas for him and Thomas failed to respond. Once he was out of the theater I could not call him back. The court said that Thomas was negligent in not responding to me but he did not engage in intentional prosecutorial misconduct."

"A few came back and talked about it."

"It doesn't matter now. His conviction was overturned."

"I know, but did you ever think that he didn't shoot him at all?" asked Tatiana.

"You mean Private Williams never shot Private Thompson? The answer to that is no. He admitted shooting his weapon while trying to shoot the Germans."

"But what if the bullet that hit Thompson was not from Andre's gun?"

"How could you know that? Or how would you prove that? That never came up. The bullet in Private Thompson's back was from Williams' weapon."

"Are you sure?"

"Yes. Although there was one thing that we couldn't figure out. It was the issue of the serial number on the paperwork for the rifle issued to Andre."

"I remember something about it," recalled Tatiana.

"There was something wrong with the number, but since the bullet came from his gun, we didn't pursue it further."

"Do you happen to have any files related to the case in this office?"

"As a matter of fact, I have some documents you can look at. There's nothing confidential about them."

"Thank you, and thank you for helping Clara Thompson," said Tatiana. As she began to leave the room, she turned around. "You know, like I said before, maybe we are focusing on the wrong thing. We are focusing on the facts of the case. Maybe we should focus on Capt. Thomas. He might be the key to this whole trial."

Weinsteain said nothing.

Chapter 4

WEINSTEIN LEANED BACK IN HIS chair and thought about what Tatiana said. Why did Capt. Thomas prosecute Private Andre Williams?

Did Capt. Thomas act improperly in Williams's trial? He had always thought that Thomas genuinely believed that Williams was guilty of shooting Thompson because of the fire and death of Andre's family when the two soldiers were kids. But this caused Weinstein to speculate something else— something he didn't want to think about. He would put that out of his mind. Did Thomas prosecute Williams because he was black? *Anyone who rises to the level of the federal judiciary could not be a racist,* he thought to himself.

He thought about Tatiana's belief that Andrew never shot Booker Thompson at all. If. Capt. Thomas knew that and prosecuted Private Williams anyway, then Capt. Thomas deserved to hang.

"Not a real hanging, of course," Weinstein thought to himself as he walked out of the library. "No matter what Thomas does, he always lands on his feet and gets away. I bet he doesn't land on his feet this time."

Chapter 5

Tatiana's story about the foreclosure of Aunt Clara's home ran in the morning and evening editions of the *Birmingham Defender's* paper. In the evening edition, Tatiana secured a quote from one of the defendants who purchased the home after the foreclosure and was about to be sued.

"I think Jesse Weinstein is just trying to make a name for himself by going after innocent investors," said a representative for the mortgage company. Weinstein drove to Birmingham to file the suit for Andre's Aunt Clara. The case landed in Judge Thomas's court. They would meet again.

Weinstein drove to the *Birmingham Defender* to see Tatiana and drop off his files from Andre Williams' trial and to give her a copy of the lawsuit he had just filed.

"Here is the lawsuit. You didn't get it from me," he said quietly. "It is a publicly filed document. Can I quote you?" asked Tatiana.

"Yes. I think this is horrible situation, but we have a glimmer of hope."

"Got, it."

"Look at the file number on this. You won't believe whose court this case was filed in."

"Whose?" asked Tatiana. "Judge John Thomas."

"You mean the same John Thomas that handled Andre's court martial?"

"Yes."

"Is that a conflict of interest?"

"Not at all. Just a coincidence."

"While you are here, I wanted to ask you about the court-martial. Did you bring the files with you from active duty?"

"Yes. Here they are." Weinstein opened up his brief case and pulled out a brown file with papers. "They are all about the Williams' trial. Everything I have is here. The only thing I can point to is that the serial number on Andre's gun did not match the one that was issued to him, but the bullet came from his weapon."

"Is there anything else about the trial you can tell me?" asked Tatiana.

"You might want to see if you can interview the French women and people at the church he went to after the shooting. They might remember something," said Weinstein.

"Should I talk to Captain Thomas? Would he talk to me?"

"Probably not. I wouldn't bother. I only think—" Then Weinstein stopped. "You think what?" asked Tatiana.

"I think he was hiding something."

"Why do you say that?"

"I wondered why he prosecuted the case. Williams was innocent to me. I thought the case would be over at the dismissal stage. I put Andre on the witness stand and the whole case imploded on me and he looked guilty. Thomas knew how to make an innocent man look guilty."

"I think the fact that he didn't know who the priests and nuns were, and he said they were black when they were actually white was what lost the case for him. I didn't believe Andre's story. How can anyone look at photos of white people and say they are black people and then think that that was what he remembered? That is too weird, even for me. I will never be able to accept his explanation for that,"said Tatiana.

"That was a crushing blow. I will never put a client on the stand like that again.But I think Thomas was hiding something—some deep dark secret. Something he doesn't want anyone to know about," said Weinstein.

"What could that be?" asked Tatiana.

"I don't know. I've thought about the trial a thousand times and it still comes out the same. I feel a sense of obligation to him after what he went through. That's why I'm defending his aunt. I think I am responsible for him," said Weinstein.

"Don't think that."

"Don't quote me on what I just said," said Weinstein.

"I won't."

"I think he needed to be held accountable."

"Williams needed to be accountable?" asked Tatiana.

"Thomas needs to be held accountable."

"What do you mean by that?" asked Tatiana.

"Thomas always manages to land on his feet. He never accepts responsibility for anything and he's never really held accountable," said Weinstein.

"I'm not sure what you are talking about. Do you have a grievance against him?" asked Tatiana.

Weinstein paused for a moment. "I guess I do. Sometimes I think conducting an investigation and exposing the truth is all that needs to be done to hold someone accountable. There is no need for punishment. The American legal system is adversarial. You can destroy witnesses and people along the way with innuendo and suppression of facts until the truth finally percolates to the top like some mystical spirit from all of the carnage. It is something that neither side can grasp."

"You sound like an old sage, but you are still very young. The legal system can't always be like that," said Tatiana.

"No. I guess not. I didn't mean that in all cases. There are some cases that should not be handled like criminal cases, but instead as more of a disciplinary or administrative proceeding."

"I can understand that."

"Good luck with your story about the burglar bar company. It's a sleaze ball company and they need to be held accountable."

"Yes. They should hang for what they did to Aunt Clara."

"Yes, they should."

"I will let you know what I find out in France," promised Tatiana.

Chapter 6

"I'M SO GLAD THAT YOU decided to take my case," Brandeesha said to Jesse Weinstein in his Montgomery office. "Mr. Williams says a lot of nice things about you."

"Thank you," said Weinstein.

"You two were in the army together?"

"Yes. We went through quite a lot together."

"I appreciate your helping me out."

"Thank you for coming to Montgomery."

"Seeing that you were doing it for free and all, I felt I needed to come here and make you come to Birmingham. You see, it's my kids. My ex's mother took them from me after the divorce when I couldn't take care of them. Now that I'm remarried I want to take them back. She said she was only taking them temporarily and now she won't give them back. My ex doesn't care about them and she shouldn't be raising them. They are my kids."

"That doesn't sound right. First I want you to know that I have never handled a divorce case or a custody case. All my experience has been in the military and involved federal law that is much different than state court domestic relations. As long as you are willing to accept that, then I will take your case."

"That is fine with me, Mr. Weinstein," said Brandesha.

"Are you able to pay me?"

"I can pay something monthly," said Brandesha.

214

"Tell me some of the facts."

"As I said, I let my ex's mother take care of them temporarily after the divorce. I moved in with her and paid her rent and childcare. My ex was there but he didn't have a job and didn't pay anything. Now that I'm on my feet she doesn't want them to leave. She gets money from the state. She would lose that if I took them back. Once I got the job at the newspaper, I wanted them back and she won't give them back. My ex doesn't want them to go back because he doesn't want to pay child support. He says it is just alimony and that he is not going to pay alimony to support me and my new husband."

"You are pregnant now it appears?"

"Yes. I'm due in late October," said Brandesha. "I want to get all together."

"I think we might need a social worker to see if you have a better home environment than where they are living."

"You do what you have to do," agreed Brandesha. "I will be in touch."

"Thank you, Mr. Weinstein."

"You are welcome."

Chapter 7

WEINSTEIN FILED THE MOTION TO modify Brandeesha's divorce decree for her to regain custody of her two children.

The case was filed in Judge Thomas's court, a court that had authority over family law matters. Judge Thomas loathed family law cases and imagined himself as a United States District Judge. He would get there some day.

"Another case filed in Thomas's court. I can't imagine what that will be like," Weinstein thought to himself.

In his short time on the bench Judge Thomas had developed a reputation. Weinstein checked with attorneys about Thomas and his reviews were all over the board. One said he was exceptionally unflexible and a "robot application of the rules. He has poor temperment and poor judgment combined with shoot from the hip prejudgment." Another said that his temperament was good and it was a pleasant experience to have a case in his court. He treats you like a normal person and not a hated lawyer. You can't go wrong having him as a judge."

Weinstein wondered whether Thomas had experience in civil matters since his prior work had been in federal criminal prosecution. One attorney told Weinstein that Thomas was "very cordial and earnest, but completely lost in civil matters. He does not understand the basics of civil discovery."

Weinstein knew Thomas better than anyone. He knew that Thomas would never be content being a state district judge.

He knew Thomas to have a temper and lashed out frequently at attorneys and witnesses. Thomas's federal service gave him a feeling of superiority over attorneys who practiced state law. It was a feeling tantamount to arrogance.

"Nice to see you back in the states after the war," said Judge Thomas to Weinstein as he appeared in court.

"Thank you, Judge."

"I thought you were going back to Illinois after the war?"

"I was offered a job in Montgomery that I couldn't turn down," said Weinstein.

"That's great. I hope to see you in my court more often."

"Thank you, Judge."

"Now the case we have here is *In re: Megan and Daren Jones,*" said Judge Thomas.

"Your Honor. I represent Brandesha Yancey. She and her husband Will are here today. Mrs. Yancey seeks a modification of her divorce decree to seek custody of her two minor children, the daughter and the son."

"And what do you say, Mr. Feldman?"

"We oppose the motion, Your Honor, brought by the attorney from Montgomery. If he practiced in Birmingham, then he would have known that his motion required a certificate of conference and he needed to tender his financial income statement on his clients and his list of recommendations to the court based on Local Rule 1.01. Since he failed to do that, I ask that the motion be denied and that he and his client be sanctioned for wasting my client's time and expenses to us appear today."

"Is it true that you did not secure a certificate of conference and you did not tender your financial papers and recommendations to opposing counsel and file them with the court, Mr. Weinstein?"

"Yes, Your Honor. I was unaware of Local Rule 1.01," admitted a nervous Jesse Weinstein.

"That's no excuse, Mr. Weinstein. I should have expected better from you. Had you bothered to read the local rules, then you would have known the requirements of the court."

"I'm sorry your Honor, I relied on the procedural rules from the Alabama Legislature. I didn't realize that local court could add new rules to that."

"Seeing that you are from Montgomery instead of Birmingham, I will give you this one mistake and look the other way."

"Yes, Your Honor."

"I ask that the attorneys go in the conference room and confer and bring all the documents to my bailiff when you are finished—including your exhibits and witness lists. After I have reviewed them I will call the case."

Brandeesha was so nervous that she had Cub drive her to the trial. Cub relished the chance of seeing Judge Thomas and Jesse Weinstein go at it again and sat in the courtroom observing.

One of Brandeesha's witnesses, George Billingsley, was in the courtroom as was her expert, Janice Stein. Weinstein found her at the temple where he worshiped and she agreed to help out for free.

"Mr. Billingsley, you've heard my admonishments to the other witnesses under the rule. You have to wait outside now, too," said Judge Thomas.

"I understand, Judge. It's just part of the game," said Mr. Billingsley. "No, sir, it's really—Mr. Billingsley, I'd like for you to hold on for just a second, and I'd like to admonish you that this is not a game. This is a civil trial in a district court. And I'd sure appreciate it if you don't insult the proceedings again. Thank you," said Judge Thomas.

"No problem, Your Honor," said George Billingsley.

Weinstein was grimacing. He didn't know what to say. His first witness was in trouble with the Judge before he testified. He didn't know why Billingsley referred to the proceeding as a "game." It wasn't anything they discussed.

Weinstein stepped out of the courtroom to talk with Mr. Billingsley. "Mr. Billingsley, I don't think you should come back to the hearing. This judge is upset about something and he typically is upset as I understand it. I think it would be best if you do not worry about coming to testify. I can get by without you," said Weinstein.

"Ok. I didn't mean it was a game. I just meant that I knew the rule about the witnesses not being in the court room. I know it is not a game," insisted Billingsley.

"I know. Don't worry about it. There isn't much that you could add to the case anyway."

"Ok."

Weinstein called Brandesha to the witness stand. He had her describe her life story, how she had changed and how she had found a new job with the *Birmingham Defender,* how she married a new man and was building a great home life. Judge Thomas was not impressed.

Then it was Mr. Feldman's turn. He had something in store for Brandesha. He could prove that she was not truthful during earlier stages in the case where he sent her questions to answer. Brandesha had to admit that her earlier answers were incorrect.

"Do you agree today that your answer earlier was incorrect?" asked Feldman. "I agree that I am aware now that they were incorrect when they were sent," said Brandesha.

"No, ma'am, that was not the question," said Judge Thomas intervening. "What was the question?" asked Brandesha.

Judge Thomas was upset with her entire testimony and thought she was dodging Mr. Feldman's questions.

"And I have had just about all of this I can stand. Listen to the question he asks and answer it. Don't just make up something that you want to say. Got it?" said Judge Thomas.

"Yes, sir."

"Ask your question. Answer it," said Judge Thomas, motioning to attorney Feldman and then to Brandesha.

"You were mistaken when you answered?" asked Feldman.

"I agree that I did not say what I meant to say," said Brandesha.

"Stop. Stop. See, you're not listening to me," said Judge Thomas. "Okay."

"He said, 'You were mistaken,'" said Judge Thomas.

"No, sir. I mean yes, sir," said Brandesha.

"—and you said, I agree that I did not say . . .," said Judge Thomas. "Okay," said Brandesha.

"You're answering the question you want to answer, but you're not answering the question that he's asking," said Judge Thomas.

"Uh-huh," said Brandesha.

"You're not the President of the United States," said Judge Thomas.

"What?" asked Brandesha.

The attorneys in the courtroom didn't know what to say. They had no idea what the judge was referring to. Weinstein suspected that the judge meant that only the President of the United States could get away with not telling the truth. *Was there a president of the United States who did not tell the truth in a court proceeding?* Weinstein thought to himself. Weinstein wanted to ask that Judge Thomas declare a mistrial and recuse himself for judicial impropriety, but if he did then the judge might retaliate further. He had no idea how dangerous Judge Thomas was becoming and how dangerous family law cases could be. *I hate family law cases*, Weinstein thought to himself.

Weinstein thought about his conversation with Tatiana. Why was Thomas being so hard on Brandeesha?

Then Judge Thomas looked at Brandesha and admonished her: "You are in an Alabama courtroom, and you will answer the question you're asked. Got it?" said Judge Thomas.

"Yes, sir."

Feldman went on with his cross-examination. "You admit that you lied earlier?"

"I admit that it was not correct as I remember it today," said Brandesha.

"Ma'am, let me stop you right here," said Judge Thomas.

"Uh-huh."

"We're going to take a break so you can get in a huddle with yourself and think about what you remember and what you don't," said Judge Thomas.

"Okay," answered Brandesha.

"I have had just about all of the selective memory I'm interested in here. You're under oath in a district court, and if you're asked a question and you remember an answer, you had best, by thunder, give that answer. You got that straight?"

"Yes," said Brandesha.

"And if you don't remember, you don't remember," said Judge Thomas.

"Okay," said Brandesha, about to cry.

Feldman continued.

"Do you apologize for anything you have done?" asked Feldman.

"I have apologized," said Brandesha.

"Do you remember what you said on a prior occasions?"

"I don't remember what I have said."

"Ma'am, let me stop you again," said Judge Thomas.

"Uh-huh,"

"Don't you play this cat and mouse game on me. I listened to that all morning. Now, do you want to take an opportunity to take a little break, take a deep breath, and decide what you remember, or not?" asked Judge Thomas.

Brandesha began to cry. She couldn't believe how Judge Thomas was treating her. He was worse than the attorney Feldman, whose questions were simple and direct. But the judge was injecting himself into the trial and abusing her as if he were assisting attorney Feldman.

Judge Thomas felt no remorse for her. Weinstein was clueless what to do. He knew that federal judges could ask questions but had no idea that a state judge could ask questions when there was no objection pending before the judge.

"I'm going to bind this witness over and give you an opportunity to call additional witnesses. And I'm going to order her to remain here today until we get to the bottom of—of what her testimony is. Her memory is not serving her well today, and perhaps she needs to think about it a little bit. Call your next witness," ordered Judge Thomas to Weinstein.

"We call Janice Stein," said Weinstein.

"Ok Ms. Stein, you have been sworn today and are under oath."

"Yes, Your Honor."

Weinstein went through some preliminary questions with her and then offered her expert report that said that the children should be in the custody of Brandesha.

"Ms. Stein, have you prepared a report?"

"Yes."

Weinstein went through the report with her before attempting to offer it. He knew that Feldman would object to the report going into evidence. Judge Thomas let the report come into evidence.

"Let's talk about the family that the children would have with Brandesha and her new husband," said Weinstein to his expert.

"Ok."

"That family life is real important, isn't it?"

"Certainly is," said Stein. "I could recount my family life story if you want to hear it."

"Recounting that is important, isn't it?" said Weinstein.

"It is," said Stein.

"Excellent answer," said Weinstein, bolstering his witness.

"Mr. Weinstein, you get about one more of those before it starts getting expensive," said Judge Thomas.

"I'm sorry, Your Honor," said Weinstein, annoyed by the Judge's admonition.

"I suggest you correct your tone a little bit," said Judge Thomas.

"Okay. I'll do my best, Your Honor," Weinstein agreed.

"Do your *very* best," said Judge Thomas.

"Your Honor, I'm just trying to do my job and examine this witness."

"Mr. Weinstein, sit down and do your job. Don't explain yourself to me further."

"Thank you, Your Honor."

Then Weinstein went through Stein's report page by page, being careful to get as much evidence in the record as he could.

"Mr. Weinstein, can I read this over lunch?" asked Judge Thomas.

"I'm sorry, Your Honor?" Weinstein was confused by the judge's question.

"Can I read this over lunch?" asked Judge Thomas.

"Absolutely, Your Honor," said Weinstein.

"Do you trust that I will?" asked Judge Thomas.

"Absolutely, Your Honor," nodded Weinstein.

"If I might, because you've been having Miss Stein read it to me all morning—or since you've been examining her, that's about all she's done. And I was wondering if I could read this and you could examine her as to issues that I couldn't read from what she's written," said Judge Thomas.

"Your Honor, yes, but that really is my direct of Miss Stein."

"Well, go right ahead," said Judge Thomas.

"And then I'll move along, Your Honor."

Weinstein closed his evidence. The opposing counsel had no evidence to offer.

Judge Thomas ruled: "I am not very happy with this case. I'm going to deny the motion. I seriously came close to awarding sanctions in this case against the Petitioner, but in the interest of justice I will not."

Weinstein was astounded by the judge's behavior and ruling. Not only that, but he took the case on a pro bono basis and he could have been hit with costs by the judge when he wasn't being paid.

"I'm sorry about the way this turned out," apologized Weinstein to Brandesha.

"That's ok. But that judge. I don't know how he gets away with acting like that," said Brandesha. "He didn't act like a judge. He acted like a corrupt cop working the nightshift. Like I was under arrest or something."

"Try not to think about him," said Weinstein. "There is something else going on with him that you don't know about. Something deep inside that he has been dealing with a long time. I tell you what I'm going to do. I will appeal this case," said Weinstein.

"An appeal?"

"Yes, we can ask a higher court to review the case," explained Weinstein.

"Do we have a case?" asked Brandesha.

"Of course, we have a case," said Weinstein, consoling her. Weinstein experienced his first defeat as a civil trial attorney.

Chapter 8

———— ❧ ————

CUB DROVE BRANDEESHA BACK TO the paper in the company car. She cried most of the way back while Cub tried to comfort her.

"It will be all right. You will get your kids back. Soon they will get old and will come back to you on their own. And when they get to be teens, you won't want 'em around anyway. You will want your ex to get them off your hands for a while because they'll be so difficult that you will send them back," said Cub.

"I would never do that," sniffed Brandesha.

"Wait until they turn fifteen or sixteen. You won't even recognize them as your own kids," said Cub.

Brandeesha began to cry even more.

They arrived at the paper and Brandesha went to her desk, where she continued sobbing the rest of the day.

"My gosh, Mr. Nelms. I couldn't believe the judge at that trial. He was the most abusive person I have ever seen. How did he ever get appointed? I saw him try the case against Andre in Paris. He was bad as a prosecutor and even worse as a judge," Cub said to Nelms. "We need to do a story about him, Boss."

"We are not publishing a story about a corrupt white Judge. They will shut the paper down. We let this one go," said Nelms.

"We need to do something," said Cub.

"Those family law judges get mad sometimes during these divorce cases. They have tempers and start acting as bad as the couples going through the divorce. It's all that they hear and after a while they go crazy on the bench just like the parties in the case."

"Yes, but this one went too far," argued Cub.

"So, what are you proposing?" asked Nelms.

"We have to write something," said Cub. Cub walked around the room, thinking to himself. Then he stopped. "How about an editorial?"

"To say what?" asked Nelms.

"What if we don't even mention him. What if I write something about what makes a good judge. Something that won't point to him directly and then let the readers draw their own conclusions."

"That's ok. I can see that. I just don't want to take on one judge directly."

"I won't write anything that is bad," promised Cub.

"You are right. Write something something good that doesn't mention the judge directly."

"You got it, Boss," said Cub as he walked out.

"Cub," called Nelms. "I want our paper to be healthy. I want our city to be healthy. We tell stories not told in other newspapers. My paper tells it like it is. We don't endorse. We are objective and want to be healthy politically. I'm seventy-five years old and have had many experiences. I relate them to what goes on today and in our segregated society. This is very important to understand," said Nelms.

Cub looked at him in agreement.

Nelms was familiar with divorce cases. He had become wealthy owning the *Birmingham Defender* and his wife divorced him, taking half of the value of the newspaper. He would never marry again after that and would be alone. Brandesha would look after him like she was his daughter.

Andre went to see Brandesha.

"He was awful," said Brandesha.

"You mean Captain Weinstein?" asked Andre.

"No, the judge. It was the worst thing that I have ever been through in my entire life."

"What happened?"

"Every time I tried to say something, the judge interrupted me and said that I was not answering the question that the attorney was asking me, but I was answering what I wanted to answer. He said he was going to keep me in the courtroom. He told me I wasn't the President of the United States."

"The President of the United States? What did he mean by that?" asked Andre. "Was he talking about Truman?"

"I have no idea," said Brandesha. "Are you aware of any U.S. president who didn't tell the truth in a court case? What did that have to do with me?"

"I don't know," said Andre. "I wonder how these American presidents come into our lives. How was Weinstein in court?"

"Did he know that judge before?" asked Brandesha.

"Who was the judge?"

"His name was Judge Thomas."

"Judge John Thomas?" exclaimed Andre.

"Yes, that was his name. There was something between the Judge and Mr. Weinstein. I don't know what it was, but he hated Mr. Weinstein."

Brandesha cried at her desk. Andre was stunned and didn't know what to say.

Chapter 9

⸻

"TONIGHT SHERRY, EUGENIE IS TO take a letter that Clisson wrote to her and read it aloud, directly to Clisson," said Betty.

"I can do that," said Sherry. "Don't laugh at me Andre."

"I won't," said Andre.

"Here goes," said Sherry. Sherry, reading Clisson's letter:

> **EUGENIE** *My love, I cannot tell you how things are changing. Your love is changed. Your heart has been stolen from me, worse this feeling is too harsh. You've been tricked. You were still virtuous despite my absence in the wickedness of man. My thoughts are all confused.*

Sherry:

> **EUGENIE:** *But he is wrong. I love no one else. But I cannot take this vengeance that he seeks against this man. He has to decide what he really wants. A life with me to continue to battle these demons and to seek vengeance against others. If that is how he feels me must decide on his own. I'm not going to run my feelings into the wind, into the sea or up a flagpole. He must decide if he will solve his quest for vengeance or consider his problems solved.*

"At this point you will sing your song to Clisson. You are exchanging letters so this will be your song to him," directed

Betty. "The song is a little complicated. Sherry, do you want to tell the cast where you got this song?"

"Andre wrote it at boot camp," said Sherry.

John rolled his eyes.

"Booker said it was worst song he had ever heard," said Andre. The cast laughed.

"Booker hated all music," recalled Mary.

"Ok, let's hear it," said Betty. "Now this song is supposed to be a substitute for a soliloquy. Shakespeare had seven soliloquies in Hamlet. I love soliloquies. Since we can't say them, you can sing them." Betty sang the word 'sing.'

Sherry took out a sheet of paper with the words. "Do you want me to read it or sing it?"

"Read it tonight and we will practice the song tomorrow night," said Betty.

"Ok. Here goes," said Sherry, singing the song a cappella:
If that's the way you feel ...

Sherry then sang the next verse, going up a higher note for each line until she reached an octave higher than where she started.

Sherry scaled the octave perfectly.

"That is the worst song I have ever heard," said John. "The Catholics are going to think this is one crazy church."

The cast laughed.

"If Sherry thinks it is good, then I'm sure this is a good song," said Betty.

"It is good. I like how it scales an octave," said Sherry. "Then the song has an orchestral part that takes off after that. We will need violins for the play."

"Violins? Where will be get them?" said Betty. "Let me ask the cast. Do you think this song fits the play?"

"It is the worst I've ever heard," said John. "I heard you the first time," said Betty.

The cast laughed, except for Andre and Sherry.

After rehearsal, John pulled Betty into a room behind the stage. "Can you believe that song?" complained John.

"I don't see Napoleon Bonaparte riding off to battle and singing, *'If that's the way you feel'.*"

"Probably something between lovers, I guess. If that's what she wants, let her have it and let her make a foll of herself, " said Betty.

"You are right! Let them make fools of themselves!" agreed John. "I'm not in the habit of running my fears up a flagpole."

"And I'm less concerned of your secrets than about why you carry on," said Betty. They laughed together quoting lines from the song.

Sherry was walking down the hall and overheard Betty. She peered in the room. "I thought I heard you two."

"Yes, I was just telling John how great you sounded," said Betty.

"I can't wait for everyone in the church to hear it," said John. "Uh-huh," said Sherry.

Chapter 10

ANDRE AND TATIANA TOOK A train to o New York City and then took a flight to London. The transatlantic flights from New York to London were on a daily occurrence. From London to Paris they took the train to Dover where the night train is loaded on a large ferry. The train is split in half to equalize the ferry. Then it crosses the English channel to Dunkirk and then the train is reassembled and continues its trip to Paris.

"I never talked to you about the trial. I was there covering it," said Tatiana, sitting next to Andre while on the final trip into Paris.

"I saw you there," said Andre.

"I thought your testimony on the witness stand was strange. I'm sorry to say that now. But since you were acquitted, I could see that it was just a mix up and you should not have been charged with anything. The prosecutor turned a losing case into a winning case and your lawyer turned it into a winning case on appeal. That was some great lawyering," said Tatiana.

"Thanks. I'm over it. The prosecutor is now a state court judge."

"I know that. You are not over the trial or the war. I know why we are on this trip," explained Tatiana. "How do you want to do this? I'm supposed to write travel articles while you investigate. What are you going to do?"

"I want to go the site and retrace my steps, maybe talk to the French women that were there."

"What do you think they will say?"

"I don't know. Maybe they saw something."

"The other soldier named Private Ellis said he saw the shooting and he shot his weapon, too. That did not come out at the trial."

"Where did you find that out?" asked Andre.

"Mr. Otwell came to see me at the paper. He was doing a story on that integrated unit you were in and he said that Private Ellis told him that. He said they were transferred out of the theater and could not testify. Do you know why they weren't called to testify at trial?"

"I gave the names to Mr. Weinstein and he tried to find them but he said they had been transferred out of the area and could not be brought back for the trial," said Andre.

"Ok. It sounds like you know what you are doing. I want to at least see the Eiffel Tower at some point during our trip," said Tatiana.

"Been there," said Andre.

"You've been to the Eiffel Tower?" asked a surprised Tatiana. "No. Not really," I dreamed I was there.

Upon arriving in Paris, they took a train to St. Raphael..

Chapter 11

AFTER HIS EXPERIENCE WITH BRANDEESHA'S case, Weinstein was concerned about Aunt Clara's suit being in Judge Thomas's court. He decided to file for a jury trial. He would never let Judge Thomas decide a case based on his judgment.

At trial, Aunt Clara testified and told the story of how a man came to her door and promised to install burglar bars on her home. She had experienced break ins and felt unsafe. She signed the paperwork but she never made any monthly payments.

Weinstein tried to identify with a jury of white and black jurors. The South was still new to him and his presentation was awkward. Aunt Clara told Weinstein to quote from the Bible during his closing and Weinstein too her advice and quoted the 23rd Psalm. He was determined to win. He walked to the jury box and in his final closing he said:

> *The Lord is my shepherd, I shall not want,*
> *He makes me lie down in green pastures,*
> *he leads me beside quiet waters,*
> *he refreshes my soul.*
> *He guides me along the right paths*
> *for his name's sake.*
> *Even though I walk*
> *through the darkest valley,*
> *I will fear no evil,*
> *for you are with me;*

your rod and your staff,
they comfort me.
You prepare a table before me
in the presence of my enemies.
You anoint my head with oil;
my cup overflows.
Surely your goodness and love will follow me
all the days of my life,
and I will dwell in the house of the Lord
forever.

Aunt Clara yelled out, "Praise Jesus" while Weinstein was quoting the Bible. To Aunt Clara, Weinstein had done his job. The jury was unimpressed and dumfounded, wondering what the Twenty-Third Psalm had to do with Aunt Clara not paying for the burglar bars. The jury was more sophisticated than Weinstein thought. While they sympathized with Aunt Clara, they thought that the company had a right to recover its debt.

The jury retired to deliberate. They were confused with the jury charge that Judge Thomas gave them. They had a chance to award damages to her for the loss of her home, but the mortgage company was owed a debt. The jury granted zero damages but awarded legal fees in their verdict. That meant that she lost the case because the law did not allow for legal fees unless there was an award of damages. Aunt Clara received nothing.

Weinstein was deflated. He wanted to know why the jury awarded legal fees but no damages. Judge Thomas called the counsel up to the bench.

"Tough luck on the case. I know you wanted to win. You should have won," said Judge Thomas to Weinstein. "But I want to add that I never quote from the Bible in oral arguments or refer to it during a case. I think you were too involved in this case. You were in the loop. You have to be out of the loop. You have to be detached from your client's case. You should know that after our case in Paris."

"Thank you, Judge. I know. I was personally involved in this case," responded Weinstein, taking the admonishment in stride. This time he couldn't blame his loss on Judge Thomas.

"Thank you, Your Honor," said opposing counsel.

After the trial, Weinstein and Aunt Clara stood outside the courtroom waiting to hear from the jurors.

One of the jurors told him, "She didn't pay for the burglar bars, so the company had no choice. But we felt that you should be paid for your work. You did a good job."

"Did you not understand the jury charge? You had to award damages in order to award legal fees," said Weinstein.

"I didn't know that. Why didn't you tell us that!" complained one juror.

Then she began to cry. "I can't believe what we did."

"We could have put something down there. Why didn't you tell us!" Another juror said.

"We needed to know what we were doing! You didn't tell us!" added another juror.

"The law doesn't work that way. It says you only answer questions. It can't advise you of the effect of your answers," said Weinstein.

"We wanted her to win. But since she didn't pay the company back we didn't think she was entitled to damages," said another juror.

Deflated, Weinstein drove Aunt Clara out to the home at St. Peter's. Sister Camille told him to bring her there after the verdict. She would stay with the nuns until they could make other arrangements.

"I'm sorry it did not work out for you," said Jesse Weinstein. "I don't know why the jury did what they did."

"It is ok. I will manage. You did the best you could, Lawyer Weinstein. I liked how you quoted from the Bible. They needed to hear that. That won the case for me."

"That was mistake. I should have never brought up religion during a trial. I have a lot to learn about civil jury trials," said Weinstein. "It sure is different than the trials I had as JAG officer."

Weinstein lost his first jury trial as a civilian lawyer. He was learning.

Chapter 12

AFTER ONLY SIX MONTHS AS a judge, Thomas learned there was an opening for a newly created United States District Judge position in Huntsman, Alabama. He would have the inside track because of his military background and his experience as a sitting state district judge. He was a natural selection.

Weinstein attended Judge Thomas's swearing in.

"Congratulations on your new position. Federal service once more. I bet it's like being in JAG again," said Weinstein.

"Yes. No running for office. A lifetime appointment. I hope to see you in my court again," said U.S. District Judge John Thomas.

Weinstein grimaced. "*I hope not,*" he thought to himself. "*A District Judge? I can't imagine what he will unleash on the federal judiciary.*" Then he left the reception. "*I can't believe I said that. I can't seem to forgive that judge.*" Weinstein realized how important relationships between attorneys were, and how important it was to have a good relationship with a judge. Attorneys were known to know many people and could influence society a great deal.

Chapter 13

———— ❦ ————

ON SEPTEMBER 30, 1948, GOVERNOR Thomas Dewey was in Salt Lake City, Utah, where he delivered a speech:

> *I deeply appreciate the rare privilege and honor of speaking to the American people tonight in this great Tabernacle built for the worship of God.*
>
> *I wish to talk with you tonight about our greatest domestic issue. It is the problem of peace of the world. It is one which should only be dealt with entirely without partisanship and I the highest real of statesmanship . . .*
>
> *The business of statesmanship is to anticipate and solve international problems before they become crises, and to solve crises before they become wars. Statesmanship is the sum total of domestic and foreign policies which make a country strong enough, consistent enough, and respected enough so that it can live at peace in the world. Crisis is the failure of statesmanship and war is the ultimate bankruptcy of statesmanship.*

The next day on October 1, 1948, President Truman gave a speech at Charleston, West Virginia:

> *For the past two weeks, I have been visiting the people of this country. I have met thousands of people and spoken to hundreds of thousands. I think I have*

been seen by at least 2½ million people in this country.

I have a vital message to bring to the people of the United States, and tonight I want to bring that message to you.

The heart of my message is this: The national election this fall will decide matters of grave importance to every man, woman, and child in the United States.

Itwillaffectthesecurityofyourjobs,yourhomes,andyourf uture.

You have a choice between the Democratic Party and the Republican Party . . .

The working men and women in this country could not do much to help themselves, because the strength of their unions had been broken by the reactionary labor policies of the Republican administration.

- The Republican bubble burst in 1929, and when it burst:

- There was no minimum wage to cushion the blow.

- There was no unemployment compensation to carry the working man's family along.

- There was no work relief program to help people through the crisis.

But the party of privilege was ready to carry big business through the crisis. It created the Reconstruction Finance Corporation for that purpose. The banks, the railways, the insurance companies; they got relief, but not the American people.

For the unemployed, it was Hoovervilles and soup kitchens. Veterans were encouraged to go into business for themselves selling apples.

That is the Republican record. Most of us well remember it. The Democratic part of the record begins in 1933, when the Democratic Party began to build prosperity for business, labor, and agriculture.

Chapter 14

WHILE ON THE TRAIN, ANDRE went to sleep. He remembered at boot camp when Booker and Ellis got in a fight about something. Ellis and Booker were similar. Ellis grew up in Atlanta, Georgia, a town of mystery and violence. Ellis had a chip on his soldier and was an angry soldier. He came from a town that in 1948 added eight black men to its police force at a time when one-quarter of the Atlanta policemen were members of the Ku Klux Klan. He grew up during Jim Crow where he black people were second-class citizens. They couldn't ride in the front of the bus or eat in most restaurants. Ellis hadn't forgotten how he was treated.

"Man, you are crazy!" said Booker as he got out of bed and took a swing at Ellis from behind.

"Whoa there," said Ellis. "You want a piece of me?"

"I'll get a piece of you yet," countered Booker. "Knock it off," said Andre.

Then they heard Drill Sergeant Bob Mills coming. All the recruits stood at attention as Mills came walking down their hall. The thin and wiry Mills would be their parent for the next twelve weeks.

"Now there are two rules you obey here. One, you obey me. Two, you obey the army. If you obey those rules you will get through here in no time. If you don't, then you will be back here with me again and again until you get it right. I know what goes on in here. I know your every move. It appears that someone here is a wise cracker. It appears that another wants to fight. What's your name, boy?"

"Private Ellis, sir."

"What's your name, boy?"

"Private Thompson, sir."

"You know, I smell a fight here. Yes, I see a fight here. Do you see a fight here?" asked Mills.

"No sir," said Booker.

"I think I see a fight. Yes. I think I see trouble here. You two are going to fight. Tomorrow Private Thompson and Private Ellis are going to box in the ring. You will settle it then."

They boxed the next day. It was a brutal fight. No one knew who won.

Ellis and Booker had no more trouble.

Chapter 15

ANDRE OPENED HIS EYES.

"Are you awake?" asked Tatiana. "Yes."

"When I was covering the trial I wasn't that sympathetic to you," said Tatiana.

"You weren't?" asked Andre.

"No. I saw things as black or white, so to speak. Oliver and I disagreed over the trial. He thought I was judgmental. I thought he was over-identifying with the soldier," said Tatiana.

"I'm glad he took a personal interest in me."

"During the trial, when the prosecutor showed you those photographs and you said that you didn't know who they were. Did you really mean that?" asked Tatiana.

"I just woke up and you bring that up," sighed Andre. "Does this bother you to talk about it?"

"Yes."

"I'm sorry. But I can't help from saying that when you were on the witness stand and the prosecutor Thomas gave you those photos of the priests and nuns. You said you didn't know who they were and you said they were *black* nuns and priests. You totally lost me at that point. I thought it made you look guilty or you were hiding something. How could you say they were black when they were white?"

"I knew they were white. I was not answering the question he was asking. I was answering the question the way I wanted to answer it. I wanted to believe they were black. I'm told if you believe it then it can be real."

"I think those photos hurt you at the trial and it looked like you knew more than you were talking about."

"That has to be the third time you said that."

"I will change the subject," said Tatiana. "Okay."

"What does Mr. Nelms have you working on?"

"A bunch of names to look up, like Hugo Black."

"Hugo Black? The Supreme Court Justice?"

"Yes, and some others. Black was a Klan member and a reporter found out about it and won a Pulitzer Prize for his research."

"I didn't know that."

"It shows how we have to investigate people and not take what they say at face value."

"It does."

"Some people stupidly got involved with the Klan and lived to regret it," said Andre.

"Like the Communists. Mr. Nelms has me reporting on Communists' influence in Hollywood and in the government. I've researched the House Un-American Activities Committee."

"Are the Russians influencing the government and Hollywood?"

"There are some communists in Hollywood, probably not many. It is blown out of proportion," said Tatiana.

"Really?" asked Andre.

"Yes. Some people believe that the Communists are influencing our elections, the government, Hollywood. Truman has instituted loyalty oaths for all civil servants," explained Tatiana.

Chapter 16

THE CHURCH AT ST. RAPHAEL was in the distance.

"Is that the church?" Tatiana asked.

"It is," said Andre. "I never thought I would see this place again."

"Let's check it out. Beautiful architecture. They don't build churches like this in America."

The two disembarked from the train and walked to the church. Tatiana knocked on the door and Sister Martine answered.

"Sister, do you remember me? I was the soldier who collapsed here a few years ago," Andre reminded her.

"I do," she replied in broken English. "Father Patrick, come here. The American soldier has returned. He has someone with him."

Father Patrick came to the door. "Come in. Tell us why you are here. Sister, can you offer them something?"

"My name is Tatiana Smith. I'm with the *Birmingham Defender* and I'm doing a travel story. Andre told me about this site. I thought it might make a good travel story or an article about what life is like after the war."

"Where do it begin?" said Father Patrick.

"Let me show you around Mrs. Smith, and Andre and Father Patrick can get reacquainted," offered Sister Martine, taking Tatiana's arm.

"What can you tell me about this church?" asked Tatiana. "Have you spent your entire career here?"

"Yes, as a servant of Jesus Christ," said Sister Martine.

"Were you here when Andre came to the church and collapsed?"

"Yes. The soldier collapsed on the front door. We took him in because we knew the Vichy police would take him."

"You are the young soldier who came to us during the war. I recognize you now," greeted Father Patrick.

"I came back to see if you could tell me what you remember back then?" explained Andre.

"You made it home safely?" asked Father Patrick.

"I did. I would like to retrace what went on back then. It's taken me a long time to get here," said Andre.

"Let's see," recalled Father Patrick. "Sister Martine found you at the door and we brought you in. The Vichy police appeared to be curious about you and wanted to know if you were in here."

"What did I say?" asked Andre.

"You said you went to school," said Father Patrick. "It was an exclusive private school for black children."

"I can't believe I said that," said Andre, shaking his head. "What name did I give it?"

"It was St. Matthias," Father Patrick remembered. "We looked for it by name but could not find one."

"That was a mistake. The name of the church is St. Peter's. I was relaying only a dream."

"Yes, it was a confusing time. Things did not seem as they appeared," said Father Patrick. "What brings you here now?"

"I came to make peace with my past. These places and memories are still with us."

"That is good," nodded Father Patrick. "Did I say anything else?"

"You wanted to go to confession," said Father Patrick.

"Did I go?" asked Andre.

"No. The Vichy police came by then," said Father Patrick.

They talked further until Sister Martine and Tatiana returned from their tour of the church.

"It is good that you are here," said Sister Martine.

"Why is that?" said Tatiana.

"The young man has come to make peace with his past. That's what he was doing when he came here the first time."

"He was?" asked Tatiana.

"Oui, Madame. He was looking for home."

"You mean St. Matthias—the wealthy private school for black students?"

"Oui, Madame. But this time, he is searching for something else."

"Like what?"

"His future."

Chapter 17

WEINSTEIN VOLUNTEERED TO ASSIST IN a pro bono case through the Montgomery local bar association referral program. His first case was a federal habeas corpus petition for a Negro defendant who had committed a burglary of a habitation. He was convicted in state court in Alabama and his conviction was affirmed at all Alabama state appeals courts.

Weinstein read the record and observed that during the closing arguments, the prosecutor raised questions about why the defendant did not explain certain evidence. Weinstein couldn't believe that the case came to him. It reminded him of the trial of Private Andre Williams and the way that Captain Thomas misplaced the burden of proof during his closing argument. He remembered Thomas's closing arguments in the Williams trial:

> "And now in a short period of time, the case will be handed to you. You're going to go back into that deliberation room with that presumption of innocence; that presumption of innocence; that presumption of innocence that the defendant is cloaked with while we have been trying this case—that presumption, when you go back in the room behind you, is going to vanish when you start deliberating. And that's when the presumption of guilt is going to take over and..."

Then he remembered how Thomas tried to correct his error by giving his own curative instruction to the jury—as if he were the presiding judge of the case:

> *"I'm sorry. I didn't mean presumption of innocence. Private Williams has nothing to prove, and it is our obligation to prove the case beyond a reasonable doubt."*

Weinstein wondered how Thomas could misplace the burden of proof. Every lawyer knows there is no presumption of guilt in a criminal case. Thomas said on the record during the Williams trial that his statement was intentional, which must have meant he made the statement, but did not mean what he had said.

He thought of Thomas's suspension for neglecting to pay his bar dues. Then Thomas, during Andre's trial negligently failed to respond to his request to have witnesses available who might corroborate Andre's story. They ended up being transferred out of theater and Weinstein couldn't interview them. Now this case and the reviews by some some attorneys showed that Judge Thomas had poor judgment. They all seemed to add up that there was a character flaw with Judge Thomas. But what was it? No one had ever pieced all this together. Maybe Tatiana was right. The focus now should not be on the facts of Andre's case but on Thomas: *Why did Thomas bring the case against Williams in the first place?*

Chapter 18

WEINSTEIN FILED THE WRIT OF habeas corpus petition, alleging a complaint of prosecutorial error that violated the defendant's Fifth Amendment right. Of all things to occur, the case was assigned to United States District Judge John Thomas.

Weinstein slapped his forehead. "Of all the courts to be in. This is my third case before him and it involves the same kind of mistake that Thomas had committed in Private Williams trial!" he thought.

Weinstein was convinced that Thomas would have to recognize the prosecutor's error and since the Williams' conviction was reversed, he would have to apply a similar analysis.

"He is going to have sympathy for the prosecutor," thought Weinstein to himself. "That's what happens when the government appoints prosecutors as judges. They have no sympathy for the defendant. A defense attorney will never be appointed as a judge."

At oral arguments before Judge Thomas, Weinstein pointed out that the record showed the error of the prosecutor in his closing argument:

> "Search of his residence. A hidden jersey. Why is that a hidden jersey? Why didn't he tell us why Sergio Rodriguez hid that jersey? Why didn't we hear about

that? Why is that jersey hidden in the garage in a box underneath newspaper?"

"Your Honor, the fact that the prosecutor asked that question shows a clear violation of my client's Fifth Amendment rights," argued Weinstein. "The record shows the following by the prosecutor:

> *Ladies and gentlemen, I'm talking about, why didn't counsel explain to us—he explained to us that that jersey was in the garage, something about it not having blood on in the garage. And he didn't tell us why it was..."*

After arguments, Judge Thomas retired to his offices and said he would come back in thirty minutes to announce his verdict. As Weinstein expected, Judge Thomas was sympathetic to the prosecutor. He announced his ruling:

> "It is my obligation in a habeas corpus case to grant it if any claim that was adjudicated on the merits in State court proceedings unless the adjudication of the claim resulted in a decision that was contrary to, or involved an unreasonable application of, clearly established Federal law, as determined by the Supreme Court of the United States; or resulted in a decision that was based on an unreasonable determination of the facts in light of the evidence presented in the State court proceeding. State court decisions are to be given the benefit of the doubt. I find that the prosecutor's comments viewed in context can only be seen as a fair comment on the state of the evidence since the prosecutor's question did not

refer directly or indirectly to the defendant's failure to testify."

Weinstein rose to interrupt Judge Thomas. "You mean his comment *'why didn't he tell us why Sergio Rodriguez hid the jersey and why didn't we hear about that'* was not a comment on his failure to testify?"

"Counsel don't interrupt the court!" yelled Judge Thomas. "I'm sorry, Judge."

"I was saying that the Fifth Amendment prohibits the prosecution from commenting on a defendant's failure to testify by forbidding either comment by the prosecution on the accused's silence or instructions by the court that such silence is evidence of guilt."

"Thank you, Your Honor," said the U.S. prosecuting attorney. Weinstein wanted to respond and began to rise from his seat.

"Counsel, stand down!" commanded Judge Thomas. He then read from a prepared ruling:

> "Courts will not reverse when the prosecutorial comment is a single, isolated incident, does not stress an inference of guilt from silence as a basis of conviction, and is followed by curative instructions. A prosecutor may comment on the defendant's failure to present exculpatory evidence as long as the comments do not call attention to the defendant's failure to testify. Comments on the failure of the defense, as opposed to the defendant, to counter or explain the testimony presented are also permissible. A prosecutor's indirect comment violates the Fifth Amendment

if it is manifestly intended to call attention to the defendant's failure to testify, or is of such a character that the jury would naturally and necessarily take it to be a comment on the failure to testify. This petition is denied because the prosecutor did not directly or indirectly comment on Petitioner's failure to testify."

Disgusted, Weinstein rose and said, "Is this something like the presumption of innocence will disappear and then the presumption of guilt will take over when you go into the jury room?" Weinstein was referring to Thomas's closing argument in Private Williams' court-martial and was comparing the two cases. "You are referring to the Williams' court-martial, aren't you?" asked Judge

Thomas. "I knew you would bring that up at some point in this case."

"Yes. The same analysis applies," said Weinstein.

"No, it does not. And one more outburst like that and it will become expensive," rebuked Judge Thomas.

"What are you two talking about?" asked the curious U.S. Attorney, watching the second private war between Thomas and Weinstein play out with no clue as to the history between the two.

"Just a score we are still settling from the war," explained Weinstein.

"Hold on there," said Judge Thomas. "I know what you are implying. You are trying to compare this case to the Williams' court-martial back in Paris where I made a mistake during the closing arguments."

"Isn't it the same?" asked Weinstein.

"No, it's not. My error in the *U.S.A. v Williams* case was was the misplacement of the burden of proof at closing arguments. I admit I slipped up and misplaced the burden of proof in closing arguments. I was tired that day as I recall, I tried to correct the error," said Judge Thomas.

"You even gave your own curative instruction to the court members," said Weinstein.

"I can't imagine you misplacing the burden of proof, Judge Thomas. You are always so good at what you do," said the U.S. Attorney.

Judge Thomas smiled at the U.S. Attorney and his fondness for Judge Thomas. Weinstein was disgusted.

"I did. I admit it and then I corrected myself during my closing," Judge Thomas recalled.

"But the Board of Review said that a curative instruction by you and the judge in that case was not sufficient," said Weinstein.

"Can I speak?" asked Judge Thomas to Weinstein. "Yes."

"That case is not similar to this one. That was not a Fifth Amendment case. That case is not on point. This is a Fifth Amendment case. Case law is clear that a prosecutor's indirect comments that do not manifestly intend to call attention to the defendant's failure to testify is not a violation of the law," said Judge Thomas.

"Your Honor, the question about why he didn't tell us about the jersey could only be answered if my client testified," said Weinstein. "You basically made it so that nothing could be explained unless the defendant got on the witness stand to explain it, where my client does not have the burden to prove anything."

"The question *'why didn't he tell us why the defendant hid that jersey?'* was used as a rhetorical device to call attention to the possibility that Petitioner hid the jersey, thereby showing Petitioner's consciousness of guilt," said Judge Thomas.

"The court is saying that the prosecutor's statements about the defendant not explaining the answers to the prosecutor's questions about the jersey was just a *'rhetorical device'*? The prosecution is shifting the burden of proof to the defendant to provide answers to the prosecutor's questions when the defendant does not have a burden to prove innocence. Isn't that exactly the same thing you did in the Williams case? You shifted the burden of proof to the defense, Your Honor."

"No! It is not the same," yelled Judge Thomas. Then he calmed down and it became quiet in the courtroom. No one said a word. At least two minutes went by in total cold dead silence in the courtroom while the attorneys waited for Judge Thomas to speak.

"It is not the same. The prosecutor clearly used *"he"* to refer to defense counsel's failure to address the issue. It was a comment to reflect the defense counsel's deficiency in addressing the issue, not an indirect attack on your client's decision not to testify. The comment was not of such a character that the jury would naturally and necessarily take it to be a comment on the failure to testify because the prosecutor's use of the word 'counsel.' They were not used impermissibly and did not convey a direct or indirect reference to the defendant's failure to testify. I find that the Alabama Court of Appeals and Alabama Supreme Court's denial of the claim neither contrary to, nor an unreasonable application of, clearly established Supreme Court law.

Accordingly, I am recommending that the habeas corpus relief be denied. Good day. You are dismissed."

Judge Thomas stood up and exited the court.

"All rise," said the bailiff as he exited. The attorneys stood up.

"What were you two talking about?" asked the confused U.S. Attorney as he walked over to talk with Weinstein.

"An old score being settled," explained Weinstein. "Sounds like he settled it."

"Yes, he did. He always has the last word. He always lands on his feet. He will never admit a mistake," said Weinstein as he was packing up his briefcase.

"What?" asked the U.S. Attorney.

"Forget it." Weinstein walked out of the courtroom.

Returning to his office after the hearing, Weinstein opened a letter on his desk. It was from the Alabama Court of Appeals for his appeal of Brandesha's case. While researching the case he found a similar case like hers in which a judge made abusive remarks to the litigant just as Judge Thomas had made towards Brandesha. The court wrote that it distinguished that case because the remarks made by the judge were made to a jury whereas the remarks that Judge Thomas made were made in a non-jury trial as closing remarks. The court held that the error was not reversible error and did not indicate bias or prejudice that may have led to an improper judgment.

Chapter 19

———— ⌘ ————

ANDRE AND TATIANA RENTED IN St. Raphael and drove through the French countryside, surrounded by farms and cattle on either side where groves of trees became woods. Andre recognized the road that he turned on when he was confronted by the Germans during the war. The thought of that drive made him shudder.

"What do you hope to find on this trip?" asked Tatiana.

"One of the soldiers said that they were there and saw the shooting. Maybe I was not the only one who fired a gun."

"The reporter Roy Otwell suggested there were others present when you were here. He said to look for the serial number on your weapon," Tatiana asked. "I knew there was an issue there but since they proved that the bullet came from my gun we didn't pursue it."

"Did you ever see the weapon after the trial?"

"No. It was gone after I got up."

"You didn't find it afterwards?" asked Tatiana. "No."

"You mean when you sent to the church you were unarmed?"

"Yes. What are you getting at?" replied a curious Andre. "What if someone switched weapons with you?"

"How could that happen?"

"Roy Otwell said that Private Lanny Ellis took your weapon after the shooting because his weapon no longer worked," said Tatiana. "You didn't know that at the trial. If the bullet that hit Booker came from Ellis's gun then that means he shot him and not you."

"I hope you are right."

Further ahead was the wooded area he remembered. Tatiana got out and followed Andre after they parked alongside the road. Andre found the tree he had hidden behind.

"There were Germans there" he said pointing."

"Where?" asked Tatiana.

"Over there," said Andre pointing into the woods. "That is where the shooting happened. I was here."

Tatiana had a hard time walking through the woods in her black sweater and brown skirt. The grass and the ground was wet and covered her shoes as she plodded on. The two made their way to the tree that Booker had rested against.

"There's the tree. Booker was right here."

Then he walked a little further.

"Here's the sink hole. I was in here after the bomb hit, and no one realized it."

Tatiana and Andre were looking in the sink hole when someone suddenly tapped Tatiana on the shoulder.

She screamed.

"I'm sorry," she said. "You startled me." It was one of the French ladies named Laurence.

"Qu'est ce que vous faites?" she asked.

"God, you scared me," said Andre. "Parlez vous anglais?"

"Oui, parlez vous anglais" said the lady.

"I'm sorry. We are on a mission. It is about something a few years ago. It was a shooting that happened here? I was in the army back then," said Andre.

The other lady came out of the home and the door slammed. "Comment allez vous?" asked Tatiana.

"Je vais bien," said Margaux.

"Parlez-vous Anglais?" asked Tatiana.

"Do you remember me? I was one of the soldiers here in 1945," said Andre. "Let us come into the home and talk," invited Laurence.

They went into the home and the older lady took out a bottle of wine. They sat down.

"Where are you from?" asked Laurence. "We are from Alabama, America."

"We are from St. Raphael," said Margaux.

"Why do you live out here?" asked Tatiana.

"My family lived here. We farmed. We have rabbits, and lambs. That is all that we need. Why are you here?"

"I came to see where my friend was shot," said Andre.

"We know the story. He came to the home and we thought he was a German. It was dark. Then there was the bombing. We've rebuilt the home," said Margaux.

"Did you see me?" asked Andre.

"We ran off after the bombing. You stayed with the other soldier and then another bomb came," said Margaux.

"You remember," said Andre.

"The other soldiers took the soldier away," said Laurence.

"You saw the army come and get him?" asked Tatiana.

"Oui. They took him on a stretcher."

"Do you remember anything else? Such as were there soldiers here before the soliders that took him away?"

"There were other soldiers," recalled Margaux.

"How many?" asked Andre.

"There were other soldiers around your friend. Two, maybe three. One was checking on him. They stayed afterwards with him."

"That was right after the shooting?" asked Andre. "Oui."

"Can you describe who came afterwards?"

"One was tall and heavy set and muscular," said Margaux.

"Do you remember a scar on his neck?"

"I didn't see that close."

"Was he a black soldier?"

"Oui."

The women described Private Ellis and others with him.

"Anything else that you remember?"

"Nothing," said Margaux.

"Nothing," agreed Laurence.

Chapter 20

———— ❧ ————

IT WAS AUGUST OF 1944, and Andre and Booker were war-torn and weary. They had spent the last two years of the war in North Africa, Sicily, and Italy. They were scheduled to soon return home, but first they would participate in Operation Dragoon in a plan to free southern France. The two soldiers were among many being transported on Navy ships to the area between Marseilles and Nice, France. Two hundred yards from the shore, a German bomb destroyed their ship. Andre and Booker escaped and swam to shore, fighting for another six days with other troops that survived the sinking of the ship.

The bombing continued, and the American platoon advanced further into a wooded area. In the darkness, Andre and Booker became separated from their platoon. They knew that they were not too far away and would eventually reconnect. They were hungry and began to look for food.

Booker entered a house and the frightened French women inside feared that Booker was a German soldier, unaware that he and Andre were Allies. When Booker attempted to clear the women from the house, one began beating him with a rake.

Suddenly, Andre saw movement in the nearby trees. Germans! He pointed his weapon at the German soldier and fired, but a bomb directly hit and destroyed the women's home, knocking Andre off his feet and causing him to miss his target.

Moments earlier, a group of soldiers searching nearby for Andre and Booker heard the commotion at the French women's home. They saw movement in the woods as well and watched from behind the protection of trees. Private Lanny Ellis saw the Germans that Andre had seen. He lifted his rifle and then he and Andre shot at them almost simultaneously.

Still unsure of the danger, Ellis and his buddies decided to remain behind the trees and watch what would happen. He saw that Booker had been shot and was lying on the ground. He could see that Andre was taking care of Booker, checking his wound. He watched the two talk, then saw Andre walk away when they began to argue.

More bombs shook the air, and Andre disappeared. Unaware that Andre had fallen into a sink hole, unconscious, Ellis could only see that Booker was alone. "We have to go now," Ellis motioned to the soldiers who were with him. The American soldiers approached Booker and could see that he was still alive. Ellis looked into the woods and saw no Germans. He investigated the wound on Booker's back. He knew that his shot hit Booker. His target were the Germans, but he had missed.

He noticed a rifle on the ground and picked it up and it was in working order. His weapon would no longer worked.

"Where is Williams?" asked one soldier. "He must have made it out," said another.

"Do you think he was taken prisoner?" asked another.

"No. They would have taken all the weapons. There are two here. That means he left without his weapon. Why would he do that?"

"Let's look for him," said Ellis. The military evacuated Booker. After a brief search, they were unable to find Andre and returned to their platoon.

Chapter 21

———— ❦ ————

THE GIRLS BEGAN TO ARRIVE at St. Peter's. The sisters were determined that this session would go smoothly.

"We are so glad that you came this weekend," greeted Sister Camille.

"Thank you for coming this weekend. You will have so much fun," said Sister Laurie.

"God has blessed us with your presence," added Sister Aude.

"There she goes again," said Violet.

"Shut up," said Leondra.

"Are we going to camp in our tents?" asked Tasheeka.

"Yes, you will. You will be warm," said Sister Camille.

That evening Sister Camille, Sister Laurie, and Sister Aude made dinner for Aunt Clara and Jesse Weinstein, who had stopped by to check on Clara. After dinner, the nuns convinced Weinstein to stay the night on the couch downstairs to avoid a drive home in the dark.

"I hope you are enjoying your stay with us, Clara. We pray that you can find a home soon," said Sister Camille.

"Maybe I should become a nun," volunteered Aunt Clara. Weinstein grinned behind his napkin.

"You would be a great nun," said Sister Laurie.

"I never thought about it until now," said Aunt Clara.

"Pray to God and live a good life. God will see that you have everything you need," said Sister Laurie.

"I believe that Jesus will answer all of your prayers," said Sister Aude.

Chapter 22 ·

AUNT CLARA WAS IMPRESSED BY Sister Camille's frequent discussions about using your mind to visualize what you want in life and to bring to fruition what you dream about. Looking around the home, she spent her time in the basement cleaning it out to make it useful for something.

Aunt Clara found an old chair and sat and pondered. What did Jesus have in store for her? Could she find her life useful at her age? She began to sing and hum to herself.

Then she saw something. Was it in her mind?

"If you are here come out. I can feel you . . . you are here . . . Oh my gosh . . . Oh my gosh . . . you were . . . you were harmed . . . you were harmed for sure . . . No . . . No . . ."

She put her hands over her eyes and screamed.

Sister Camille, Weinstein, Sister Laurie, and Sister Aude heard the scream as did Violet, Tasheeka, and Leondra, who were camping the closest to the home.

"What was that?" asked Sister Laurie.

"It came from the basement," said Sister Camille.

"Jesus protect us," Sister Aude prayed.

They walked downstairs step-by-step. There was Aunt Clara, sitting in a chair facing the wall.

"Clara, Clara," said Sister Camille. "You need to come upstairs. You really shouldn't be down here."

"Aunt Clara, we have a place for that upstairs that would be much better for you," said Sister Aude

"Jesus said go to the closet and pray," said Aunt Clara.

"He said nothing about a basement," said Sister Laurie.

"Let's get her upstairs," said Sister Camille.

Weinstein took her arm and led her upstairs to her room. The nuns put her in her bed.

"Sister Laurie, would you get her some milk?" asked Sister Camille.

"I will," said Sister Laurie.

She returned with the milk.

"Thank you, thank you," said Aunt Clara. The nuns left the room.

"Sister Camille, I don't think she was praying. I think she was doing something else," confided Sister Laurie.

Chapter 23

LATER THAT EVENING THE GIRLS built a fire to cook their meal outdoors. Sister Aude came out of the home and sat down on a seat to watch the girls gather kindling. Leondra started the fire with a few matches and small twigs. She blew softly and the fire slowly began to fire. Violet and Tasheka placed additional sticks of wood in it. Then the girls placed a metal grill over the fire and began to boil water in a small pot.

"Sister Aude, what did you do before you came to St. Peter's?" asked Violet as she stoked the fire.

"I dreamed of going to China to help the poor. I was a volunteer in a Christian missionary group," said Sister Aude.

"What made you think of that?" asked Leondra, peeling potatoes.

"I read a book about Gladys Aylward who went to China. I wanted to do the same thing. She was unqualified but made the trip anyway. She never gave up."

"Who is she?" asked Tasheeka.

"A young Christian missionary. She read Genesis 12: 1-2 and was called to go to China," said Sister Aude.

"What does that verse say?" asked Violet.

"Now the Lord said unto Abram get the out of thy country, and from thy kindred, and from thy country, and from thy kindred and from thy father's house, unto a land that I will show the: I will make thy name great; and thou shalt be a blessing."

"Did you go to China?" asked Leondra.

"No, but I became a nun after that. I was called by Jesus," said Sister Aude. "Have you girls chosen the foreign language that you are required to take to graduate from St. Peter's?"

"I did," said Tasheeka.

"What is it?" asked Sister Aude.

"Latin."

"Latin? That is amazing. There are many people who study Latin that someday it will be spoken again," said Sister Aude.

"The Romans will not rise again, but I can say that I have a book of my first one thousand Latin words," offered Tasheeka.

"What have you learned?" asked Sister Aude.

"Things like *cubiculum*, *vesibulum*, *sessorium*, and *vasa coquinaria*," said Tasheeka.

"She's always talking like that," said Leondra.

"Have you picked a second language?" asked Sister Aude to Violet.

"I picked French."

"Great. I can say a few words."

"I've memorized a few paragraphs from a book. I can pick a name and put it in the paragraph," said Violet.

"Like what?" asked Sister Aude.

"I can take someone's name and insert it in the paragraph. Like Sister Camille. I can use her name as an example. Here goes. *Camille ne veut pas aller à l' école.*"

"Camille does not what?" asked Sister Aude.

"She doesn't want to go to school!" Violet translated. The girls laughed. "Here's another. *Camille est avec Nounours sous sa couette bien au chaud. Elle n'a pas envie de se lever, pas envie d'aller à l' école. Elle a juste envie de rester au lit encore un peu, puis de jouer et de se glisser à nouveau sous la couette avec ses livres préférés.*"

"Hey girl, that sounded real," said Tasheeka.

"You girls are funny," said Sister Aude. "What about you, Leondra. Have you chosen a language?"

"I haven't. I might pick Spanish. Who knows? *Cómo está usted?*" said Leondra.

"I am fine. Gracias," Sister Aude. "I better get back to the house. You girls have fun out here and don't get into trouble."

Sister Aude left.

"That woman is really serious," said Leondra. "I've never met anyone like her."

Chapter 24

THE SISTERS, WEINSTEIN, AND AUNT Clara retired to bed. Later that night Aunt Clara got out of bed and went back to the basement. Becoming comfortable in the home, she sat in the same chair and faced the wall. She closed her eyes and began calling the spirits. She began to practice her Voodoo like she did in Jackson. She called and called. The house became cold inside.

Sister Camille was in her bed and woke up from the temperature change. Then she heard the sound of someone walking. She closed her eyes, and when she opened them up there was a grizzly looking bearded Civil War soldier in his uniform, looking at her while she was sitting in the chair in the basement. She was about to scream and then decided she must be dreaming. The image disappeared.

Sister Laurie was in her room and the same thing happened to her. Another bearded Civil War soldier looked at her from the end of her bed. She couldn't believe what she was seeing. She was about to scream when her parakeet squawked, "Jesus is watching you." She froze. The image disappeared.

Jesse Weinstein was downstairs sleeping on the couch. Something woke him up and he opened his eyes. There was the young mother who was the original owner of the home. She was in a white night gown and her face was white as if painted with makeup. She looked like a zombie.

"I would like to shrink your head," she said spookily to him.

Weinstein gasped in disbelief and covered his eyes with one of his hands.

The image disappeared.

"A nightmare," he said to himself as he got up.

Then he heard a scream upstairs. It was Sister Aude. The same thing happened to her as the other sisters. Another Civil War soldier appeared at her bed. Her scream was loud enough to be heard by the girls outside.

Sister Camille ran to Sister Aude's room.

"What happened, Sister Aude?" she asked.

"I saw a soldier. A Civil War soldier," said Sister Aude, trembling and her voice cracking in fear.

"I did too," gasped Sister Laurie.

"And I did as well, I have to say," said Sister Camille.

"The devil is in this house," said Sister Aude.

Jesse Weinstein heard the scream and went upstairs. "What is going on? I thought I heard a scream," he said.

"You wouldn't believe it," said Sister Camille.

"We all saw ghosts — Civil War soldiers."

"But you didn't. What could it mean? All three of you are having the same dream?" asked Weinstein.

"I don't know," said Sister Camille.

"I can't explain the ghosts but I know that something terrible has happened or is going to happen. Is there any memorabilia in this house? Any old pictures, books?" asked Weinstein.

The nuns looked and found an old photo album. There were photos of the owner and a portrait of lady and her two daughters in white flowing dresses and hats. It must have been taken in the 1860s.

Chapter 25

———— ❧ ————

"WHAT WAS THAT?" SAID TASHEEKA. "Did you hear someone scream?"

"I did," said Violet."

"It was a scream," said Leondra.

The girls crawled out of their sleeping bags and tent and decided to walk to the home. Slowly they crept up on the squeaky front wooden porch that surrounded three sides of the home. None of the other girls would get out of their tents. They opened the door to the home and went in slowly. The old wood floors squeaked as they walked.

"It is so cold in here," shivered Violet.

Directly across from the front door was the door to the basement and the stairway to the second floor. The door to the basement was open.

"Let's go down there," said Violet.

All three walked down to the basement. Step by step they walked while the rickety stairs squeaked each time they took a step.

"This is so weird," said Violet.

"Like some kind of weird movie," added Tasheeka.

"The Wolfman is coming!" warned Violet.

"You two be quiet," shushed Leondra.

When they reached the bottom of the stairs, they saw a woman sitting in a chair facing the wall.

"Who is that," whispered Violet.

"This is really scary," said Tasheeka. But slowly they approached the figure.

Step by step.

Violet turned the chair around. It was Aunt Clara.

"I've been doing some Voodoo down in Jackson," she said to them.

The girls screamed and ran back upstairs and outside to the front porch. It was the scariest thing they had ever seen.

"What was that?" asked Sister Camille.

"It was a scream. Sounded like some of the girls," said Sister Aude.

"I will go down and see," said Sister Laurie. As she walked partially down the stairway she could see the girls on the front porch. She walked down and opened the door.

"What are you doing here? You girls need to go back to your tents," asked Sister Laurie.

"We heard a scream," said Violet.

"It is fine now. Go back to your tents," said Sister Laurie as she closed the door and walked back upstairs.

The girls remained on the front porch. Violet remembered Aunt Clara. "That was Aunt Clara. What is she doing here? Stop. We need to go back down there."

"Go back down there? Are you crazy? There is no way on God's green earth that I'm going back down there," said Tasheeka.

"No. Just stop. Let me think," said Violet.

"You want to go back down there?" asked Leondra. "Yes. I know her. She wouldn't hurt a fly," said Violet.

"Ok. You must be psycho if you want to go back down there to that basement. Sister Laurie told us to go back to our tents. Come on, I'm going back to my tent," said Tasheeka.

"I'm going back down there," said Violet, walking back in the home. "Can you believe she wants to go back down there," said Tasheeka to Leondra.

"Be quiet. Let's go. What is she going to do? Turn us into frogs?" asked Leondra.

"Now I *know* I'm not going down there," said Tasheeka.

"Come on," said Leondra, pushing Tasheeka into the home.

"That was the scariest thing I have ever seen. I thought I was going to die. I can't believe we are going back down there," said Tasheeka as she was walking down the basement stairs.

"Aunt Clara. I thought you died a long time ago," said Violet approaching her.

"It's me. Is that you, Violet?" asked Aunt Clara.

"It is."

"Oh, my precious Violet. My precious. I used to rock you like a baby," said Aunt Clara, giving Violet a hug.

"I haven't seen you in years," said Violet.

"I'm so glad to see you now," said Aunt Clara.

"What are you doing here?" said Violet.

"I came here to live since I lost my home. I come down to the basement to pray."

"You lost your home?" said Violet.

"Yes. I lost it and the nuns let me stay here until I can get on my feet," said Aunt Clara.

"These are my friends, Leondra and Tasheka."

"It's nice to meet you. How long are you staying?" asked Aunt Clara.

"Until the camp is over," said Leondra.

Sister Laurie came to the top of the basement stairway.

"Are you girls down there? You mustn't go down there. You need to go back to your tent."

"Yes, ma'am," said the girls almost in unison.

"I'll talk to you tomorrow," said Aunt Clara.

On the way up the stairs, Leondra asked, "Is she really your aunt? She looked kinda crazy to me. And what's with that '*Voo doo down in Jackson*' stuff. She's got to be crazy saying that."

"Oh, that's nothing. She used to say that all the time. She said she could call the spirits. No one knew why she did that. She was just the crazy aunt," said Violet.

"In the basement," said Tasheeka. They all laughed.

Chapter 26

TATIANA AND ANDRE WENT THROUGH Weinstein's notes and compared the documents on the serial numbers of the weapons. The answer was simple. The serial number on Ellis's weapon matched the serial number on the weapon that discharged the bullet that shot Booker.

"Do you realize what this means?" asked Tatiana.

"The entire trial was for nothing," said Andre. "How come we didn't figure this out the first time?"

"No one was looking at that angle," said Tatiana. "You admitted shooting Booker so the question was whether it was friendly fire or negligent homicide. No one even thought of the possibility that someone else had shot Booker Thompson."

"Thanks to Mr. Otwell's investigative work, we would have never known this," said Tatiana. "He learned this through following up with witnesses who did not testify at the trial."

"They were transferred out of the theater," said Andre.

"Why did that happen?" Tatiana thought to herself. "Why would Captain Thomas have allowed Ellis and others to be transferred out of the area before they were questioned? Did he really act negligently in allowing that to happen?"

Andre said nothing.

Chapter 27

THE NEXT DAY JESSE WEINSTEIN left the old home and went to the public library in Birmingham. In the genealogical section he found Civil War records and an article about raids conducted by renegade black and white Buffalo Soldiers shortly before the Civil War ended. The Union rounded them up after the war and executed them. One story involved soldiers killing the young widow and her two daughters. Her husband was a Union soldier who died at sea. The article was about the same home that the nuns had restored.

Weinstein took the article back to Sister Camille.

"Sister Camille, you should see this," said Jesse Weinstein.

"What is it?" she asked.

"It is a story about the former owners of this property. In 1865, this property was home to a lady who was raped and killed by some Buffalo soldiers. Her two children were there and saw it."

"What an awful story," said Sister Laurie.

"What are the Buffalo Soldiers?" asked Sister Camille.

"God have mercy on us and protect us," said Sister Aude.

"Thank you, Sister Aude. Now, you were saying?" asked Sister Camille.

Jesse Weinstein continued. "They were an unusual group of black and white soldiers who fought for the Union. One group went off the range. They were rogue and went around destroying the southern plantations as revenge on the south.

The Union caught up with them and stopped the destruction. This group raped and tortured the owner of the home."

"I heard a rumor about this home but I didn't believe it," said Sister Camille. "Four of them were executed at this home in 1865. A military trial was conducted and they were executed."

"God have mercy," said Sister Camille.

"God in Heaven protect us," said Sister Aude.

"That's called the law of war," said Jesse Weinstein.

"Did it say who conducted the military trial?" asked Sister Laurie.

"It doesn't. It says that they were hanged in a tree outside the home after a battle took place to stop them," said Weinstein. "I know this might sound crazy, but didn't you say that you saw a soldier at your bed?"

"I hate to admit it, but I did," said Sister Camille.

"And isn't that what the other sisters saw as well?" asked Weinstein.

"Yes, they saw that too," said Sister Camille.

"And I saw a lady in a white evening gown. I opened my eyes and she was looking right at me like a zombie. I know this sounds weird, but do you suppose those were just images of these people that lived here and we were dreaming about them?" asked Weinstein.

"It had to be a dream. There's no way that it could be real," reasoned Sister Laurie.

"I can't believe that I'm even thinking about this," said Sister Camille. "I've always hated horror movies and now I'm dealing with one."

"Let's think. The only thing that has changed in this house is that Aunt Clara has come to stay. She's been listening to

Sister Camille's talk about using your imagination to find your true purpose," said Sister Laurie.

"Are you suggesting that it is Aunt Clara who has been imagining these things and bringing these people back to life here?" asked Sister Aude. "Maybe we should cancel the retreat until we figure out what this is all about."

"It's too late for that. They are already here. We can't just send them home. On Saturday, Andre's church is going to put on their play on Halloween," said Sister Camille.

"You're having a play here on Saturday night?" asked Weinstein. "I need to head back to Montgomery."

"You can't do that. We need you now. Please stay through Sunday morning and the children off. We need protection. You heard about what happened last time the Klan came? We put the play out here in the country on a Saturday night to keep the kids off the street on Halloween," said Sister Camille.

"That's perfect timing it appears. The ghosts start showing up right before the play," said Weinstein.

Chapter 28

———— ❦ ————

"FATHER WEBSTER, I NEED TO report a strange occurrence last night at the Sister's home," said Sister Camille, walking into Father Webster's study.

"What do you mean?" he asked.

"Sister Laurie, Sister Aude, and the lawyer, Captain Weinstein—well I hate to say it, but we all saw ghosts last night!"

"That's preposterous," said Father Webster.

"If it had been just me I would agree with you, but all of us had the same experience. I know how this sounds but believe me I am not making this up. Maybe someone is trying to play a trick on us right before Halloween. With the Klan out there anything is possible."

"Do you think this was some elaborate trick by the Klan to scare you so you cancel the play?" asked Father Webster.

"It could be."

"Father Sanders and I will come down and check around. We don't want anything done to interrupt the events here."

"There's something else," said Sister Camille. "The strange events started after Aunt Clara came to stay at the house with us."

"Are you saying that she has something to do with it?" asked Father Webster.

"I hope not, but it is strange that nothing happened prior to her coming to the home. You know Father, she was the one who accidentally burned down Andre's home and initially led Andre here. She led the young men to believe that one or the other one caused the home to burn down."

"That's a terrible thing to leave them thinking that for all of those years."

"I think she died a thousand times over that."

"You are right that this is a concern. Perhaps she shouldn't be staying at that home with the children."

"Father, we caught her downstairs doing something. Sister Laurie said she was not praying."

"If anything else happens down then let me know and we will find another place for her to stay."

"I will Father," said Sister Camille.

"You know Sister Camille, when you talk about imagination and realization about your dreams you need to be careful. It is quite a powerful message and without understanding it fully. People can misunderstand what you mean by it," said Father Webster.

"What do you mean, Father?" asked Sister Camille.

"It is good to visualize your dreams but you have to do more than just imagination."

"Of course. I understand that."

"I know you do. But the people listening to you might not. They might take what you say and then think that they can do whatever you want simply by thinking about it."

"I'm sorry if that was what I was saying. That is not what I meant," said Sister Camille.

"You are right Father. I will make it known that what I'm talking about is much more than dreaming. We have to have faith *and works* to achieve our dreams," said Sister Camille.

"We are to strive to be saints. You have to have a plan, much like a business plan for success for use in one's personal life. Prayer, service, sacramental life, identifying weaknesses, and surrendering these challenges to the Lord and let him guide the way. It is much more than just visualizing as if the world will bring you anything that you think about," said Father Webster.

"I understand, Father," said Sister Camille. "There was something attractive about simply asking and receiving. Somehow, I was drawn to it as if it was magnetic. Like some kind of universal attraction. Like I was in my vortex."

"I know it is seductive, but the concept is confusing the parishioners as if the word of the Lord implies that it brings material possessions and profits simply by thinking of it. That is not biblical. Many a traveling preachers have preached the same thing for centuries. They take the words 'The Lord is my Shepherd, I shall not want' to mean that God will bring money and material possessions into their life. That is not scriptural."

"That is not what I meant, Father. I only meant our thoughts to be used in a spiritual manner."

"I know that is what you meant. My hope is that Aunt Clara hasn't misinterpreted what you have been saying and is the one causing the confusion in the home," said Father Webster.

Chapter 29

JUDGE THOMAS DECIDED IT WAS time to come clean and make peace with his soul. He couldn't live with himself any longer. His bouts with Jesse Weinstein in court reminded him of his prosecution of Private Andre Williams in 1945. Thomas knew he deliberately went after Williams with the court-martial. No one knew Judge Thomas's dark secrets. He was brutal to Williams on purpose. He went after Brandesha for the same reason. And he favored the prosecution over the defense in Weinstein's habeas corpus proceeding. He wasn't going to let the obviously black and guilty criminal defendant go free because the state prosecutor blundered.

Thomas went to the 12:15 mass at the downtown St. Jude Chapel and then to confession afterwards. He was the real Catholic. *Andre Williams was not*, he thought as he remembered the trial.

"Forgive me Father, for I have sinned."

"What sin is that?" asked the priest.

"I've abused my position as a judge. I love the law. I love the profession of law. I love my position as a judge. But I've abused my power and the trust that was given to me."

"And how have you done that?"

"I've prosecuted people who should not have been prosecuted."

"What else?"

"I've judged people harshly who did not deserve it."

"Anything else?"

"I've hated people I should not have hated."

"Is that it?"

"Yes. That's it."

"Why do you do these things?" asked the priest.

"I don't know. I do it without thinking. It's like it's unexplainable. I hate them for no reason. I was born to hate them."

"You hate who for no reason?"

"I'm sorry. I didn't mean that. I meant that I have hated without reason."

"That is wrong," said the priest.

"I know. That's why I'm here."

"Do you hate a certain kind of person?"

"Yes."

"Can you describe this certain kind of person?"

"I can't, Father. It's too painful to admit."

"Do you intend to sin again?"

"I do not."

"Do you intend to sin against these persons or to a certain people?"

"I will not," said Judge Thomas.

"Then sin no more. What do you intend to do to make peace with these people?" asked the priest.

"I will resign my position as a judge." The priest said nothing in response. "Yes, I'm going to resign," Thomas repeated.

"In that case, you have learned your lesson. Now say your contrition and go make peace with your enemies and sin no more."

Judge Thomas left the chapel and walked back to his office. He could never confront or admit his mistakes to the litigants he dealt with in the past, but he had to be at peace with himself.

Chapter 30

Ellis and Coggins were sitting in their car across the street from the courthouse watching for Judge Thomas to leave work.

"He leaves at 5:15 p.m. every day and walks out the door. He makes his juries leave at 5 p.m. They have families to go home to. They can collect an extra day off and jury pay if they have to come back the next day instead of staying late," said Ellis.

"His car is in the parking lot on the side of the building. I will follow him and talk to him before he leaves," said Coggins.

Judge Thomas walked out of the courthouse with his briefcase. Coggins got out of the car to approach him as the judge walked down the sidewalk.

"Judge Thomas, my name is Bill Coggins. I'm with the FBI."

"Yes? What do you want from me?" asked the judge.

"Do you mind coming with us down to our offices?"

"What for?"

"We have some important cases that involve some litigants in your court that you might be able to shed some light on," said Coggins.

"How long will it take?" the judge asked. "Probably about an hour," said Coggins.

"If it is necessary. I'm always interested in helping out the FBI."

Thomas sat in the back seat with Coggins by his side. Ellis looked back from the driver's seat and nodded his head.

"I'm Lanny Ellis."

"Are you also with the FBI? Ellis said nothing.

"Judge John Thomas."

Ellis drove outside of Birmingham towards the Klan hideout only a half a mile from St. Peter's. It was in an old shack in the countryside.

"I didn't realize the FBI had colored agents," said Thomas to Ellis. Ellis did not respond.

They drove further into the country.

"You said you guys were with the FBI and we were going to your offices. Why are you taking me out to the country?"

"We found a suspicious hideout in the countryside that we are checking out and were wondering if you know anything about it." explained Ellis.

"Okay, but it sounds strange to me," said Thomas.

Ellis drove off the highway and down a dirt road. He stopped at an entrance that was locked up.

"We have to walk from here," said Ellis.

"Do you have permission to be on this property?" asked Thomas.

"I am a federal agent. I can investigate," said Coggins.

"No search warrant?" asked Thomas.

"We are not going to search. We can come on the property if we have reasonable suspicion of a crime. If we need a search warrant we can get one," said Ellis. "You could give us one, couldn't you?"

"I could," said Judge Thomas.

They walked through the woods until they came across the Klan hideout.

Ellis looked at Thomas for a reaction. Thomas was nervous but Ellis couldn't tell whether there was any noticeable reaction from him.

"Have you ever been here before?" asked Ellis.

"I haven't," said Thomas.

"See Judge Thomas? My job is to investigate the Klan. We found this hideout here that we believe belongs to the Klan. Do you remember the raid on the girls' summer camp at the Catholic school up the road?"

"I read about it," said Thomas.

"This is where they planned it and then they drove up the road to the church. We think they are going to do it again on Saturday night when the church hosts an event up there on Halloween. We are here to stop it," said Ellis.

"Can you help us by identifying anyone in the Klan?" asked Coggins.

"I don't know anything about this place," said Thomas. "I don't know anything about the Klan."

"That's interesting, Judge. What I find in my research is that a lot of these Klan members are really outstanding local white citizens. They join this group thinking it does some good things and then they find out the dark side of it. There have been some real famous Klan members before who joined thinking this was a good organization, only to find it is a racist organization. Some jump quickly before they ruin their reputation. The bad apples stay like a bunch of rats. That is our job—to eliminate the rats and the Klan."

"Good luck," said Thomas.

"We were wondering if you see anything in here that might help us identify these people?" asked Ellis.

"I don't see anything that I'm familiar with," said Thomas.

"You could help tip us off to the ones that come in your courtroom or lawyers who practice in your court that you might suspect as Klan members," said Coggins.

"I don't know any Klan members. I don't know anything about this place," said Thomas.

"That's not what I've heard," said Ellis.

"What have you heard?" asked Thomas.

Ellis grabbed Thomas and threw him down on the ground. Coggins gave him a rope to tie his hands and legs. Then the men hung Judge Thomas upside down.

"How does it feel now, Mr. White Man, to be strung up? You white boys have been doing this for years. How do you like it now, Mr. Judge?" tormented Ellis.

"I haven't done anything to you. You don't know me," said Thomas. Ellis had no idea that Thomas had repented and was a changed man.

"You've been doing this your entire life. You've been trying to destroy us for 100 years," said Ellis, his anger unleashed.

"I don't know what you're talking about," said Thomas. "Yes, you do!" yelled Thomas.

Thomas took his gun and slapped Thomas across the face. The he punched him in the stomach and two more times in the face.

"That's enough," said Coggins, stopping Ellis. "You are going to kill him."

"You don't like it now, do you? You should see how the white man killed my grandfather and strung him up to a tree and hung them for doing nothing more than stealing a chicken. He had nothing to eat," said Ellis.

"We have to go. I think I hear cars," said Coggins.

"Take him down. Take off his clothes and put this on him," said Ellis. He hit Thomas in the head, rendering him unconscious.

Ellis found a Klan suit in the back. He and Coggins put the white robe and hat on him.

"We are going to have to carry him out of here. I know where we can take him. There is an old house near that Catholic church. We can put him in the basement for now. It's not far away," said Ellis.

Ellis and Coggins carried Thomas to the home that Sister Camille and the nuns were renovating. They entered the back way through stairs that went down into the ground to a door to the basement.

"Did anyone see us?" asked Ellis. "No," said Coggins.

"Let's just wait here for now until we can find a way to get out of here without being noticed," said Ellis.

Chapter 31

VIOLET DECIDED TO VISIT AUNT Clara in the old house. Aunt Clara was resting in her room on the second floor.

"Oh, my precious. I was so happy to see you. Where are your friends?

"They are outside."

"Why don't you go get them. I made a cake and I would like to give them some of it."

"That's great. I'll go get the other girls and bring them back," said Violet.

Aunt Clara got out of bed and dressed. She needed to go to the restroom that was shared with Sister Laurie's room. She opened up Sister Laurie's door and looked around. She walked to the window and saw Violet with Leondra and Tasheeka. After talking to her friends, Violet led the girls back to the home.

"Jesus is watching you," squawked Calista, Sister Laurie's parakeet.

Aunt Clara screamed at the unexpected voice. She looked around and didn't see a soul. Then she realized the voice came from the parakeet.

"You are so cute. You won't scare me next time," said Aunt Clara.

The girls nocked on Aunt Clara's door.

"Oh, my precious girls," she cooed, opening the door.

"You scared us to death last night," said Tasheeka.

"I thought I was going to die," said Violet.

"You're chicken. It was nothing," said Leondra.

"Let me go get the cake," said Aunt Clara.

The girls inspected the room and Tasheeka walked through the bathroom. She opened the door to Sister Laurie's room, wondering what the room of a nun looked like.

"Jesus is watching you," screeched Calista.

Tasheeka screamed and ran back to Aunt Clara's room.

"What's wrong with you?" said Leondra.

"Someone's in the other room," said Tasheeka. "Who is it?"

"I don't know," said Leondra.

The girls walked together through the bathroom and into the next room. Nothing.

"No one is here," said Leondra.

"Jesus is watching you," squawked Calista again.

The girls screamed and flew back into the other room just as Aunt Clara entered with the cake.

"Who is in the other room?" said Violet.

"That's Sister Laurie's parakeet," laughed Aunt Clara. "The same thing happened to me."

"Whew," said Tasheeka. "I thought I heard a ghost."

"This is great that you brought us a cake, Aunt Clara," said Violet.

"Where do you want to sit down?" asked Leondra.

"Let's go to the attic. There are all kinds of things up there. Pictures, dolls, antiques," said Aunt Clara. She led the way to the attic through a pull-down ladder. They crawled up, being careful not to drop the cake.

"What a playground," said Violet.

"Wait, I'll be right back," said Aunt Clara, climbing down the stairs to get matches from the kitchen.

The girls went through the boxes in the attic and found a small box. They opened it up and there was a photograph of a young mother and her two daughters in flowing white dresses and bonnets.

"Who are these people?" asked Violet.

"Probably the prior owners of the home," said Leondra.

Aunt Clara returned with matches and candles and the girls placed them on the cake. Aunt Clara lit the candles.

"This is great, Aunt Clara!" said Violet. "I remember you cooking like this when we were kids."

The girls blew out the candles and Aunt Clara put the smoldering match down on the floor.

"What is that photo?" asked Aunt Clara.

Violet showed her the picture of the lady and her daughters.

"Let me see that. I've seen them before!" exclaimed Clara. "You haven't seen them," said Leondra.

"What are these other pictures?" asked Aunt Clara. "How horrible."

"What's horrible?" wondered Leondra.

"The photo of the soldiers being executed. There are four men hung from a tree," said Aunt Clara.

"Where?" said Leondra.

Leondra sifted through the photos. There it was: a photo of the hangman and four men hanging on a wooden scaffold. Union soldiers stood all around.

"Gross," said Leondra.

"That makes me sick," said Violet.

"Oh, my Jesus. I hear them and I recognize them. I've heard them call," said Aunt Clara.

"Let's go," shivered Leondra.

"We will talk with you later," said Violet to Aunt Clara. The girls left the attic and went downstairs.

"Your aunt is crazy," said Leondra to Violet.

"She's weird, but not crazy," said Tasheeka.

Aunt Clara remained in the attic, once again calling the spirits.

Chapter 32

———— ❦ ————

MARYELLEN WALKED OUTSIDE TO PICK up and read the morning newspaper. Her morning coffee was brewing and the scent circulating through the home. She sat down on the swing and perused the *Birmingham Defender*. She skimmed through the paper and noticed on the back page in the religion section that a play would be held at St. Peter's. The church suggested that families bring their kids there instead of Halloween.

"Bruce," she called from the swing.

"What dear?" he said, walking out on the porch while cleaning his hands with a rag. He had been working inside the house.

"I haven't seen Oliver or Tatiana in a while. They never come over. We should invite them over tonight for Halloween."

"Ok with me," he said.

"We need to invite my great Aunt Myrtle. She is getting so old. She hasn't met Tatiana yet," said Maryellen.

"Ok, if she wants to come, I will pick her up."

"I will call Oliver." Maryellen went inside to the kitchen and dialed Oliver's number at the newspaper.

"Oliver, this is your mother. Is this a good time?" she asked.

"I can't talk right now," he said.

"But I haven't seen you in such a long time. I would like to see you and Tatiana. Your father misses you and has been asking about you," said Maryellen. "What has been going on? What are you doing tonight?"

"We are going to a play at the Catholic church. One of the reporters is in the play. Tatiana is going but she doesn't know it yet. Why don't you come with us? We can talk on the way."

"I would love to do that," said Maryellen. "I need to tell you that my great Aunt Myrtle is coming over tonight. Bruce is picking her up. Can she go with us?"

"Why not? We can all pack in the car," said Oliver.

Excited, Maryellen went outside to see Bruce. He was sitting on the porch swing drinking coffee.

"Bruce, I spoke with Oliver and he said we should all go together to the play. I'm so excited."

"What? A play? You can count me out. I have work to do," said Bruce.

"No, you don't. You haven't seen Oliver and Tatiana in a long time. I haven't seen them either. You are coming. Maybe we will find out if she is pregnant. Can you pick up Aunt Myrtle say, around 3 pm?

That way she can be here when we leave," said Maryellen.

"Alright. I will do that."

"Thank you, my sweetheart. You know you are my sweetheart," said Maryellen.

"I am?" Bruce asked.

"You know Bruce, I can say this. Through all of our forty years together, I can say without a doubt that we are close."

"We are close," he repeated.

"We are friends," Maryellen said.

"We are friends," said Bruce.

"And our love never ends," she said.
"It sure don't," he said to her and smiled.

Chapter 33

— ❧ —

"Do we really have to go to the play?" asked Tatiana to Oliver. "I'm so exhausted from the trip to France. I just want to stay home and rest."

"I promised Andre we would attend," said Oliver. "Nelms and the rest of the staff are going to be there."

"I guess I'd better go," she said. "As much as he studied his lines during the trip to France, I don't know how he is going to be able to do the play."

"Mother called today and she and Dad are coming to the play. We have to pick them up," said Oliver.

"They are coming with us?" asked Tatiana.

"Yes, and with my great-great Aunt Myrtle who is 105 years old."

"One-hundred and five years old? I want to see her," said Tatiana. "Did Mr. Nelms say anything about me covering this play tonight?"

"No, you don't have to. Brandesha is back on entertainment. The paper is underwriting the play to donate money for the girls' camp and keep the kids off the street during Halloween," said Oliver.

"That's a nice thing to do," said Tatiana.

After Oliver knocked on the door, Maryellen opened the door and cried, "Oh Oliver, oh Oliver, look at you! Where is Tatiana?"

"She's in the car. We don't have time to come in," said Oliver.

"Oh, all right. Let me get Bruce and Myrtle." Myrtle walked slowly to the door.

"Do you remember Oliver?" asked Maryellen. Myrtle said nothing.

"She hardly says anything anymore and can barely move around. We have to be careful going out there," said Maryellen.

"It is nice to see you, Aunt Myrtle. It has been a long time," said Oliver, raising his voice. Myrtle looked at him and said nothing.

Bruce came down. "Are you sure you want me to come to this tonight? I have work to do."

"Hi, Dad. You aren't getting off that easily," reprimanded Oliver. "I know what you are thinking. I already tried it but it didn't work."

"Where is Tatiana?" asked Bruce.

"She's in the car. We have to go. We can talk on the way out to the church," said Oliver.

"Ok, ok. Let's go see how those Catholics do things," said Bruce.

"This isn't the Catholics, Dad. This is the First African Baptist Church putting on a play at the campgrounds of the Catholic Church."

"I didn't know they mixed the religions like that," said Bruce.

"It is some kind of ecumenical effort," said Oliver.

"Ok. Whatever. Here goes," said Bruce. "It's good to see you, son."

"It's good to see you, Dad," smiled Oliver.

Chapter 34

—————— ❧ ——————

TATIANA BROKE THE NEWS TO Oliver on the drive to St. Peter's, while putting on her makeup in the car, looking into her compact.

"Oliver I need to tell you what we found out on our trip," said Tatiana. "What is that?"

"I don't think Andre shot Booker Thompson."

"What?" asked a stunned Oliver, stopping the car suddenly. "You smeared my makeup, Oliver!" cried Tatiana.

"What did you say?"

"I was saying that I don't think Andre shot Booker Thompson. It wasn't his weapon that shot Thompson. It was Private Ellis's weapon. They both were shooting at Germans, just like Andre said he remembered, but it was Ellis's weapon that shot Booker. This proves that the entire incident was nothing but friendly fire, an accident."

"There were Germans out there when Andre shot?"

"Yes, and he wasn't the only one who saw them. The other private named Ellis saw the shooting. Ellis shot at them and then took Andre's weapon since it no longer worked. They assumed that the other weapon was Andre's weapon and therefore he had shot Booker. The rifle that shot Booker belonged to Ellis."

"That's so simple. Why didn't they figure this out the first time?" asked
Oliver.

"They were not focusing on that. They were focusing on why he shot his weapon."

"What are you two talking about?" asked Maryellen, leaning forward to hear the conversation.

"Nothing Mother, just work," said Oliver.

"Well, let us talk too. Your Aunt Myrtle is celebrating her 106th birthday next month. Can you believe that?"

"No. Congratulations Myrtle," said Oliver.

"Yes, congratulations to you Myrtle. That is really something," said Tatiana. "That means you were born in 1832. I can't believe I know someone who goes back that far. Do you remember who was president? Do you remember Abraham Lincoln?" Myrtle motioned.

"She remembers him," said Maryellen.

"That is unbelievable," said Tatiana. "I want to do a feature story about you."

"We are here. There's Ed and Brandeesha walking up. Brandeesha is covering the event tonight," said Tatiana.

"Ed is having her do the story. He's coming. There is talk that the Klan might make another move so we will be ready for it," said Oliver.

"Surely they won't do that," said Tatiana.

"Don't count on it, this being Halloween and with rats like that, anything is possible," said Bruce.

"You don't believe in ghosts, do you?" asked Oliver. "Of course not," said Tatiana.

Chapter 35

⟁

"GOOD LUCK WITH THE PLAY," said Betty to Sherry.

"I know you didn't like Andre's song," said Sherry.

"I do. I know there was competition between Andre and John over who would play thte lead, but in the end, I think it was best that you and he played those roles. John wasn't right for Clisson and Andre will play a better military general. John is better as the part of stealing Clisson's wife."

"You are right," Sherry agreed.

"And I think your song will be good tonight," said Betty.

"It will be. Andre is so exhausted. He and the other reporter from the paper came back from their trip to France and they are still recovering from the trip," said Sherry.

"I know. Ok, break a leg," said Betty.

Sister Laurie walked out on the stage to welcome the crowd. The time for the play had arrived.

"On behalf of Father Webster and St. Peter's Catholic Church, thank you all for coming to see the play presented this evening by the First African Baptist Church. We are always thankful for the work of our Protestant friends. Thanks to Rev. George Williams, the pastor, and to Betty Jones, the youth director, the choir and the actors. They have been working hard. Thank you to Mr. Nelms, the publisher the *Birmingham Defender,* for sponsoring this event tonight. Sister Aude will open with a prayer," she said.

"Let us pray. The Lord is a God of justice, who knows no favorites. Though not unduly partial toward the weak, yet he hears the cry of the oppressed. The Lord is not deaf to the wail of the orphan, nor to the widow when she pours out her complaint. The one who serves God willingly is heard; his petition reaches the heavens. The prayer of the lovely pierces the crowd; it does not rest until it reaches its goal, nor will it withdraw till the most high response. He judges justly and affirms the right, and the Lord will not delay. In your name, we pray. Amen." Sister Aude gave the sign of the cross, as well as some of the Protestants.

"She always talks like that," whispered Violet.

"Shut up," hissed Leondra.

"Now without further ado, we present *Clisson and Eugenie,*" announced Sister Laurie.

The choir sang an overture accompanied by a piano and three violins. The curtains opened.

Andre entered along with Sherry and Mary. They were dressed in the French fashion of the early 1800s.

> **CLISSON:** *May I escort both of you to your country home? I would like to see you sometime.*

Andre exited stage left. Eugenie was looking at Clisson as he left.

> **AMELIE TO EUGENIE:** *You know you must learn to hide your feelings when you are displeased with a man.*

> **AMELIE:** *Eugenie, can you come to the spa with me today?*

> **EUGENIE:** *I can't go.*

AMELIE: *Don't make me plead my case with you.*

EUGENIE: *I must ask you then are you wanting to the spa for you, for me … or for the gentleman?*

AMELIE: *We were invited by the gentleman. I can't go.*

EUGENIE: *You were invited by the gentleman?*

AMELIE: *We were both invited by the gentleman.*

EUGENIE: But it is you that must go.

The play continued and the actors delivered their lines flawlessly. Betty was relieved. "They did it!" she said to John.

John said nothing.

Chapter 36

MEANWHILE, ELLIS AND COGGINS WERE in the basement with Judge Thomas, who was beginning to regain consciousness.

"Where am I?" asked Judge Thomas.

"We are here to put you on trial for the crimes against humanity by the white man," said Ellis. "How do you plead?"

"I'm not pleading to anything," said Thomas.

"Ok, then I'll string you up," said Ellis. He put the rope around Thomas's legs and then pulled Judge Thomas by his legs.

"Don't do that!" cried Coggins.

"It doesn't matter what I plead. You have no jurisdiction over me. I ask for an attorney to represent me," said Thomas as he was lifted upside down.

"He wants an attorney to represent him?" laughed Ellis. "No attorney for you."

Elllis pulled off the mask. "Now Mr. KKK, Mr. Judge. Mr. Klansman. That is your name now. Your name is Mr. Klansman."

Coggins laughed but was uncomfortable. He and Ellis were to only ask Thomas if he could provide names of Klansmen. With Thomas being a federal judge, Ellis would face criminal charges and Coggins would be complicit with him.

"Torture works," continued Ellis. "I've asked around and I'm told it works. Mr. Klansman, this is the soldier that likes to try other soldiers. How does he look now?" said Ellis.

"Ellis, you can't do this," said Coggins.

"You see Mr. Klansman, Mr. Judge, Mr. U.S. Army JAG officer, I'm putting you on trial," said Ellis.

"For what?" asked a bewildered Judge Thomas.

"As a representative of the white man and for your crimes against humanity," accused Ellis.

"I haven't done anything wrong," Thomas retorted.

"Yes, you did!" yelled Ellis, hitting him in the face with his gun. "You killed my grandfather for stealing a chicken."

"I did not," argued a weak Judge Thomas.

"Yes, you did. Your race killed many black people for nothing. For being black. For being brought over here to work the fields. Do you know what it is like to work the fields from sunup to sundown?" said Ellis.

"No. I don't."

"No. You don't!" yelled Ellis, punching Thomas in the stomach. Thomas let out a growl from the hit.

"That's enough Ellis. We are to investigate and find out who the Klan is. That is all. No one authorized this," said Coggins.

"Judge Thomas, I am sorry he is doing this. We were to only question you to see if you could identify the Klan," said Coggins. Coggins took his knife out and tried to cut the rope to free Thomas but Ellis hit him knocking him against the basement wall.

"No one has to authorize this. I authorized this. He is guilty," said Ellis. "Guilty of what?" said Coggins as he fell to floor in a sitting position. "For being who he is," said Ellis.

"That's not a crime," said Coggins.

"Do you know a Private Andre Williams?"

"I remember him," said Thomas.

"I bet you do!" said Ellis hitting Thomas in the face with his gun.

"That's enough!" said Coggins getting up and grabbing Ellis and pushing him away. Ellis took his .45 caliber weapon and pointed it in Coggins face. Then he backed a few spaces and had both Thomas and Coggins in his range, moving his gun from one to the other.

"That's not enough," said Ellis.

Ellis turned to Judge Thomas and stood just inches away and put his .45 caliber weapon to Thomas's face.

"Judge, Williams says you put him on trial for no reason," said Ellis.

"I didn't put him on trial for no reason," said Thomas.

All of the sudden there were noises in the house from actors and choir members using the first floor of the home as backstage for the play.

"I'm cutting him down," said Coggins. Ellis didn't stop him.

Chapter 37

—————— ❧ ——————

ANDRE WENT BACKSTAGE WHERE SISTER Camille, Sister Laurie, and Sister Aude were helping with the play. Aunt Clara was there, too.

"So far so good," said Sister Camille.

"That was great," said Aunt Clara.

"I didn't know you were back here," said Andre.

"You've come a long way since I tucked you in bed that night years ago. Look at you now," said Sister Laurie.

"Jesus has blessed you so much," said Sister Aude. Andre smiled.

"It's your time to enter," said Sister Camille.

Eugenie and Amelie walked down the aisle while Clisson was completely enamored with Eugenie. They delivered their lines for the first scene.

> **CLISSON:** *May I escort both of you to your country home? I would like to see you sometime?*

The next scene was Eugenie and Amelie talking of the new gentleman.

> **EUGENIE:** *What's the matter with him? How somber and pensive he is! His glance has all the maturity of old age, but his physical appearance reveals the language of adolescence. Has he been to war?*

AMELIE: *Yes, he has been at war and is not recovered. He looks to one of us for comfort. We must attend his needs.*

Then Clisson approached Amelie.

CLISSON TO AMELIE: *My darling. I am so happy to see you. I have been at war for years and I feel at home with you. I do not remember anything that happened before. I remember only now. There is no future. There is no past. There is only now. The future is what we believe it can be. You must have the feeling of your wishes being granted.*

EUGENIE: *I'm not going to listen to this. I'm so tired I have to go back home. I'm going to break his neck.*

The next scene was Eugenie at home recovering.

EUGENIE: *Ask the doctor to come in.*

As rehearsed, John entered stage left with a doctor's bag and walks past Clisson, saying nothing to him.

AMELIE: *This is Monsieur Clisson.*

The doctor examined Eugenie while Clisson and Amelie watched at the edge of the bed.

EUGENIE: *We have heard so much about you, Clisson. I understand that you have been at war for the past few years.*

CLISSON: *I have been at war fighting throughout the great lands and now I am home ready to for home and to pursue my dream of a writer. I plan to write novel. A love story.*

EUGENIE: *A love story.*

CLISSON: *Yes. A love story.*

They looked at each other.

Chapter 38

—⟨∞⟩—

"WHAT DO YOU THINK OF it so far?" asked Brandeesha to Nelms.

"Where do I jump off? I have no idea what's going on up there or what they are saying. You know the new youth are growing up in this world. They are going to hell. I can't figure out who is doing what to whom. Andre is supposed to be a French general and he is with two women and he is starting to like the other one. That is so French," complained Nelms.

"You're bad," said Brandeesha. "Can I quote you?"

"No."

The play continued:

CLISSON: *You have kept secrets from me.*

EUGENIE: *My beloved, I do not wish to burden you with my pain. My soul is full of ghastly premonitions.*

CLISSON: *My soul is full of dreams. Some I do not know if they are real or not.*

EUGENIE: *I am troubled by a cloud before me. My panic could only be justified if it is because you have stopped loving me. If that happens then take my life.*

CLISSON: *My dear Eugenie, I swear to you that I will love you forever.*

EUGENIE: *Then remove this past of yours, this past wickedness that has strangled you for so long, your* *need to find vengeance. This need to find this man or this past that has harmed you. Tell me you have come to terms with it.*

CLISSON: *I have come to terms with it. I have learned the true cause and I suffer that I spent years re-living the past of which was no fault of mine. I have been ordered to Paris. I must leave. This is an important mission. Justice will be served and those who have caused an offense to the country will be executed.*

EUGENIE: *You must not be brutal Clisson. Nothing comes from brutality.*

CLISSON: *I will not be brutal. It will be duly reported that justice will be served! I will send my aide Beville to watch over you.*

Clisson kissed Eugenie and exited stage left.

"Are you sure Napoleon Bonaparte wrote this play?" asked Tatiana.

"Beats me," said Oliver. "I have no clue what they are saying."

The play continued and then Eugenie sang a song to Clisson.

> *Si c'est ce que tu ressens, ne change pas d'avis*
> *Cette fois, ça ne me dérange pas*
> *Si c'est ce que tu ressens, laisse tomber*
> *Décidez ce que vous voulez vraiment …*

As she sang each line of the song she went one note higher than the next. Then the violins played an impressive section in the song. The crowed was overwhelmed with Sherry's ability to sing each line until she reached an octave higher than where she began. Listening to the song offstage, Betty and John watched and fumed.

"What are they doing?" asked Betty.

"I don't know. During practice, that was the worst song I've ever heard, but in French she has me liking it. Look at the crowd. They even like it. How can they like a song that sounds like that?" asked John.

"Things are not going as planned. I think Napoleon Bonaparte will rise from the grave and punish us for what we are doing," said Betty.

Act I was finished.

"There will be a fifteen-minute intermission," announced Sister Laurie.

Chapter 39

VIOLET, BRANDEESHA, AND LEONDRA WORKED the booth selling drinks, candy, and hot dogs. Families brought their children to the play dressed up in Halloween costumes.

Nelms and Brandesha were in line to buy a hot dog when Oliver, Tatiana, and Cub walked up to join them.

"What do you think?" asked Nelms.

"All for a good cause. I think they are raising a lot of money tonight," said Oliver.

"Why didn't you tell me this was an opera?" asked Nelms.

"I didn't know," said Oliver.

"I've heard enough already," grumbled Nelms.

Cub heard the conversation while walking up to Nelms and Oliver. "I think Napoleon would probably slay everyone up there if he saw how his play is being tortured. If I hear another song I think I will volunteer to have myself killed."

"Cub!" said Tatiana. "Don't make fun of this play! They are trying very hard and spent a lot of time and money."

"I still think I am going to die," said Cub. Everyone laughed.

"Ok, Cub. Enough," said Tatiana.

"Where did they come up with all that music? I've never heard songs like that before," said Oliver.

"You know Andre. He probably dreamed it up from the future and brought it back here," said Tatiana.

317

"It's good to see those kids up there enjoying himself," said Nelms.

"It sure is," agreed Oliver.

"Tatiana, what did you learn from your trip to France?" asked Nelms.

"We discovered that Andre did not shoot Private Booker Thompson, the soldier he was charged with shooting," said Tatiana.

"He didn't?" asked an incredulous Nelms.

"No. It was a mistake. Another soldier shot in the same direction at the same time. That soldier later switched weapons because his rifle wouldn't work after that. He took Andre's weapon and turned his weapon back in. They thought the weapon they had was Andre's when it was the other soldiers. The entire thing was a mistake," said Tatiana.

"Will they try the other guy for the same offense?" asked Nelms.

"No chance. There was no offense. It was just friendly fire during the fighting of a war. End of story," said Tatiana.

"I bet Andre is glad about that," said Nelms.

"He is. That's why he is performing so well on stage," said Tatiana.

Back stage, Betty approached Sherry and asked her, "Where did you learn the French?"

"We thought about it at the last minute." said Sherry.

"You two planned this out all along. Sneaking around and springing this on us. I know Andre. He is as sneaky as a tank. You can't do things like that. It could throw off everyone else, including the orchestra. That's not a funny thing to do, no matter how well it turned out," lectured Betty.

No one responded.

318

Chapter 40

———— ❦ ————

THE CHOIR SANG AN OPENING song, accompanied by the violinists, while the crowd returned to their seats with their food and their children. Andre entered the stage as Clisson, dressed in his uniform fit for a general with a hat in the Napoleon style.

The crowd clapped when he walked across the stage.

CLISSON: *My beloved, my wife, happy mother my children, why Eugenia are your beautiful eyes wet with tears? You're like something; your heart is closed and empty! You often are alone. You cry too when you are with the children. It is as if your heart is shut away in the corners of your soul. Wisdom and common sense seem unable to reach you. The world is covered with thick clouds, scored by lightning, thunder, torrential rain in my soul like nature, is agitated. I will go hunting and I will return.*

Then Andre began to sing a song to Eugenie, accompanied by a piano, flute, guitar, and the violins.

I believe if I was all alone …

"Another song, I think I am supposed to work the night shift tonight," said Cub.

"Cub, be quiet and stop making fun of the play. This is a serious story," said Tatiana.

"Did you hear that, Oliver? It is a serious story," said Cub.

"It is a serious story," said Oliver to Cub.

Tatiana looked at Oliver seriously and then repeated, *"It is a serious story!"* Oliver gave her an awkward smile.

"It is serious. I said it was," said Oliver.

"You said 'it is,' said Tatiana.

"That's what I said. I said, 'it was,'" said Oliver.

"No, you said 'it is.' It is, isn't it?" asked Tatiana. "That depends on what 'it' is," said Oliver.

"Are you telling me the truth? Who do you think you are? The President of the United States?" asked Tatiana.

Chapter 41

⁓⁓

AUNT CLARA STAYED IN THE home and did not watch the play. Curious about the photographs that Violet had found, she went into the attic to look at the again. Then she began to call the spirits. Sister Aude and Sister Laurie were in the front room, watching the play from behind the stage.

"Did you hear something?" asked Sister Camille. "It sounded like Aunt Clara. She's upstairs."

"Oh my goodness, Father Webster told me to take Aunt Clara out of the home and not let her spend the night again," said Sister Camille.

They went upstairs and found the ladder from the attic pulled down. "Aunt Clara, come out from there," called Sister Camille.

"Aunt Clara, you should come down," repeated Sister Laurie.

"Jesus is watching you," squawked Calista.

"Can you tell the parakeet to shut up? I'm sorry. I didn't mean that. Just quiet her down for a minute," said Sister Camille.

Sister Laurie put a sheet over the parakeet cage and Aunt Clara began to walk down.

"That is good," said Sister Camille, escorting Aunt Clara back downstairs. "Come with me and stay downstairs while the play is going on."

Chapter 42

ANDRE WALKED ON STAGE. THE crowd clapped. "Here we go," he said. The crowd laughed. "Coming at you," he continued.

"What is he doing?" asked Betty.

"He wants to be the ham," said John.

Tell everyone that I am sorry ...

"Did you know that Andre could sing like that?" asked Oliver.

"I did know that. That boy can sing," said Cub.

"I think he can sing," agreed Oliver.

"You boys stop that," said Tatiana.

"This time we mean it," said Oliver. Tatiana gave him that look. "We're not playing this time," said Oliver. "We are for real."

Andre's song continued:

I have lied, I have begged and I have cheated ...

"Now John, it's time for your song to Eugenie. You've taken Clisson's wife. Now go out and show you can sing better than Andre," said Betty.

Mary overheard Betty and hissed, "Whose side are you on?"

"I was getting John pumped up to go onstage," Betty said her. "I mean. I didn't mean that. I mean, I don't lie. I mean, a girl is entitled to have a private side and a public side." Then she smiled and walked with John to stage left.

"I can sing better than he can. Watch me," said John.

"Of course you can. Break a leg," said Betty.

"Yeah, break it in two," said Mary.

John entered the stage as Berville as the crowd applauded. His French costume glittered in the lights and the music began to play. His character professed his love for Eugenie, walking around her across the stage as she was seated, singing to her:

Eugenie, Eugenie
You're the prettiest girl I've ever seen...

"That young man can sing," said Oliver.

"That's nice," said Tatiana. "See? You can be nice."

"I meant it," said Oliver.

Tatiana smiled, putting her hand underneath is arm and drawing him closer.

"What do you think, Cub?"

"Me? Where do I surrender?" said Cub.

"Cub!" said Tatiana. "Shhhhh!"

"Is she always like that?" asked Cub. John continued his song.

Sherry kept up her part and smiled at John as he serenaded her. When he finished, the crowd cheered and he exited stage left. Betty was on the side clapping her hands lightly and smiling.

"That was so good," said Betty to John as he exited the stage. "It almost brings me to tears. I'm so proud of you, John."

"Thank you," said John. "I was nervous out there."

"That was a great job, John," said Mary, acknowledging that he did sing the song well.

Mary turned to Andre as he was about to walk onstage.

"Now it's your turn to show that guy up," said Mary. "Can you do it again?"

"I'm not competing with him," said Andre.

"Of course you aren't," said Mary.

The next piece was a beautiful love song with a grand opening accompanied by piano and violins.

> **Betty narrated:** *Now it is the final scene before Clisson   decides togointobattleafterlearningthatEugeniehasfallenforBerville.*

The lights came on. Andre was sitting in a chair, contemplating what he would do next. He had no life left after learning of Eugenie's betrayal. His aide walked across the stage and addressed him:

> **CLISSON'S AIDE:** *Sir, everything is prepared for death. The orders have been given and the battalion is ready.*

> **CLISSON**: *If this is my last day then I would report that I was not grateful. I did not give to God what was Gods. No matter what happens to you—good or bad—I am responsible for that. I have left my wife all alone as she cries for me. Letting her heart break. I have sent my trusted aide to her to lead her home. Now I must pay the prince for my ungratefulness.*

Then Clisson stood up to sing his final song.

> *There's a grand old maid across the sea …*

A French horn played a solo during the middle of the song. The beautiful horn sounded across the fields of St. Peter's. Andre looked around and saw the crowd. While the French horn was playing, his thoughts were filled with his family house burning down, he and Booker joining the army, fighting in Kasserine Pass, Booker's shooting, and the trial.

Then he remembered leaving Paris to go fight in Germany, joining the first integrated fighting unit since the Revolutionary War . . .

Chapter 43

By March 1945 in Remagen, Germany, the men of K Company had been fighting for weeks, including hand to hand combat. The German divisions had been counterattacking up the forest ridges of the Rhine River town of Erpel. Artillery from the 155 and 105 mm guns shelled the retreating Germans.

The men of K Company crossed the Rhine on the Ludendorff Bridge. The Germans wanted the Americans back across the Rhine. The next night, the men prepared for another engagement. The Germans would make their way back to the town in the evening.

The weary men of the K Company had seen so much. They were unprepared for what they would see next. A group of soldiers began to emerge from the trees. They were Americans in uniform and they were walking towards the company. The white men stood out: a white lieutenant, a platoon leader, and a white platoon sergeant. The rest were black army soldiers who were about to join the white army troops. They were the 5th platoon to an existing white company. Each infantry company had four platoons: three rifle platoons and one weapons platoon, which carried mortars and machine guns.

"Look at those guys," said Lt. Kirkpatrick. "They've never seen a black fighting soldier before."

"Looks like their heads are turning," said Private Saller.

"They are now," said Private Trimmer.

"They sure are," agreed Private Adkerson.

Kirkpatrick, Saller, Trimmer, Hawkins, and Adkerson were white soldiers and welcomed black U.S. soldiers Privates Ellis and Williams.

"Thank God you are here," said Private Hawkins to Private Andre Williams and Private Lanny Ellis as they moved in to the join the company. "In war, it doesn't make a difference what color you are."

Firing and mortar fire continued, but the white troops welcomed the black soldiers. They wanted all the help they could get.

The arrival of the 5th Platoon (5th of K) to reinforce K Company on Erpeler Ley and the assignment of other black volunteer infantry platoons to infantry and armored divisions on the western front in 1945 was a turning point in American history. It would begin the momentum that would lead the integration of the American army and American society and transform the United States over the next generation.

The next day, J company was making their way from field to field at about 1400 when they were attacked by a German patrol.

"Looks like we got careless," said Lt. Kirkpatrick.

The fields were separated by hedgerows. The giant hedges had grown for a long time without being cut and it was difficult to get through them. Their mission was to take out the German battery 100 yards away. To do that, they would have to send five or ten men into enemy territory and attack them from behind. They could not be noticed along the way.

It didn't go so easily. Two U.S. soldiers were hit and went down. Private Trimmer returned fire and hit one German. The German spun around and his rifle flew out of his hands.

One mortar round went off and J company lay down in a blanket of fire. The Germans threw grenades and the company dug in close to the hedgerows. Then they advanced. Trimmer continued to approach the German. He was not dead. Trimmer removed the weapons from him before a medic arrived.

Private Adkerson twisted his ankle in the skirmish and was attended by a medic.

"Do you have anything to help me?" he asked the medic. "No. Take these APC tablets," offered the medic.

"What will you do with the German?" asked Adkerson.

"I don't do much," the medic said. "If they're hurt bad, I don't do much either."

"Three squad! Move out! Three squad move out to the left! One squad and Two squad! Move out!" ordered Lt. Kirkpatrick.

The troops moved out to the right and down along the path as the sound of explosions penetrated the night. The Germans had retreated for the time being. "Let's wait here for now. We will move later," instructed Lt. Kirkpatrick.

Chapter 44

———— ⌘ ————

IN A FOXHOLE DURING A quiet moment, there was nothing to do but listen to the surrounding sounds for hours. Nothing would happen. Then a few in the company began to talk.

"We deer hunt in Tennessee," said Saller. "Do you hunt?"

"I do. I remember when Booker shot his first deer," said Andre. "Who is Booker?" asked Saller.

"A friend of mine. He was in the army. He's dead now." Ellis said nothing.

"Sorry to hear that," said Hawkins.

"You should come to Texas. There is all the deer you would ever want," said Adkerson. "I even bow hunt up in Oklahoma every year. Man, I can't wait to get back up there."

"Booker shot a deer like no other deer," said Andre.

"What do mean?" asked Trimmer.

"The deer had three legs," said Andre.

The men laughed quietly. Ellis pulled out a cigarette.

"You can't smoke," Saller reminded him. "The Germans will see the flame or smoke and then you're dead."

Ellis put the cigarette back in his pocket.

It remained quiet and still. Nothing happened.

"A three-legged deer, you say?" asked Trimmer.

"He had to shoot that one. I guess that's like a spike," said Trimmer.

"He had to shoot him," said Andre.

"Who knows. Maybe it lost its leg jumping over a fence. It was gone at the ankle and its antler on the same side as the leg didn't grow right," added Trimmer.

"That was probably a deformity instead of an injury," Hawkins guessed.

"Everyone has crazy stories like that," laughed Adkerson.

"I remember shooting my first rabbit. I shot the head off of it. Made me sick after that," said Andre.

"I remember when I shot my first bird. I was nine years old. I couldn't find it and then some farmer started running his plow through the field and there it was. He turned up the ground and it was there. I'm surprised his horse and plow didn't tear it up. I couldn't kill it, so I put it in the back of my shirt and it was still alive. I carried it home and put it on the kitchen table. My mother screamed. It jumped off the table and tried to fly. It just wouldn't die. My father yelled at me and he took that bird outside and pulled off its head and brought it back in and put in on the table for my mother to deal with. Then it started flapping its wings and tried to fly off the table with no head. My mother screamed at both of us after that," recalled Adkerson.

"Makes you wonder—life wasn't just intended to for us. That bird fought so hard for his life," said Ellis.

The soldiers looked at Ellis and said nothing. It was a deep thought for the moment.

"Are you some kind of priest?" asked Trimmer.

"No. I think of the ministry sometimes," said Ellis.

Then it was quiet again. The sound of war could be heard in the distance. "The Germans want to kill us and we want to kill them. The Japanese bomb Hawaii and we invade Africa. I wonder why we didn't head with what was left of our fleet straight to Tokyo after that," said Hawkins.

"Roosevelt made a deal with Churchill. He wasn't ready to take on Japan. He wanted to concentrate on Europe first. I never thought I would be fighting in Africa," said Saller.

"I thought I would be heading to Pearl Harbor," said Andre. "We arrived at Fort Bragg on November 5th and Pearl Harbor happened two days later."

"That's the last place they would bomb again, right after attacking it. Some of the soldiers were sent there to replace others. They didn't bomb just Pearl Harbor, but all the bases on the island—even over at Kaneohe where the Marines are," explained Trimmer.

"How do you know that?" asked Hawkins.

"I studied it. I'm going to join the Marines after this," said Trimmer.

"The Marines! Are you crazy! I'm going home after this," said Hawkins. "What are you going to do?" asked Saller to Hawkins.

"I'm going to Texas after this. I'm going to open up my own car repair company," said Hawkins.

"What about you?" asked Hawkins to Saller.

"I'm joining the Marines," Saller replied.

"We have two Marines here. This calls for a celebration," said Adkerson.

The sound of explosions continued in the distance. Soon Lt. Kirkpatrick returned to the platoon.

"Listen up. I thought that the Germans were retreating. They like to attack when we think they are retreating," he said.

Lt. Kirkpatrick took a stick and drew on the ground the position of the battery and the cover.

"Intel says that there is a German battery of Howitzers three hundred yards away, just waiting for the advance. They are concealed in the hedgerow. In front of it is a tunnel they use to supply the Howitzers. They have three Mk42 in sandbags as cover for them. We have to leave tonight and go back behind them and take out the MK42 and the Howtizers. Get your stuff and let's go," ordered Kirkpatrick.

"How are we going to get to them without being detected?" asked Saller.

"We have to go way around and come up through the back. All we have is just what we have here. But we have the element of surprise, the firepower, the best men, and with a little bit of luck on our side we can knock out the battery," explained Kirkpatrick.

The men gathered their M-1s and began their silent walk. Along the way, they ran across a jeep with two dead Jerrys in it. Andre grabbed the MG-42.

"Be careful with their weapons. They booby trap them if they have to leave them," Trimmer warned.

Once they were close enough to the German battery without being detected, Saller decided to climb a tree so he could see the battery. From the tree, he could see the Howitzers and had straight aim at the battery.

Hawkins, Adkerson, Williams, and Ellis spread out in the cover and waited for Lt. Kirkpatrick to give the order. After a while, Lt. Kirkpatrick gave the order to open fire. Hawkins fired right at the men in the battery. They all began to fire and quickly advanced forward.

Kirkpatrick sent Ellis and Williams forward with Trimmer. They had the element of surprise. Trimmer took a hand grenade and threw it into the tunnel, killing the Germans.

Ellis mounted the MG 42 and began to shoot. The MG-42 made a distinctive German sound that the Americans could detect. All of the sudden they could hear American M-1s being fired in their direction.

"Drop the machine gun. It's too hot to handle," ordered Lt. Kirkpatrick. When they approached, they could see the battery. They were spread out 100 yards apart.

"Two more to go and then the battery. They weren't expecting us to come from the rear," said Lt. Kirkpatrick.

Chapter 45

———— ❧ ————

THEN ANDRE CAME BACK IN the play. He was onstage and the French horn finished the solo. He continued:

And kneeling down for sadness sake ...

The crowd clapped as Andre finished his song. Cub and Oliver clapped the hardest. Tatiana looked at them.

"That was good," said Cub.

"We really liked it," said Oliver.

"Uh-huh," said Tatiana.

"We did," said Cub. "Uh-huh," said Tatiana.

> **Betty narrated:** *Clisson placed himself at the head of the squadron and had blown into the fray at the point where he would expire pierced by thousand blows.*

"I wish I had thought about doing that," said Cub. The crowd gasped as Clisson fell dead on the stage.

"You mean Andre dies and the wimp gets his wife?" asked Cub.

"Cub, you are terrible!" said Tatiana.

"Sorry," said Cub. "I can't imagine what's next."

Eugenie walked out and saw Clisson dead on the stage. She knelt down and sobbed. Clisson had gone to war to fight his enemy, only to realize that he had sent him to take care of Eugenie.

EUGENIE: *Oh Clisson. Clisson. What have I done! What have I done."*

The audience was quiet.

Then she got up and composed herself. The music began to play in the background. She sang:

When you say goodbye ...

"You better not make fun of that," said Tatiana to Cub.

"I'm not," said Cub. "I believe her. That gal can sing. I like the songs. It's the acting that is going drive me over the cliff. I would rather be hanged than have to go through that again."

Oliver, Tatiana and Cub led the standing ovation and cheers. "Now you can get back to the night desk," said Tatiana.

Chapter 46

———— ✥ ————

UNBEKNOWNST TO ANYONE ELSE, SHERRY and Andre arranged for Clisson *not* to die in battle. Andre exited stage right and came to the front of the play as if it were the final curtain call. John and Sherry were holding hands, taking a bow as the crowd cheered. Then Andre as Clisson came on stage and kicked John as Berville away and held hands with Sherry, as Eugenie. The audience gave a louder cheer.

Betty came to the stage and, attempting to speak over the audience's cheers and the choir's singing, announced, "Clisson is not supposed to live."

"We changed the ending so that Clisson lives. As for the French, well this is a French play. We can change our minds, can't we?" said Sherry.

Then they took their final bows. Andre and Sherry held hands as Clisson and Eugenie. Once the clapping subsided, Sister Camille came to the front of the stage. The crowd sat down.

"Thank you for attending tonight. As a final gesture, the First African Baptist Church will sing the Battle Hymn of the Republic."

The entire cast and crew got on stage together to sing the finale. The violin and music began to play:

Mine eyes have seen the glory of the coming of the Lord;
He is trampling out the vintage where the grapes of wrath
are stored;

He hath loosed the fateful lightning of His terrible swift sword:
His truth is marching on.

Glory, glory, hallelujah!
Glory, glory, hallelujah!
Glory, glory, hallelujah!
His truth is marching on.

I have seen Him in the watch-fires of a hundred circling camps,
They have builded Him an altar in the evening dews
and damps;
I can read His righteous sentence by the dim and flaring lamps:
His day is marching on.

Glory, glory, hallelujah!
Glory, glory, hallelujah!
Glory, glory, hallelujah!
His day is marching on.

I have read a fiery gospel writ in burnished rows of steel:
"As ye deal with my <u>contemners</u>, so with you my grace
shall deal";
Let the Hero, born of woman, crush the serpent with his heel,
Since God is marching on.

Glory, glory, hallelujah!
Glory, glory, hallelujah!
Glory, glory, hallelujah!
Since God is marching on.

He has sounded forth the trumpet that shall never call retreat;
He is sifting out the hearts of men before His judgment-seat;
Oh, be swift, my soul, to answer Him! Be jubilant, my feet!
Our God is marching on.

Glory, glory, hallelujah!
Glory, glory, hallelujah!
Glory, glory, hallelujah!
Our God is marching on.

In the beauty of the lilies Christ was born across the sea,
With a glory in His bosom that transfigures you and me.
As He died to make men holy, let us die to make men free,
While God is marching on.

Glory, glory, hallelujah!
Glory, glory, hallelujah!
Glory, glory, hallelujah!

Suddenly, while singing the last verse, the crowd could feel the air getting colder and circulating the area as if dry ice had been put around the stage.

Then soldiers dressed as Union Civil War soldiers rode from behind the home and began to surround the house and the crowd. They were like ghosts riding horses in the dim cold night. As the song was about to end, a small hole in the top of the house burst open, projecting a burst of flames from the home. The crowd assumed it was part of the act, but some women began to scream. The fire was actually a result of Aunt Clara leaving a smoldering match after having cake with the girls earlier in the day. She had done it again—accidently set another house on fire.

The crowd praised the performance. They clapped louder, but the choir was uneasy trying to sing the last verse as they realized that the top of the home was actually in flames. They had rehearsed this scene many times. They knew it was not part of the play, but they continued to sing until the song was finished. Then in an amazing display above the top of the house a dead woman, the former owner of the home who had been killed by the rogue Buffalo Soldiers, appeared as a giant image on a screen as large as a drive-in theater. At first, she appeared young, then aged to an old maid right before their eyes. The crowd gasped in disbelief.

"I'm beginning to like this," said Cub.

"Oliver, how did they do that?" asked a concerned Tatiana.

"Must be some kind of projection like the new drive-in theater. Pretty imaginative. Dangerous fireworks," said Oliver.

"I don't know about this Oliver, this seems scary to me," said Tatiana as she grabbed his arm.

"Relax, this is Halloween," laughed Oliver.

"Mr. Nelms," said a scared Brandesha. "My water broke. I'm think I'm going into labor."

"My gosh. Tatiana, take care of her," said Nelms.

"I will Mr. Nelms," said Tatiana as she got up to walk over to Brandesha.

As the face of the lady of the home disappeared, Union soldiers circled the house and now surrounded the crowd as if they were getting ready for the ending of the song. It appeared to the audience that these were actors in the play for the final scene.

"Look at that. They have Union soldiers. Quite a performance," said Ed Nelms.

Chapter 47

DURING THE PLAY, KLANSMAN BEGAN to arrive at St. Peter's in their cars began to slowly drive towards the house. They watched the play from their cars as if they were in a drive-in theater. They would strike when the play ended. Hearing the final song coming to an end, the Klansman exited their cars and began walking towards the home in full regalia as the Battle Hymn of the Republic finished.

Union soldiers were mounted on their horses and separated the crowd from the Klan. Many in the crowd looked behind and were aghast at the Klan walking towards them. They knew this was not part of the play and these could not be Halloween costumes.

As soon as the Battle Hymn of the Republic ended, the choir quickly ran off stage for cover wherever they could find it. Some went into the home. Others dispersed in the fields to St. Peter's Cathedral. Andre, Cub, and Oliver ran to the back of the home and found a water hose and a well and began pumping water into the top of the attic to stop the fire.

The Union soldiers and the Klan began to clash. The soldiers were outnumbered but they had swords and rifles. The Klan had handguns. The fighting and sounds of shots began.

Cub, Oliver, Andre, and many other men pitched in carrying water into the home and fighting the fire before it broke from the attic. They contained the fire, but it burned out the attic and part of the roof.

Tatiana, Maryellen, Bruce, and Myrtle went inside the home after the fire was contained. Sister Camille and Sister Aude helped Brandesha inside.

"We will take care of you. Your name is Brandesha?" asked Sister Camille. "Yes, thank you Jesus," said Brandesha.

"Sister Aude, get some water," directed Sister Camille.

Violet, Leondra, and Tasheeka followed Sister Laurie into her room upstairs. Violet got in the bed and covered herself with a blanket. Leondra and Tasheeka hid under the bed.

Sister Laurie looked out the second story window. "God help us. Open up the windows upstairs," she said.

"God is watching you," said Calista.

They heard a strange walking in the hall. Sister Laurie jumped in the closet and closed the door.

A Klansman with a gun opened the door to the room. It was quiet but they could hear the sounds of fighting and gunfire outside. The room was totally dark and the girls stayed very quiet. The Klansman walked around the room, looking around. Step by step, toe by toe, he walked while the floor creaked with every step.

"Jesus is watching you," squawked Calista.

The Klansman stopped. He looked around but couldn't tell where the sound was coming from. He took another step.

"Jesus is watching you," the bird repeated. He stopped again.

Sister Laurie and the girls put her hands over her mouths to keep from screaming. The Klansman turned and walked along the side of the bed. He took two more steps. "Jesus is watching you," the bird squawked another time.

Oliver was downstairs with Tatiana. He heard something upstairs. "Stay here," he said.

"Be careful, Oliver," said Tatiana.

Oliver went upstairs. He opened one room door. Nothing.

The door was open to the second room. He peered his head into the room and looked to his left. He saw the Klansman about to pull the door open to the closet.

Oliver walked behind the Klansman and hit him on the neck. The Klansman fell. Oliver grabbed him and dragged him across the room and threw him out of the back window. The body fell off the roof and down to the ground.

Sister Laurie opened the closet door. "He's still a life of God," cried Sister Laurie.

"Yes, and now God has him," said Oliver. He looked at her and then walked out of the room.

The girls got out of the bed and out from underneath it. "I thought I was going to die!" said Tasheeka.

"I thought I was going to scream!" said Leondra.

"Sister Laurie, my back hurts from lying on that bed," Violet winced. "You know what that means don't you?"

"No," said Tasheeka.

"You must be a princess," said Sister Laurie.

"That's what I thought," grinned Violet.

Jesse Weinstein entered the home as Oliver was walking downstairs. "I thought I would come to help," he said.

"Nice to see you. It's been a while," said Oliver.

Andre walked in. "Is that you, Captain Weinstein?"

"Yes, I came to the play," said Weinstein.

Sister Camille walked in. "Andre has always been a singer. Thank goodness you are all safe."

Then there was a noise from the basement. They all looked in the direction of the door to the basement. It was open.

"Andre, your aunt is down there," said Sister Camille. "She was in the attic and we got her out of there, but a then she went down to the basement. I don't know what she is up to."

"I will go get her," said Andre.

Andre walked down the stairs, followed by Jesse Weinstein. Aunt Clara was sitting on a chair facing the wall.

"Aunt Clara. Aunt Clara. Hello, it's me. I've thought about you for a long time," said Andre.

She said nothing.

"Aunt Clara. This is Jesse Weinstein. Lawyer Weinstein. We need to go." Aunt Clara looked up. "Lawyer Weinstein. And Andre. My precious Andre.

You shouldn't blame yourself for what happened."

"What?"

"The fire in the attic. It's not your fault," said Aunt Clara.

Andre looked at Aunt Clara, almost about to smile. He looked at Weinstein. "What is she talking about?" asked Weinstein. "The fire upstairs?"

"Yes. She blamed the fire of my parents' home on me, too," said Andre.

"This one too? Let's get her out of here," said Weinstein.

Then he heard a sound coming from another room in the basement. "Wait. Did you hear that?" What was that?" asked Weinstein.

"Let's check it out. We will come back to get her," said Andre. "You're giving orders now?" asked Weinstein.

"Sorry," said Andre.

They opened the door and entered a short hall. To their surprise there was a man hanging upside down in a KKK suit.

"Looks like someone caught a Klansman down here," said Weinstein.

"Is that you Ellis?" asked Andre. "What are you doing down here? And who is this that you've caught. Poor guy in his white robe," said Andre.

"Who are you?" asked Weinstein to Ellis. "Lanny Ellis," said Ellis to Weinstein. "What are you doing?" said Weinstein. "Who is *he*?" asked Ellis.

"My lawyer. Who do you have strung up here?" asked Andre. Andre pulled off the white mask. It was Judge Thomas. "Judge Thomas?" asked a bewildered Weinstein.

"This can't be right," said Andre.

"You need to stop this," said Weinstein.

"We ain't stopping nothing!" said Ellis. "He is going to pay for what he did."

"Let him go," said Andre.

Ellis jumped at Andre to stop. Ellis's gun fell to the floor. Andre went for the gun and they struggled while Weinstein cut down Thomas and untied his hands. Andre secured the weapon and shot Ellis in the leg as they struggled. Ellis stopped.

"And *that* was no accidental shooting," Andre said to Ellis.

"I'm taking the judge upstairs. He could be killed wearing this," said Weinstein.

"Thank you," said Judge Thomas.

"Let's get you upstairs," said Weinstein. "What are you doing out here, Judge?"

"I was kidnapped," said Thomas. "Is that Private Williams?"

"You know Judge, I was wondering about the trial back in France. Did you know that Private Williams did not shoot Private Thompson? Did you know about the gun switch?"

Thomas said nothing.

"You don't have to say anything. You knew there was a gun switch. You knew that the other soldiers were transferred out of theater and they would never be able to testify at his trial."

"That's not true. I didn't know that. Sometime soldiers have to use other soldier's weapons if they lose their own. It doesn't matter. The bullet came from Williams' gun. He admitted shooting Thompson," said Judge Thomas. "He admitted shooting his weapon. Ellis shot at the Germans. They were both shooting at Germans. The bullet that hit Thompson came from Ellis' rifle. He took Andre's rifle after that since his stopped working. You had to have known that. I bet you knew that Ellis and the others were transferred and were not able to testify."

Ellis jumped in. "I shot at the Germans. We both did. I can't believe you prosecuted Williams for shooting Private Thompson. There was a war going on, you crazy man."

Ellis walked over to Judge Thomas and got in his face, speaking softly. Weinstein could barely make out the words.

"I wondered why all the KKK were out there. All this time I thought they were here to harass the black girls to prevent integration with this Catholic church. But I've known all along. It wasn't hard. I did some checking. It was quite easy. All this time everyone thought you prosecuted Williams because you didn't believe his story. You know better. I know better. These Klan boys are not here to disrupt the Negro girl's camp."

"What are they here for?" asked Thomas. "This is a rescue mission," said Ellis.

Thomas's eyes got wider.

"What's going on here?" said Weinstein as he pushed Ellis away from Judge Thomas. Thomas said nothing and walked away and started for the front of the house.

"You can't go out the front. Everyone will know who you are. No one will see you if you go out the back way. Go out the front and you are dead and your life is unchanged. Go out the back and you can start your life over. You can change your life," said Weinstein.

"I haven't done anything wrong," said Judge Thomas. "I've changed."

"I know why you prosecuted Williams. Remember when you and I had that conversation about how you were treating him differently than anyone else? Now I know what you meant. This is a secret we will have to keep to ourselves," said Weinstein.

Thomas said nothing. He would not acknowledge anything. To do so would mean confirming Weinstein's speculation.

"Take the basement. There is a way out down there. The rest of the home is boarded up. There is only one way out," said Weinstein.

Judge Thomas looked at him and said nothing. Weinstein followed him to the exit where he could leave and no one would see him.

"Judge Thomas, you still have time to change," said Ellis.

Thomas looked back at him. The Klan robe was torn and he was bloodied. "Get out of this Klan robe," said Weinstein. "You belong only in a black robe."

346

"I've repented," said Thomas, finding a way through the woods. Weinstein didn't hear him.

Weinstein realized he had made a mistake lecturing Thomas. Then he went after him. Thomas stopped.

"Judge Thomas, I shouldn't have said that. Maybe you haven't done anything wrong. You refuse to admit a mistake. You always land on your feet and never seem to be held accountable. I don't think you are going to land on your feet this time," said Weinstein.

"Is that what you really think?"

"Yes."

"Then you are an idiot. No one gets as far as I do if they have poor judgment, and no one gets appointed to the federal judiciary if they are a racist or a Klan member. You have poor judgment. I've lived my entire life following the rules. I've done nothing wrong."

Judge Thomas left.

"Except you don't tell the truth," said Weinstein to himself. Thomas looked at him and said nothing.

Chapter 48

———— ⟐ ————

OLIVER, TATIANA, ED, CUB, BRANDESHA, Bruce, and Maryellen were in the home, boarding up the windows and doors to prevent the Klan from entering. Weinstein went back and entered the house from the basement. He secured the basement door and went upstairs.

Bullets were hitting the outside of the home. The war was raging. Some Klan members had advanced and were now on the front porch, putting their hands through the windows and trying to prevent the windows from being secured. As soon as one arm would reach through the window Oliver, Cub, Nelms, or Weinstein would hit their hands with a board. The men continued to board up all of the windows.

Brandesha screamed when she saw Nelms bash a man's hand extending through the window with a board.

"He needed that," said Nelms. "I've been wanting to take a whack at one of those guys for a long time."

Soon it was calm outside.

"I think I will go outside and talk to them," said Oliver.

"It's not safe," cautioned Nelms. "If we don't do something to stop the carnage, the president will call up the feds."

"I will be fine," Oliver reassured him. "We will find sanctuary in here. We need a sanctuary city."

"Oliver, no telling what will go on out there," said Cub.

"I will go with him," offered Sister Camille.

"Sister Camille, that is much too dangerous," said Father Webster. "Father Sanders and I will go out there with you. I don't think they will do anything to us."

Father Webster, Father Sanders, Oliver, Cub, Nelms, Sister Camille, Sister Laurie, and Sister Aude walked out one by one. The young girls stayed in the home.

"All of you need to calm down and get in your cars and go home. If you leave now nothing else will come of this," announced Oliver.

Father Sanders, Oliver, and Sister Camille tried to talk sense into the men. "Get him off there," yelled one of the Klansman.

"We can't have this going on around here any longer," said another Klansman. "We have to enter the home. If you stand away and let us enter, no one will get hurt."

"This is too dangerous. They can't hear you anyway," said Sister Camille. In the back was a car of Klansmen arriving late, unaware of what had been going on the last few hours. One Klansman got out of the car with a 30-30 deer rifle with a scope. "We got one. See him?"

"I do," said the Klansman.

"Now aim to the right," said the second Klansman.

"I am," said the other Klansman.

The Klansman fired. The shot went straight and hit Oliver in his arm. "Got him."

Oliver fell to his knees.

"Oh my God," cried Sister Camille as she screamed and looked down at him.

"You are not going to die. You are not going to die," she said. Oliver said nothing. There was a pause.

"Oh no!" screamed Tatiana. She kneeled down to hold Oliver. Andre, Cub, and Nelms gathered down to shield him as did Father Webster and Father Sanders.

"Should I give him his last rites?" asked Father Sanders.

"No. I'm not going to die," said Oliver.

"Put something under his head," suggested Sister Laurie.

"I'm not going to die," said Oliver.

"You are not going to die!" said Tatiana.

Chapter 49

ELLIS WAS RECOVERING FROM ANDRE'S shot to his leg. "What did you do that for?" asked Ellis.

"It's not right."

"We had him! We had him and you let him go. No telling how many bombings have been going on in our homes by guys like that," said Ellis.

"Did you see him do it?" asked Andre.

"No," said Ellis.

"Then you have nothing. This isn't the way to stop this. It will end someday. Probably when every one of the guys like him die, for all I know. You had nothing on him. You can't take the law in your own hands," said Andre.

The fighting between the Union soldiers began again. The Union general ordered another attack on the Klansman, who had spread out and taken cover behind their cars. It was a strange site to see the Union Cavalry fight on horseback with their weapons against the KKK in their outfits, using rifles and shotguns and taking aim from behind cars built in the 1940s and earlier.

The Klansmen were taking shots, picking off soldiers while the soldiers rode through the cars slashing the Klansmen with swords.

The grounds of St. Peter's became a killing field.

"My God, what is happening out there," cried Father Webster. "We have to do something," said Father Sanders.

"We've called the police, haven't we?"

"Yes," said Ed Nelms. "The police will contact Governor Folsom. He will have to call out the National Guard."

"Let's hope they get here in time," prayed Father Sanders.

"The Union is doing a good job. Maybe they will kill all of them," said Father Sanders.

Father Webster looked at Father Sanders.

Chapter 50

———— ❧ ————

ANDRE LOOKED OUT THE WINDOW and saw the Union soldiers on horseback and on the ground fighting the Klan. The Union soldiers were being picked off one by one by rifles that the Klan brought with them. *What could he do*, he thought?

Then he thought about his interview with President Andrew Johnson, the 17th President of the United States. He thought about his ride to boot camp with Booker on the train. He was reading a book about Andrew Johnson.

> *"What is that you're reading?" asked Booker, taking the book away from Andre.*
>
> *"Hey," said Andre. "Give that back to me."*
>
> *"Andrew ..." Booker read from the cover. Then he kept reading, "Andrew Johnson it says. And who the heck is Andrew Johnson?" Booker asked Andre, disgusted by the thought of Andre reading a book. "And what the heck are you doing reading a book about Andrew Johnson when you are on your way to the army? You probably got this book because you liked the first name."*
>
> *"Let me have that," said Andre, taking the book back from Booker.*

"There are no pictures in it. Forget it. I would never read a book without pictures," said Booker, returning the book.

"You won't need that. Andrew Johnson won't be able to help you now," said Booker.

Andre smiled. He remembered Booker talking to him on the way to boot camp.

"So who was he?" asked Booker. "He was one of the presidents."

"You mean like Roosevelt?" asked Booker. "Yes, like Roosevelt."

"So what about him?"

"He was the only one impeached," said Andre.

"Impeached? What the heck are you talking about? Impeached. I'm going to impeach your butt! What are you talking about impeached?" said Booker impatiently.

Andre smiled again. That was definitely Booker, pulling the book out of his hands when they were on the bus heading to boot camp.

It was quiet outside. There was no fighting. The Union soldiers retreated behind the house to prepare for another raid. Andre walked outside to the front of the home and stood on the porch. What could he do? Then he heard horses in the back. Someone was arriving on horseback. Then more horses.

"Do you hear horses?" asked Cub inside the house while looking out the window.

"I do," said Tatiana.

"Who do you suppose that is?" asked Cub.

354

"We are going to die. It's going to be Napoleon Bonaparte coming to avenge how poorly we botched his play," said John.

"Who is that on horseback?" asked Nelms.

"I have no idea?" said Cub. "He sure is distinguished looking, whoever he is. I would vote for him."

John looked out the window and said, "Look Betty, it *is* Napoleon Bonaparte!"

"Oh, my word. We are going to die. I've met my Waterloo," said Betty as she prepared to faint. Before swooning, she looked at the couch behind her, making sure she had a place to fall. Then she fainted on the couch.

"I didn't mean it," said John. "Oh Betty, Betty, what have I done."

Cub saw this display. "You were the singer out there, weren't you?" he asked John.

"Yes."

"You know, we need get you a woman." John looked at him.

Chapter 51

———— ∞ ————

PRESIDENT ANDREW JOHNSON RODE UP on horseback, surrounded by Union Secret Servicemen on horses. He stopped and then got off his horse.

The Union General got off his horse at the same time to greet the president. "Good evening Mr. President," said the general.

"What is the situation?" asked the president.

Brandesha was in labor with an occasional scream that could penetrate the walls worse than a Union cannon.

"Did someone say Mr. President?" she asked.

"Who are they saying he is?" asked Oliver. "That's not President Truman."

"Sounded like Johnson," said Cub.

"I think I heard the name Andrew Johnson. I don't believe what I'm seeing. They say he is Andrew Johnson. Like the the president after Abraham Lincoln," said Oliver.

"What?" asked Maryellen.

"Well I have a hard time saying it, but they said he was President Andrew Johnson," said Oliver.

"Did you hear that Bruce? They said it was Andrew Johnson."

"I don't believe it," said Bruce.

Suddenly Aunt Myrtle, who was sitting on the couch, got up and walked to the window and looked out.

"Yep, that is Andy Johnson," Myrtle said confidently. Then she walked back to the couch and sat down. Everyone looked at her. She was 105 years old. She would have been twenty-two years old when Andrew Johnson was president.

"Mr. President, we are rounding up the rogue soldier attacking the home.

They are wearing their Klan robes. They raided the home and raped the woman who owned the home and tortured her two daughters," said the general.

"Defend the home and destroy the militants. Take prisoner anyone who surrenders," said the president. "Prepare and convene the military tribunal to try the prisoners."

"Yes sir, Mr. President," said the general.

By the cool morning light under command of the U.S. President, the Union soldiers defeated all of the Klan members. The rest lay dead in front of the house and spread across the fields of St. Peter's.

Chapter 52

THE CROWD THAT ATTENDED THE play was gone. The only people remaining were the girls from the camp, the staff of the *Birmingham Defender,* and the clergy of St. Peter's all packed inside the home. All the cars were bloodied with dead bodies slain across them. The dead were soaked red from the dew.

Tatiana bandaged Oliver's arm and placed it in a sling. They walked outside one by one to see the commotion and the United States President.

President Andrew Johnson was strong and muscular. His clothes were perfectly fitted. He was impressive.

"That's what he really looked like?" asked Nelms. "That' him," said Andre.

"You've been doing your homework, Andre," said Oliver.

The Union general came to the front of the home on horseback. "Have the militants been destroyed?" asked the president.

"They have been, Mr. President," said the general.

Three men with cuffs on their hands and legs were pulled by a Union soldier on horseback up to the front of the home. With the help of two other soldiers, the hangman put black bags over the heads of three of the soldiers.

"These are the men who tortured and raped the woman in the home."

"Justice will be served," said the president.

Another Union soldier brought a fourth soldier. The hangman took off the hat. It was Judge Thomas.

Everyone gasped when they saw that he was not one of the soldiers. "Has the military tribunal issued its judgment?" the president asked.

"We have," said the general. "The tribunal has ruled that all will die by hanging."

"Fine. Carry out the order."

"Yes, Mr. President."

The Scottish soldier began to sing "A Ramblin Soldier" in the background to the annoyance of some. No one told him to stop.

The hangman approached the first Union soldier and put the noose around his neck. "Do you have anything you want to say?"

The soldier began to cry. "Tell everyone that I am sorry, truly sorry for all of the things I have done. I never meant to hurt nobody, no one . . ."

"Yeah, yeah," said the hangman as he pulled the black cover over his face. Some Union soldiers laughed.

"Carry out the sentence," ordered the president and the first soldier was hung.

Sister Camille saw the hanging and was appalled. "What are they doing?" she cried. "Don't they know that in Christ there is no East or West and in Him no South or North?"

The hangman approached the second Union soldier. "Do you have anything to say?"

The Union soldier with the rope around his neck looked at the crowd of soldiers staring at him and then yelled, "Tell my mother that I love her. Tell my father, rest his soul, that I always wanted him to be proud of me."

Then his face fell down and he exclaimed, "Tell him that I didn't support Buchanan. I never did. He thought I did. I never voted for Buchanan. I don't know what I was thinking... I supported the Union. I met President Lincoln..."

"Ok. That's enough," said the president. More laughter by Union soldiers.

The hangman put the sack over his head. "But I didn't vote for Buchanan. I supported the Union. I voted for Lincoln, God rest his soul," said the second Union soldier as he continued to yell.

The hangman carried out the second hanging. "He didn't vote for Buchanan," said the hangman. Some laughter.

The soldier gasped for air and his legs finally came to a stop. Then the hangman came to the third Union soldier.

"What do you have to say?" asked the hangman. The stopped singing.

"I think I'm going to faint," said the soldier in his deep Scottish accent as he began to collapse.

"Grab him," said the hangman. Two Union soldiers grabbed him and propped him up.

"Please, can I have some water?" the soldier asked.

"Give him some water," said the hangman. One of the soldiers walked off the scaffold to find some water.

Sister Laurie brought a cup of water out of the home and gave it to the Union soldier, who brought it up to the man to be hanged.

He took a drink. "Please Madam, can I have some more?" asked the soldier.

"More?" asked the hangman.

Laughter again.

"If anyone wrote that down, I want 3,000 copies of that, that I said water," said the soldier.

More Laughter.

The soldier regained his composure. Then he looked out to the crowd of Union soldiers waiting to see him hang.

"Now, I will continue with a wonderful song that was written by ..."

"Shut up," said the hangman. "Are you some kind of comedian?" The Union soldiers laughed again.

The soldier continued: "When you live your life by the devil's brew, you are already dead. I'm already dead. I died when I took that first drink. If I could live my life again I would report that I was not grateful. I did not give to God what was God's and I did not give to Caesar what was Caesar's. I was never grateful. It was my fault. I never learned that the key to life is to be grateful to the Lord thy God, no matter what happens to you—good or bad."

The Union soldiers laughed once more.

He continued: "I spent money I should not. I was after the feeling of money. It was not about the money, but how I felt spending the money . . ."

"Is there a problem? Say your peace and get it done," said President Johnson.

"No, Mr. President, we should have never given him the water," said the hangman.

Laughter.

"Then carry out the sentence without further delay," ordered the president, and the third soldier was hanged.

"I guess he met his Waterloo," said Cub. Everyone in the room gasped at Cub's remark.

"Cub, this is serious. You see what is going on out there and yet you are making this out to be a joke!" scolded Tatiana, raising her voice to Cub for the first time.

"Tatiana, I don't know what's going on out there. But that is one nutty play!" retorted Cub.

Then it was time for Judge Thomas.

Sister Camille, Sister Laurie, and Sister Aude reacted as President Johnson ordered the sentence carried out. Cub, Nelms, Oliver, and Tatiana looked at each other in disbelief. Brandesha hid her face. She could not look.

"Is that the lawyer who prosecuted Andre in Paris?" asked Cub. "Sure is. I can't believe what I'm seeing," said Oliver.

"What is he doing here?" asked Nelms.

"Oliver, do something! Mr. Weinstein! Do something!" said Tatiana. "We have to do something, anything!"

Sister Camille spoke up, "Mr. President, we must forgive. Love trumps hate."

The President looked at her and said, "Yes, but the rule of law trumps corruption."

Violet, Tasheeka, and Leondra ran upstairs to the second floor to hide as Andre approached President Johnson.

"Mr. President, do you remember me?"

"Yes, I do. I remember your interview with me at the White House," said the president.

"Mr. President, he is not guilty. I ask that you pardon him of all of his crimes. We all make mistakes. You know that, Mr. President," said Andre.

"Yes, that's true. I made plenty of them, but I can't help you here. It is not up to me. He has been tried and sentenced by the military tribunal. This is out of my hands," said the president.

"Mr. President, spare his life," pleaded Andre.

"I can't help you this time, son," said President Johnson. "Carry out the sentence."

Jesse Weinstein knew this was not right. He would intervene. "Mr. President, I'm Captain Jesse Weinstein, United States Army. I know this man. He is Captain John Thomas in the United States Army. He is one of us. We served in the war together. He is now a prominent United States District Judge. There is no way he would commit any crimes against the family in this home or the United States."

"That's not true, Mr. President," said one of the Union soldiers. "We found him trying to run off outside the back, but we caught him before he could get away. He was in the house and had even put on the enemy's uniform. We found it in the woods when he took off. He's one of them. There is no way he could be a federal judge. He's a deserter, Mr. President."

"A deserter?" asked President Johnson. "I see. So this deserter thinks he likes their way of life, obviously. 'Oh, they have a wonderful way of life.' So one day he leaves. We lost five or maybe six, but at least five people looking for him."

"That's right Mr. President, we lost five guys trying to rescue him. I'm pretty sure he has been AWOL a long time," said one of the soldiers.

The president turned to the general for a response and the general said: "Like any American, the prisoner is innocent until proven guilty. However, our army's leaders will not look away from misconduct. In the meantime, we will continue to care for him and his family."

"Did you hear that?" asked President Johnson as he turned around to face the Union soldiers. Suddenly he was

363

campaigning again for the presidency. He could feel it. No one had more energy than he did. He was the consummate stump speaker.

"He deserted," yelled a soldier in the crowd.

"So, we lose five or six of our men. They were killed. They were killed by the enemy!" said the president.

"He deserted! He deserted!" yelled some soldiers.

The Union soldiers continued to get louder and yelled as the president spoke. He had invigorated the crowd. It was like running for office again.

"They go out; they're looking for him. They knew he left!"

"They knew he left!" yelled a soldier.

All the Union soldiers raised their weapons and yelled out: "They knew he left! They knew he left!"

"Everybody with him knew he left because he was all whacked out and a believer in them, not us!" said the president back to them.

The Union soldiers roared in response.

"He deserted!" said the President.

"He deserted! He deserted!" The soldiers yelled back. Then the president brought the crowd down to a silence. "Remember the old days? A deserter, what happened?"

"No? What happened" yelled a soldier back to the president.

The president made a rifle-shooting gesture and then: "Bang! Twenty years ago, it was bang." Then he made another rifle gesture.

The crowed laughed and repeated, "Bang, bang."

Then seeing the reaction by the soldiers to him, the president began to deliver a speech that he had given in Cleveland on September 3, 1866:

"And let me say tonight that my head has been threatened."

"No," yelled back some of the soldiers.

"No," continued others.

"It has been said that my blood was to be shed. Let me say to those who are still willing to sacrifice my life…"

There was derisive laughter and cheers from the Union soldiers.

"If you want a victim and my country requires it, erect your altar, and the individual who addresses you tonight, while here a visitor…"

"No, no," responded some of the Union soldiers with laugher.

"Erect your altar if you still thirst for blood, and if you want it, take out the individual who now addresses you and lay him upon your altar, and the blood: that now courses his veins and warms his existence shall be poured out as a last libation to Freedom. I love my country, and I defy any man to put his finger upon anything to the contrary…"

"Now that is one heck of a speaker," said Nelms. "Write down what he says," looking to Tatiana. "I want to remember this." Nelms had no idea that he was witnessing the same speech that President Johnson had given in 1866.

Seeing that the crowd was getting hopelessly out of control, Jesse Weinstein once again jumped into the fray.

"Mr. President, give me twenty-four hours to secure a writ of habeas corpus from a United States District Court," said Weinstein. "I can prove he is not part of this. He is a United States citizen entitled to a trial of his peers before a jury, not a military tribunal."

"We are at war. This is an Article I court and I have the authority to carry out the sentence. He is not entitled to an Article III trial. There would never be justice if we put war criminals on trial in civilian courts."

"Let me at least try with a writ of habeas corpus. There is no use in hanging him now when I can prove he had nothing to do with any of this," said Weinstein.

"That is of no use. I have authority to suspend writs of habeas corpus. And I have the authority over military trials. I have the authority to decide who comes into this country. I will not allow a federal judge to ban what is exclusively in the power of the presidency. I cannot let one federal district judge determine what is going to be the law of the land. Carry out the sentence," directed the president to the hangman.

"Do you have anything to say?" asked the hangman. Thomas did not respond.

Weinstein walked up to him. "With your permission, Mr. President, let me ask him something," said Weinstein. "Judge Thomas, I know this is it. There isn't anything I can do now. That was a good fight in Paris during the Williams trial. Lord knows we fought in Paris during the trial of Private Williams. You never gave up. I never gave up. I never thought you would win, especially after your closing argument. You redefined criminal law when you did that. That was great. I never heard of the presumption of guilt taking over. That was a good one, Judge. I don't know how you did it. I have a question for you, although it doesn't matter now. You can answer any way you wish because it doesn't matter what you say. The truth is not going to set you free. You are going to die today no matter what you say. My question is: Judge, did you prosecute Williams in Paris because you thought he was guilty or because he was black?"

Thomas didn't answer.

"Did you go after him deliberately?" Thomas didn't answer.

"Ok. You won't answer. Did you know there were other witnesses who knew about the Williams case?"

"Yes," said Thomas.

"Did you prevent them from being able to testify?" asked Weinstein.

"No. I was negligent in not responding to requests about them and the transfer out of country, making them unavailable for the trial, but their testimony would not have changed the outcome of the trial," said Thomas.

"Wasn't that up to the court-martial to decide that, Judge Thomas?" asked Weinstein.

Thomas said nothing.

"Then let me ask you. Why did you let your bar dues lapse? Was it negligence in not paying them?"

"Yes," he said. "I forgot about paying them after leaving the state and then I realized how badly it would look to have my name publicly listed on the state's roster for being suspended. So, I did what I could to get my name reinstated."

"You wanted to be reinstated in a state where you were not going to practice law?" asked Weinstein.

"Yes. I should have kept current with both state bar associations. That was wrong of me. I needed it corrected. I was quite embarrassed about that."

"Did you accept responsibility?" asked Weinstein.

"Yes," said Thomas.

"When I was trying the Brandesha Yancey case, why were you so mad at me from the bench? What did I do and what did she do to be treated so harshly by you? Why did you ask her if she was the President of the United States?"

"I guess I was tired of hearing the same story over and over again. I hate family law cases and I lose my patience with the lawyers and the people coming in the court with all of their excuses and delays and how they don't tell the truth and how unprepared they are. They don't have to be the smartest lawyer but they should be prepared. I lose my patience when it comes to family law cases," said Judge Thomas.

"I understand that. You get tired of the same cases over and over again but to them their case is the only case in the world. You lose your patience with witnesses coming into your court. What are the witnesses to do when you lose your patience when you are on the bench? To them, their case is the most important case in the world and they don't want a judge yelling at them from the bench," said Weinstein, losing his patience with Judge Thomas. "You have no right to abuse anyone in the court."

Then he stopped. "I'm sorry. I didn't mean to say that. I didn't mean to go so far. Maybe I should be careful too," said Weinstein. "I can see how you can get carried away when you are in power."

Thomas said nothing.

"You admit you are as flawed as the lawyers and the clients coming in your court, but they are treated harshly. I understand that," said Weinstein.

Thomas said nothing.

"Lastly, during the *habeas corpus* case where we argued over the shifting of the burden of proof, did you sympathize for the prosecutor because you made the same mistake in the Williams' court-martial?"

"I didn't make the same mistake," said Thomas loudly.

"What are they talking about?" asked Tatiana.

"Looks like they have a score to settle," said Andre. "This looks like the second private war going on between them."

"Ok. Do you favor the government or the defense in criminal cases?" asked Weinstein.

"I am neutral to both sides," said Thomas. "What did you expect me to do—let out a known killer go free because a prosecutor made a mistake in his closing arguments that had no effect on the guilty verdict?" said Thomas.

"Uh-huh," said Weinstein.

"Do you have anything further?" asked the hangman.

"Nothing. I'm through with this witness," said Weinstein. The hangman put the black sack over Thomas's face.

"One last thing," said Weinstein. The hangman removed the sack. "Judge Thomas, are you the head of the Klan?"

Everyone watching gasped. "What did he say?" asked Oliver.

"Something about 'are they kin?'" said Nelms. "No. It sounded like something else," said Tatiana.

"He asked him if he was head of the Klan," said Cub.

"What?" asked Tatiana. "You mean all this time ..."

"Don't say anything," said Oliver. "It's just rumor and innuendo. It is unsubstantiated. There is no corroboration. He shouldn't have asked that question and we shouldn't report it. We have no proof. I don't want to believe it."

"We can report that he asked the question," said Andre. "It is a fact that the question was asked."

"Oliver, we have proof that unflattering things were asked about the judge and he responded. It doesn't matter whether they are true or false. They could compromise him in his position as a judge and he needs to know that the information is out there," said Tatiana.

"We have to disagree on this one. We could be accused of slander or promoting 'fake news.' We don't want to be called a 'fake news' organization."

"But Mr. Smith, what is going on out there right now is real! It is our duty to report what is happening!" exclaimed Andre.

"I had the same disagreement with Tatiana over your trial and it is happening once more. Let's not let anything like that come between us again," said Oliver to Andre and Tatiana.

Thomas looked at Weinstein and smiled. He said nothing. The hangman put the sack back over Thomas's head.

The bottom of the floor collapsed. Thomas groaned as his body bounced and settled. Everyone watching gasped as he struggled for air and his legs came to rest. Judge Thomas was hung. His life was ended. It was a brutal execution. He died the way he lived his life—in brutality. Brutality does not change another's behavior. Brutality breeds brutality. For the first time in his life, Thomas did not land on his feet.

"What's going on out there?" asked Brandesha.

"They hung the judge," said Cub.

"The one on my case?" asked Brandesha. Then she screamed out.

"That judge," said Cub.

"Push," said Sister Aude.

"You are doing great?" said Sister Laurie.

"I don't know what is going on here, but that man deserved everything he got," said Brandesha.

"Oh, my goodness, it can't end this way," cried Sister Camille. Sister Camille was stunned. Looking over the bloody battlefield spread across the fields of St. Peter's, with four men hung from a tree in front of the house that the sisters had renovated, she said a prayer: "Pray for us, so that the word of the Lord may speed forward and be glorified, as it did among you, and that we may be delivered from perverse and wicked people, for not all have faith."

Then the sound of a baby broke the silence. The sound of a baby crying could be heard across the fields of St. Peter's. All in the room gathered around Brandesha to see her baby. The bells in St. Peter's began to ring.

It was a new day.

It was a new beginning. It was November 1, 1948. The president was gone.

Chapter 53

ANDRE WOKE UP. HE HEARD a voice say to him:

You can do whatever you want. You can achieve whatever you want. The universe is yours. All you have to do is ask and it will be given to you. Seek and you will find. You will never want again. Anything you want is possible. You must have faith. You must believe. You have to work towards your path. Your dreams will become your reality.

"What happened?" he said to himself.

"How are you, old buddy?" asked Ellis. "That was quite a scare. I heard you walk out last night while I was sleeping on the couch. Next thing, I hear this plop."

"Andre, you really scared us. Lanny brought you inside and you slept like a baby all night," said Sherry.

Andre looked at Sherry. "You did a great job in the play. You sang the song well and your French was perfect. The audience liked the song. I thought they were going to hate it. Who would've ever guessed Napoleon Bonaparte wrote a story and we pulled all that together? Even Aunt Clara in another one of her moments managed to make it look like it was all part of the same play. No matter what people say about it, I still like that song," said Andre.

"Andre, you know I can't speak French. And what play? You must have been dreaming. You were knocked out from the fall you took last night, but you are ok," said Sherry.

"What?" asked Andre.

"I think you should stay home," said Sherry.

"Did you find the answer to the million-dollar question or the secret of the universe?" asked Ellis.

"What are you talking about?" asked Sherry.

"Nothing," said Ellis.

"I have to go work today," said Andre. "I have an article that I wrote for Mr. Nelms.

"Remember what we talked about last night," asked Ellis.

"I have to get to work," Andre said.

"Well, at least let me put a bandage over the cut on your head," said Sherry. As Sherry put the bandage on his head.

"The universe never says no to you," he said.

"What are you talking about?" she asked.

He smiled. "I was thinking when I came to see you on the porch before I joined the army. The universe brings you want you think about," he explained.

"You're crazy. Be still," she said as she applied the bandage to his head.

As he dressed for work, Andre realized that all he had dreamed was nothing more than memories and negative emotions being played out. The horror of the war being raged at St. Peter's, the executions, the unethical acts of Judge Thomas, the mistakes of Jesse Weinstein, Brandesha's dislike of Tatiana, the actions of Lanny Ellis, the white Klan racists were all tests to see what path he would take afterwards. If he dwelled on hatred, jealousy, the faults of others, then those negative emotions would become permanent fixtures in his own life. They could even change his physical appearance. If he focused on what was healthy, natural, and beautiful, then he could attract those thought currents into his life.

Andre came to terms with the knowledge that Captain Thomas was not a racist and genuinely believed that a crime had been committed. Thomas had acted with his own good conscience, even if he had poor judgment. Thomas was a leader but not a good leader.

He remembered Lew and Alvin at the barbershop and how they said they were taught to be racist. Andre said they were born that way. President Andrew Johnson was a slave owner and never saw slavery as a moral issue and had deep seated racism. In a strange way, he sympathized with those who were born on the wrong side of history. They were symbols of the unforgiving past and he believed things would change.

Andre discovered that his dream did help him find the truth regarding the shooting of Booker Thompson. Sometimes there's real truth in a dream. He didn't shoot Booker; Ellis did, and there would be no investigation. This would be a secret he would have to keep to himself. Finally, he had to remember that no matter what happened to him, he had to be grateful to the Lord thy God for it.

Chapter 54

ANDRE ATTENDED THE MORNING MEETING with Mr. Nelms, Oliver, Tatiana, and Cub. Brandesha walked in the room. She was elegant, thin, and fit. Andre was stunned at her appearance. She wasn't pregnant.

"What are you looking at?" Brandesha asked him. "You're looking nice this morning," said Andre.

"He knows what to say," said Brandesha as she exited the room. Her voice penetrated the walls of the room while the chairs moved.

"How was your night? Is that a bandage on your head?" asked Oliver to Andre.

"Yes. I hit my head. It's nothing. I'm fine," said Andre. "I'm glad you are fine," said Oliver.

"That looks serious, Andre. Did you go see a doctor?" asked Tatiana. "He doesn't need a doctor. He's tough," said Cub.

"I'm ok. Really," reassured Andre.

"Are you looking forward to working on the paper?" asked Tatiana. "Yes," said Andre.

"We have class today," said Cub.

"Sorry I'm late," said Nelms, walking in his office. "Andre, do you have your story?"

"I do sir. Here it is." Andre pulled out his story from his folder and handed it to Mr. Nelms.

"Let me read this," said Nelms. "Looks long. How many words?"

"I don't know," said Andre.

Nelms read:

In January of 1948, the full moon was the closest to the Earth in its orbit. Big and bright, many would never see a supermoon like it again in their lifetime.

"That sounds good," said Nelms. "Nice lead."

"That *was* good," said Tatiana.

"Yes, pretty good start," agreed Oliver. "Sure is," said Cub. Then he continued:

> World War II was over and Alabama soldiers were home. Some had readjusted to civilian life. Some had not. Alabama and its elected citizens were making news inside and outside the state.
>
> After the Republicans took control of both the Senate and House of Representatives in the 1946 elections, President Truman began to build support for his candidacy in 1948. He courted black Americans by favoring civil rights, higher minimum wage, and national health insurance. He also drew a hardline policy against the Soviet Union.

"I can accept that," said Nelms. Then he continued:

> Truman's actions were not without controversy and ramifications from some Southern voters. He recognized the new state of Israel and desegregated the armed forces with Executive Order 9981, establishing the President's Committee on Equality of Treatment and Opportunity in the

377

Armed Services that committed the federal government to desegregating the military.

Truman was changing the nation, but some in Alabama were not going along with the change. Alabama adopted the Boswell Amendment ..."

"I'm glad you put that in there. You remembered," said Nelms.

... that allowed registrars to deny voting rights to those who might not understand the U.S. Constitution. Although the law applied to both whites and blacks, its obvious purpose was to deny African American citizens from voting in the Democratic primary—the only place where it mattered.

"Why did you go into journalism, Mr. Nelms?" asked Tatiana interrupting Nelm's reading of Andre's story. Everyone looked at him.

"I guess it was my love for the common man. I wanted to turn the world around."

Nelms continued to read Andre's article:

No matter how qualified a black voter might be, the local registrar could deny a citizen's right to vote through questions asking for an interpretation of the United States Constitution or through purges of voters who did not respond to inquiries of voter eligibility. The NAACP filed suit on behalf of ten plaintiffs against the Board of Registrars for violations of the Fourteenth and

Fifteenth Amendments to the U.S. Constitution based on the amendment.

"Uh huh," said Nelms.

Alabama's new colorful governor, Jim Folsom, made headlines when 30-year-old Christine Johnston filed a paternity suit alleging that he was the father of her 22-month-old son ...

Alabama delegates walked out of the 1948 Democratic National Convention in Philadelphia, Pennsylvania, to protest Truman's civil rights policies ...

Truman won the nomination at the Democratic National Convention in July of 1948, choosing for his running mate Kentucky Senator Alben Barkley.

The Republicans nominated New York Governor Thomas Dewey for President and Earl Warren for Vice President.

Satchel Paige joined the Cleveland Indians as a rookie pitcher at the age of 42.

Mahalia Ashley Dickerson from Montgomery received her law degree from Howard University in Washington, D.C.

Ralph Abernathy was 22 years old and back from serving as Platoon Sergeant in the army in London.

Nat King Cole married Maria Ellington and moved to an allwhite Hancock Park neighborhood in Los Angeles, prompting protests from white neighbors.

Alice Coachman won the gold medal during the 1948 Olympics in London for her leap of 5 feet 6 1/8 inches, making her the first black woman to win the gold.

Things were changing in Alabama. Alabama and Auburn would renew the Iron Bowl, a rivalry so intense that the teams had not played together for forty years.

"I like it. You reported on everyone I mentioned, but it's way too long.

Did I give you a word limit?"

"No," said Andre.

"Less is more, but it's good. You need to cut it down to 500 words. We can work this in the paper. Congratulations, Andre," said Nelms. "You will have a by-line. From proofreader to writer."

"Congratulations," said Tatiana.

"Congratulations," said Oliver.

"Good job," said Cub.

"Now, what's going on with the election?" asked Nelms.

"Well sir, the papers say that Dewey is going to win," said Oliver.

"He isn't going to win. He doesn't believe he will win. To win you have to believe in yourself and that you have already won," said Nelms.

Andre had heard that before.

"You think the president can win even with the polls saying he won't, Mr.

Nelms?" asked Tatiana.

"The voters aren't going to reject Truman. We can't trust the polls. We have to question the people. We have to go back to old fashioned reporting. We have to go into the community and find out what is really going on with them. If we rely on the polls for our stories, we are never going to understand the American people and will be out of touch with them. We can't be daydreaming and let the world pass by," said Nelms.

They all looked at him.

THE END

NOTES

Chapter 15
The examples of Father Sanders in the journalism class comes from an article by Paula LaRoque, *The Quill*, The Society of Professional Journalists (July/August 2015).